TELEPORT 3

JOSHUA T. CALVERT

1

James lay on his back, enjoying the gentle tickle of the grass against his bare skin. The stalks were damp enough not to be scratchy, but dry enough so as not to cause a chill. The temperature was very comfortable, so he was neither sweating nor shivering.

He closed his eyes and saw an orange-red glow behind his eyelids that created a warm wall, inviting and relaxing. A light breeze blew in the distance and gently brushed against him. A lightness spread through him, lifting the burden he had become so accustomed to. Only now was he fully aware of it. Like an avalanche of suppressed fear, anger, and tormenting thoughts that could steal a grown man's mind, they swept through his stomach and chest... a ball of unspoken reactions that he had never acted upon, either because he hadn't had time in the hectic necessity of survival or because he hadn't wanted to unnecessarily frighten his friends.

The avalanche brought with it a wave of nausea, a leaden heaviness in his guts that rose convulsively within him and settled as a lump in his throat. He swallowed and calmly inhaled the fresh air through his nose, felt it fill his diaphragm, which gently rose and fell, unaffected by the emotional hurricane causing his autonomic nervous system to run at full speed.

He settled in to listen to his breathing, that foundation of life, and experienced it as an attentive but uninvolved observer, the lump in his throat eased. Immediate panic became a mere stirring, which he accepted and saw as the fleeting physical reaction that it was. He allowed his body's innate intelligence to detach itself as a deep sensation of peace slowly spread through him.

The fact that he was not wearing a stitch of clothing and that the others lying in the grass around him were similarly naked did not bother him. A half a year ago he never would have thought that he would one day be able to walk—or lie—around in front of others like an unashamed European. Yet their time with the Tokamaku, who dealt with nudity as one should, namely naturally, had changed him. Added to this was the closeness he felt toward his team, his *friends*. It was an intimate closeness forged out of their shared confrontation with illness, death, the adverse conditions they had faced, and the absolute cohesion necessary for survival. They had become like family to him, and it was only when they had nearly died while battling Altan-117, the Kazerun hacker-possessed Servitor on Al'Antis, that he had realized that he would die for each and every one of them if he had to.

"Isn't this wonderful?" Mila asked from beside him. Her voice brought him back from his thoughts. She lay close to him, her shoulder and thigh touching his upper arm and thigh. His right hand and her left were clasped tightly. "Birds are chirping, the sun is shining—or rather, the *suns* are shining—and the sky is a fabulous turquoise."

"I'd feel even better if there were trees here, but yes, you're right."

"What do you mean?"

"There are no trees or shrubs, just endless meadows, and yet birds *are* chirping all around us."

James listened, letting the avian chatter and melodies wash over him. Every bird call seemed to awaken something raw and evolutionary in people that came with life and security. It just felt good to let those ethereal sounds affect him: gentle melodies of delicate creatures that had not allowed gravity to pull them down, but had overcome it millions of years ago to soar through the air. He tried to remember how he must have looked at them when he was a small child, before he had been told that this mysterious creature fluttering above him, beating its wings, was a "bird." As soon as he knew their name and was told what they were, they had somehow lost their magic, the unknown mystical, and he had seen only seen them as "birds" since, and not the indescribable being that had so enchanted him.

"Every explanation is merely a label we give things we basically don't understand," he said aloud. "We only imagine that we comprehend because we give them names, but we actually know absolutely nothing about them. Not where they come from, why they exist, or what it must feel like to be them."

"Are we still talking about the birds?" Mila asked.

"Maybe," he said as vaguely as he felt. "We haven't seen any vegetation here for them to hide in, yet we hear them singing around us—and it's wonderful. I don't have an explanation for it, but for the moment, I don't need any. I'm content to just enjoy how good it feels."

"We do that far too rarely."

"Exactly." He turned his head and kissed her forehead

without opening his eyes. Her hair tickled his nose and she smelled faintly of grass. What a gift these simple sensations were! He didn't have to question it, just welcome it gratefully, and that made it that much more precious and profound.

Slowly he opened his eyes and looked up into the turquoise sky. A lone white cloud drifted alonglike a sheep that had lost its flock.

Like us, he thought and looked at Mila. *Far from our flock, which we can no longer see, lost in a sky that no longer seems hung with dark clouds. A decidedly friendly sky.*

"Do you think it worked?" he asked.

"I don't know. I expected something different, I guess." Mila fell silent, enjoying a peaceful moment. She seemed to hope he would not disturb it with impatient inquiries. Finally, she continued, "Seats, for example."

"Mmm."

When he had closed his eyes in his seat on the Ark's teleporter platform on Al'Antis, his body had been bruised, a battered shipwreck that his last reserves of strength had barely managed to keep afloat above the bottomless abyss where he thought he would perish. The pain had bordered on the unbearable, filling half his world. The smell of ozone and dust lingered in his nose, although it now seemed like a distant dream, just as one could hardly imagine the cold rain of winter on a sunny summer day.

He had closed his eyes… and woken up here, but not as expected, in a seat arranged with his companions, in a room housing a new teleporter. No, he had emerged—or awakened?—here, just like his friends, in the middle of nowhere, with no sign of any the technology necessary for teleporting.

But after his first use of the teleporter on Earth, he had decided not to seek explanations in mere musings about an afterlife or some kind of illusion. Yet there had to be an explanation that he just couldn't see yet—or didn't want to see. For all he knew, their trip to Al'Antis had been real, and if it wasn't, then there was no way whatsoever to look past the illusion, the dream, or the metaphysical phenomenon holding them captive. This realization made it clear that pondering any such scenario would be completely useless, for then he would have to question his entire life and consider it no more real than an insubstantial phantom.

He wasn't willing to go down that road because he wanted to keep his sanity, if only that.

"We just showed up here as if we'd always been here and were just taking a nap," he said, sighing.

"Do you think it's *their* planet?" Mila asked. "The origin planet? The home of those mysterious *Elders* Nasaku told us about, those the Al'Anters have been searching for so long?"

"I don't know, and I dare not hope, though I really wish it is so. A few answers might do us all some good."

"At least we're still alive, so that's a good start. At least we're able to hear answers if anyone has any to give. For a moment, I thought that we were through."

"I thought so too," he said slowly, "but it doesn't matter now." He squeezed her hand. "All that matters is that we made it and we're here. We're breathing, we have each other, and we haven't lost anyone."

Slowly, James sat up. His back tingled pleasantly where the blades of grass had gently dug into his skin. It felt like someone was peeling a massage mat off him. Justus, Meeks, Adrian, and Mette still laid fanned out in an irregular semicircle in front of them, their feet almost touching. It was a picture of relaxation and relief that warmed his heart once more.

They seemed to notice, despite their closed eyes, that

something had changed, and one by one they stirred. Adrian was the first to sit up. He exhaled long and loud, an extended sigh that seemed filled with a mass of pent-up emotions that were now being released.

"Good to see you're okay again," James said, and for the first time since he could remember, he saw the Russian smile. It was not a cynical smile, not a disapproving one, nor a resigned one, but a *genuine* smile. It suited him extremely well. It took away some of the shirt-sleeved seriousness that always surrounded him like a nimbus of professionalism.

"Likewise. Your jaw…" Adrian shuddered. "Let's just not do that again."

"No more killer 'bots," Meeks agreed, wiping the grass from his bald head and winking at Mette, who rose onto her elbows beside him, looking almost sleepy. "No more irradiated planet."

"Whoever built those teleporters," Justus said, looking down at himself suspiciously as he sat up, "has a strange penchant for nudity."

James eyed the German, his sinewy muscles moving like snakes beneath his skin. They were still stately, but they no longer looked like they had come from a cover model gracing an issue of *Men's Health*. Nor was his complexion tan, as it had been back on Earth; it was pale, as it had been on Al'Antis.

"Interesting," he muttered, loud enough so all eyes turned to him. He noticed and pointed at Justus. "I'm not sure what happened, whether the teleport worked. But if it did, we know one thing for sure: our Al'Antis selves were teleported, not our Earth selves. We're pale, Meeks no longer has a gut, and Mette is slimmer than I am."

He watched Mila run her fingers through her full head of hair, and the others, like him, consciously scanned her skin for abscesses, swellings, or redness. After arriving at this place, perhaps half an hour ago, they were simply relieved to be sprawled on the grass and hadn't given it a second thought.

"We're just like we were on Al'Antis, but healthy and strong," Meeks said, nodding. "My goodness, this is getting weirder and weirder. Anyway, the teleport from Earth to Al'Antis went differently than this one."

"What do you mean?" wanted James to know.

Meeks thrust one foot forward and spread his big toe from its slimmer neighbor.

"There, see that?"

James looked closer and shook his head.

"No."

"Exactly. When we arrived on Al'Antis I was pretty pissed off because my damned athlete's foot came with me." The engineer pointed to the skin between his toes, which looked healthy and pink. "I thought, if someone can manage to build a thing like that, surely they can manage to leave something as annoying as a damned athlete's foot where it belongs. Surely a machine of such intelligence should be able to distinguish between what's useful and what's not useful, malignant versus benign."

"But what if taking away what makes people who they are is malignant in general? Including diseases," Mette mused.

"Athlete's foot? Come on!"

"My grandmother was a horrible old witch. She always kicked me and my little brother under the table when we went to her house for dinner. My parents worked a lot, so they always dumped us on her. She was an angry old woman who didn't have much joy in her life since my grandpa died in a car accident. He was run over by a drunk, and I think that made her angry at God and the world. Today, I can kind of understand that, and I feel sorry for her.

"When I was twelve, she got pancreatic cancer. Not a nice thing, I can tell you. Her breath smelled like carrion and the wrinkles around her eyes got even deeper. The doctors gave her six months to live. In the end, it was thirteen—more than a year." Mette paused and looked off into the distance, smiling. "Thirteen months in which I got to know a grandmother I had never had before. All at once, she became extremely gentle and good-natured, as if suddenly transformed. I didn't even know what had happened to her, but she gave us presents, took us to play miniature golf, ordered us pizza when we wanted it, she even watched all the movies with us that she had always found so terrible, and she showed genuine interest in us.

"I had just turned thirteen, and before she died, when she could barely speak, I will never forget what she said to me then as I lay crying by her bedside, begging her not to die. Children give their love quickly and completely, like a dog that always returns even after even the hardest beating. She said: 'Child, it's quite all right.' Of course, I wasn't going to let it go at that and railed that I hated her cancer. I cursed it with the desperation of a teenager. But she would have none of that and told me that cancer was the best friend she had ever had because it had shown her what was really important and how precious every breath could be. She had loved the thirteen months with the cancer far more than all the years of bitterness before. I didn't understand it then and I'm not even sure I do now, if at all—though perhaps I do on an intellectual level. I guess you can only understand it if you've stood in front of that abyss yourself. But what I learned from that painful experience—my grandma died with a smile on her face—was that circumstances make us who we are. You might argue that it's our reactions to them that decide what we become, and that may be true, but circumstances are always the trigger."

"Fate," Mila said thoughtfully, nodding to herself.

James, knowing the pain of the loss that lay dormant in her memory, felt a wave of compassion rise within him. "That which is greater than us. Fate, chance, God—it's all the same, no matter what we call it. Whether it directs or follows an intelligent design, as we must assume at least to some extent after all we've been through, does not matter. There are things over which we have no influence, over which we have no control. Maybe that's what gave your grandmother her peace: the final realization that she had no control. External circumstances made her, or allowed her to, give up her illusions of being in control of her fate. That can be very liberating."

"Actually, I just had athlete's foot," Meeks grumbled, raising his hands defensively when he saw the others scowl. "What?"

Mette was the first to smirk and laugh. Eventually, they all joined in.

"Glad I could cheer you up!" The American sketched a slight bow and sat.

"She's right," Adrian said after he stopped laughing, rubbing his strong chin. "Your missing foot fungus tells us something about the Elders and their teleporters—if only about their philosophy, their worldview."

"'Don't interfere' can hardly be it," Meeks said. "The creation of six identical solar systems alone is an act of intervention beyond all imagining. And then there are the teleporters connecting everything. Everything they do and leave behind is the definition of intervention, of change."

"You're right about that, with one caveat: they clearly

don't exercise influence on anything that concerns humans since that point in creation when evolution took its course. Otherwise, they would not have allowed the Kazerun to destroy the Al'Anter. They might have intervened when the experimental teleporter was built on Al'Antis."

"Yes," Adrian agreed. "If it's true that each planet has its own Avatar and they're similar in their core programming, then they have instructions only to observe, not intervene."

"But Nasaku *did* intervene," Justus pointed out.

"Yes, but something happened to the Avatar that I find difficult to describe." James thought back to the first flower that had opened and bloomed under the sun on Al'Antis, that precious moment in the steady breathing rhythm of the plant that had brought such an ethereal change, short-lived and ephemeral, and yet it had represented a change that had gone far beyond the colors of the flowers that brought the concept of beauty to the planet. "It fundamentally changed beyond its programming, whatever that may have been."

"All right, so they may not be consciously intervening, maybe they follow something like a prime directive," Meeks suggested.

"Prime directive?" asked Mette, confused, and got an eye roll in response.

"*Star Trek*? Sorry, but so we can remain friends, I'm going to pretend I didn't hear that." A fleeting smile crossed his face to emphasize his good-natured jest, then he turned back to the others. "But even with a prime directive, it's different here. We're unscathed now, even though we were harmed before."

"What if it only affects acute trauma?" James grabbed his jaw and winced inwardly.

"Athlete's foot!"

"Oh, yeah. Right."

"But we're not dealing with the normal teleporter network here," Adrian reminded them. "So we can assume that the rules and guidelines have changed, too, or no longer apply. If we assume that it worked and we've traveled to the master teleporter, then we did something that, at least superficially, was not intended by its builders."

"Or there's a malfunction," Mila said, and all eyes turned to her. All of a sudden, James found the breeze a little cooler, and his skin broke out in goosebumps.

"Malfunction?" he asked.

She held up one finger of her right hand. "Well, we don't see any teleporter here"—she raised a second finger—"there are no seats"—she extended a third finger and looked at Meeks—"and we're stuck in our Al'Antis bodies, but there's no longer the foot fungus that was present there. Seems to me like some things here are different than we expected. Admittedly, our prior experience isn't sufficient for making sound deductions, but we did learn enough to have some reasonable expectations that have been unfulfilled on many levels. I'd say there was a malfunction."

2

James shaded his eyes from the light of the two suns. It was more out of reflex than that they were actually blinding. One glowed a soft shade of orange, the other had a red tinge, like what you could get by laying a thin red cloth over a lamp. On its own, it might have created a strange twilight, but as a double star with its brighter partner, it created a pleasant and lively atmosphere and the grass appeared lush and luminous. It stretched over a hilly landscape as far as the eye could see. The endless expanse of fresh ankle-high stalks formed wave-like patterns in the wind that seemed perpetually in motion.

"Looks a bit like the Shire," Meeks said.

"It does. Only the hobbits are missing. It wasn't so deserted in the Shire," Mette agreed.

"And there'd be beer and tons of food." Justus spun in a circle and shrugged his shoulders.

James nodded. "Definitely the Shire. I couldn't have thought up a more beautiful place."

"If Gandalf came around the corner now, at least we'd

have someone who could answer a few questions for us and we'd know we weren't stranded in a vast nothingness."

"The questions never end," Mila objected. "Whether there is a Gandalf or not."

"Who is *Gandalf*?" Adrian asked seriously.

"Are you kidding me?" Meeks rolled his eyes. "What did you read where you come from? Grummelov the Red?"

Mette and Justus chuckled, but the cosmonaut just frowned.

James indiscriminately stretched out a hand. "How about we go that way? Seems as good as any other direction."

"Why not?" Mila replied, then pointed to the flattened grass between them. "But we should mark this place so we can find our way back."

"Why? There's nothing here that wouldn't exist anywhere else around here: grass and even more grass."

"As long as we don't know whether we appeared here by chance or in accord with some law, we should mark the spot," Adrian said, supporting his countrywoman. "We could dig a cross into the ground with our hands."

They did just that: six naked adults tore out grass and used their hands to shovel the moist soil until there was a two-by-two-meter cross that would be visible from afar, especially since there was also a large pile of dirt now standing next to it. James looked down at his dirty hands and reflexively wiped his forehead, only to blink in amazement when he looked at the back of his hand afterward.

"What is it?" Mila asked.

"No sweat."

"Pardon?"

"I didn't sweat a drop, though the work was actually

quite strenuous." James said, then murmured, "Or at least it should have been."

"Hmm, I didn't find it exhausting at all."

"Exactly. Isn't that strange? We dig up the ground with our hands and don't break a sweat, don't even feel fatigued. That's strange, at least in my world."

"He's right," Adrian said, pointing up at the two suns, which were far enough apart that with his hand extended in front of him they could fit between them. "My skin isn't burned, either. It's usually irritated and red after just ten minutes in the sun."

James eyed the chalky white Russian, who had been extremely pale even before their time with the Tokamaku and had experienced virtually no direct sunlight since. Yet they had been here for over an hour, unprotected, without shade, and with no clothing. On Earth, they would have started showing the first signs of serious sunburn and feeling the effects of sunstroke, but none of them had any such symptoms here.

"I guess we've got some more unanswered questions," James said. "The best thing to do is to go and see what's between the hills. What do you think?"

Everyone nodded, and so, after wiping their hands on the grass and patting them clean, they set off. The ground was, as expected, extremely soft and pleasant underfoot, a sharp contrast with the alternating quagmire and sharp-edged rocks in Al'Antis's Death Zone when they had fallen out of that teleporter. Everything there had been hostile to life and filled with a tragic melancholy. Here it was the opposite: the light was warm and friendly, the sky was turquoise with white clouds scattered here and there, the smell of humus and chlorophyll filled the fresh air and tickled their nostrils, and the chirping of birds accompanied them like a melody of life and familiarity. It was almost kitschy, as if they were in the middle of some Scottish Highland ballad composed of notes of bliss and contentment that had been purposely heightened so even the slightest negative emotion was impossible.

"I always wanted to build a house in a place like this," Mila said as they walked leisurely eastward—at least it felt to James like they were walking east—and climbed the first hill, beyond which the landscape stretched onward, just as before. He didn't know what he was expecting to see. A city? Different vegetation? Maybe just a single tree, some sign that there was something else here besides grass and invisible birds.

"In a place without earthworms?"

"What's that supposed to mean?"

"When we were digging the marker," he explained, "I didn't see any earthworms. Fertile earth is usually full of them. When I was a kid, I filled whole canning jars with them because I wanted to relocate them. I was disgusted by them until my parents made me play in the dirt. I was in one of those playgroups for difficult children. We were taught that the whole grass and forest ecosystem wouldn't work without earthworms because they dig myriad tiny tunnels in the soil through which fluid and nutrients pass. The vegetation here seems to do just fine without them."

"Maybe this planet has found another mechanism," she suggested.

"Maybe." He knew he didn't sound convinced, but he didn't want to burden her with his suspicions either. They had earned the right to enjoy their present carefree mood for a little while without obsessively looking for the catch. He had resolved to think more like an Al'Anter, even though it had been difficult while on their ruined home planet. Not a day had gone by in that place without it showing him what could happen if one was too naive. "This house you imagined, what did it look like?"

Mila smiled and took his hand.

"I wanted to build it in New Zealand, where *The Lord of the Rings* was filmed. Rolling hills like this one, lots of sunshine and lush greenery as far as the eye could see. Rustling trees, birds chirping in your ears, and not a trace of concrete, just stone and wood and maybe a hobbit hole with round doors and windows." She snorted. "Isn't it amazing that you can miss a place you've never actually experienced?"

"I know what you mean," he said. "I had the same feeling when I saw the movie. Everything there had an aura of carelessness and peace that touched me even through the screen. Until now, I always thought it was just my imagination because the images trigger in us exactly what our lizard brain sees as homey and safe, as a perfect hunting ground, or something like that."

"As unattainable because it's too perfect," Mila summarized.

"Yes. After all, when you watch a movie, you don't smell the manure pile just out of sight, you don't feel the splinter that lodges under your toenail as you walk across the meadow, you don't feel the mosquito bites, you don't feel the sweat as you work, and you don't hear the buzz of the wasp that's been bothering you all day." James gestured around with his free hand. "It's just like it is here. There's nothing disturbing, which is really... *remarkable*."

"You're living proof that the first Matrix didn't work."

"What?" he asked, giving her an irritated sideways glance.

"*The Matrix*, the movie. Neo asks why the Matrix is so

imperfect, there's violence and war, poverty, and all that stuff. That's when he gets to hear the unvarnished truth, that people just couldn't come to terms with a perfect world. I think that's the fundamental problem with our existence: we always have to look for the fly in our soup because that was an evolutionary advantage; Seeking out danger before it bites us in the butt. Survival is a fragile thing."

"Then I am absolutely in flow with evolution."

"You might be, but this place isn't."

"That's what I'm saying..." He paused when he noticed the others had stopped.

They were standing atop one of the uncountable hilltops, looking ahead. James followed their gaze and blinked a few times. His mouth went dry. About a hundred meters away, on the sprawling grassy plain, he saw a dark cross amid all the greenery.

"How is that possible?" breathed Mette. "Have we been walking in circles?"

"Apparently," Adrian muttered, his face somber.

"How?" James asked. "The hills form a clear profile that's easy to see. It's not like everything is identical. So how can we have gone in circles?"

"There's only one way to check. We split into three groups of two and walk in three cardinal directions for as long as we have so far. I would guess about ten or fifteen minutes."

Which is exactly what they did after they arrived at their crudely dug cross and assured themselves that the size and texture matched what they had left behind. There was no doubt, which only served to intensify the uneasy feeling in James's stomach.

"We didn't go in circles," he said as he and Mila set out to explore their chosen point of the compass.

"I didn't feel that way either, but that's probably how it always is when you're walking in circles, when you don't have enough landmarks to guide you. It can happen quickly even in a forest. It happened to me a lot in Siberia when I was a teenager, even though I grew up there. It's even worse in the tundra."

"But in a landscape like this?"

She didn't answer and they walked on in silence, focused on maintaining a straight line and looking to see if they could make out any spots in front or beside them that indicated footsteps in the lush grass. They found none. After a few minutes, James stopped abruptly.

"Do you see that?" He pointed to the two roughly human outlines on a hill in the distance. They were barely visible, and he had to squint to be sure, but they were definitely identifiable as people.

"No, what—oh, yes there is. Somebody's there!" Mila said, half startled, half delighted.

Side by side, they started running as if on command, only to stop after fifty meters on the next hill. Their shoulders sagged with disappointment. Adrian and Mette were coming straight at them. Between them on the circular plain was the cross they had left behind. Justus and Meeks appeared from the left. They were now back at their starting point.

"All right, there's clearly something fishy here," Meeks said. "I must confess that I didn't want to think about it, but now I'm worried."

"What is it?" Mila asked. "No matter where we go, we always come back here. I don't need to tell you that that's physically impossible."

"There's something else." Adrian pointed upward to the two suns. "They haven't moved an inch since we got here."

"Maybe this planet's in a bound rotation?" Mette suggested.

"Impossible." Justus shook his head. "Bound rotation in a binary star system is rare, though usually not impossible. But the reason that can't be the case here is the wind and temperature. In that case, we'd be on the day side, and it would be constantly irradiated, effectively grilling us, while the night side would be freezing. Violent storms would be blowing into our faces right now, created by the temperature amplitude at the equator."

"Good, so another glitch in the Matrix." James looked at Mila. She did not smile at his remark and looked paler than before.

"Maybe the world of the Elders is different than we expect or can explain," he said. "After all, they did manage to seed six solar systems in the Milky Way over four billion years ago and kick off six evolutions, at the end of which there were always humans. A few days ago, I would have said that was absolutely inconceivable, and I'm not even a scientist. Isn't it possible their homeworld follows laws they themselves determined?"

"I think anything is possible. The word 'inconceivable' hasn't been part of my vocabulary since I went through that teleporter." Meeks growled like a grizzly bear, a deep, rolling sound.

"We should take our time and think this through," Adrian said. "We're in no hurry or acute physical need, and there's no immediate danger."

A moment later they were sitting around their cross and James was picking at individual blades of grass from the sods they had piled up. He held them in front of him as if they were utterly fascinating structures and eyed their cellular structure, which on close inspection he could make out as a pattern of vaguely rectangular squares surrounded by minute gaps. Was it a blade of grass like on Earth, or was there something different about it from what he remembered? Had he ever even looked at one close enough to be sure? It looked exactly as he imagined it should, but he wasn't a biologist. What if it was artificial, like in the Matrix? Sight and feel might be identical, but their origin was not. On the other hand, that was also certainly true of Earth and Al'Antis. What was natural or even normal about the two planets?

His friends talked for hours about various scientific theories to explain what they simply could not explain. He didn't understand half of what they were saying, and the longer their discussions went on, the more complicated and convoluted their vocabulary became, as if they were climbing a tower of scientific semantics in an attempt to reach a summit that didn't exist. When he spoke the thought aloud, however, they merely gave him looks that were a mixture of pity and impatience, so he held back and continued to look at his blades of grass. They smelled fresh when gathered in a bunch, but of nothing when he sniffed individual ones, which struck him as odd. But it had been the same at home. Hadn't it? Had he ever smelled a blade of grass?

At some point—it must have taken hours and his head was spinning so much—they agreed that they couldn't even say with certainty whether they had left Al'Antis at all. Justus had theorized that they were in a virtual cache of the experimental teleporter because their surroundings were extremely inviting and downright fantastic to look at, and that was something that had occurred to the Al'Anters. Mette did not believe it and objected that they could then also be dead and in the afterlife, just to prove that they could not completely exclude any theory at this point, however abstruse it might sound.

As a consequence, Adrian might also be right when he proposed that they were on the world of the Al'Anters, but which functioned according to other rules that did not follow a linearity that humans thought and experienced in their environment. Or Meeks, who suggested that they were in Mila's subconscious because she had always dreamed of such a landscape. After the others had shared similar fantasies of their own, James had merely shrugged and said that might be part of her subconscious, too.

"There is no such thing as the subconscious," James had explained to them. "That's outdated psychology. Our minds are shallower than we think, more like a coherent structure of recurring thoughts and automatisms that we don't always perceive."

They fell silent for a while until Justus spoke up.

"Do you feel tired?"

"No," Meeks answered, followed by the others in turn. James had just noticed the same. They had been here for a long time, maybe half a day—at least it seemed so to him. The suns were still in the same place, and there was no sign of approaching dusk.

"It's not getting dark," he said mostly to himself, squinting up at the turquoise sky. "And we're not getting tired. I still feel amazing."

"Mmm-mmm," Meeks said, agreeing with him. "I'm not hungry or thirsty at all. Normally, I should be able to eat half a pig by now."

"I am picking up increased stress levels from you," said a new voice, and they startled like a flock of birds abruptly changing direction.

A man in a white robe stood next to them. He was old,

had a full head of silver hair and a long, messy beard. His eyes were large and kind, and his nose strong and round at the tip. He was altogether an impressive figure with the body of a man who had led a comfortable life.

"Shit!" Meeks exclaimed. Adrian jumped. "Where did he come from?"

"I didn't mean to frighten you," the stranger said, raising his large hands placatingly. His voice had a pleasant resonance and was calm. "Please, do not be afraid."

"Where did you come from?" Mila asked, looking around almost feverishly, as if more figures might suddenly appear out of nowhere.

"I come from heaven," the man answered kindly, giving her a warm smile. "There is no reason to be afraid of me. I am here to take care of you and make sure you want for nothing."

James exchanged a look with Mila and swallowed.

"Okay, now it's getting really weird." Meeks tried to grin, but it belied a mixture of sheer panic and indifference, like that of someone who no longer felt like asking questions.

"Who are you?" Adrian asked tensely.

"Oh," the stranger went on, smiling. "I'm God."

3

James just stood there speechless, just like the others, staring at "God." He could not form a thought let alone words.

The old man with the wild beard pretty much fit the stereotype of the childish image of God that he had had when he was little. "God" folded his hands in front of his stomach and regarded them calmly and serenely.

"I'm sorry, my children, I didn't mean to unsettle you."

"Unsettle?" Adrian was the first to regain his speech. He stated decisively, "You are not God."

"No? Why do you doubt me?"

"Because there is no God," Mette jumped in.

"How do you know?" God said. "Do you have any proof of that?"

"No, but there is no proof that he exists either. And certainly not because someone shows up and tells me he's God." The Dane blinked and shook her head. "Are we really having this conversation right now?"

"Therefore, your belief that I don't exist is also just that: a belief. Either you believe I exist or you believe I don't exist.

Thus, everyone has their own religion, right?" God leaned his head back and laughed in a full-throated bass. "Do you require proof?"

The stranger snapped his fingers and they collectively flinched when a bolt of lightning struck the ground next to him out of nowhere, splattering grass and earth. The air crackled with the static discharge. A second finger snap and the suns began to move. The sky rapidly dimmed, then grew so dark that the stars stood out as a twinkling blanket in the firmament, and finally became bright again with a double sunrise unparalleled in beauty. If only it had not happened so quickly...

Gaping, astonished, James stood with his friends, unsure whether to be afraid or to rejoice after witnessing such a miracle. All this time they had been looking for something —or someone—that would make this place seem not so lonely and strange, and then "God" showed up?

"Who are you?" James asked again, after regaining his composure.

"God," the stranger repeated, winking at him, amused.

"Tell us the truth."

"My goodness." God sighed throwing his hands in the air and looking disappointed. "Okay, I'm not God. The concept is amusing, though, I must say."

James exchanged a glance with Mila.

"Then who are you?" Adrian demanded. "What are you?"

"I am the master of this construct. Well, actually, I *am* the construct." The bearded figure sat on the grass and smoothed his white linen robe. "Almighty as the Father."

Another chuckle and giggle.

"Why did you..."

"Ah. I was looking at your memories, and when you

started to get unhappy, I thought I'd better show myself to you so you wouldn't go mad. Using the data available to me, I concluded that a simple god figure in the form of a kindly grandfather might be the best choice for making first contact between us." The construct shrugged. "You haven't tried to kill me, so I think I was right in my assumption."

"God?" Meeks shook himself like a dog trying to rid its fur of water before rubbing his temples.

"Each of you had a similar image stored away in your childhood memories. I saw your prayers and such. Before you switched to the next faith, atheism, of course."

"Where are we here?" Adrian asked. "And what is 'the construct'?"

Then everyone began talking over one another, as if an emotional dam had broken.

"Is this your home planet?"

"Are you an Elder?"

"Are you an AI?"

"What kind of 'construct'?"

"Are we real?"

"Is this real?"

"Are we dead?"

"Slow down, slow down." The construct raised its hands defensively and smiled. "I thought the God thing was pretty funny, but apparently you fellows don't feel like laughing. I'll try to answer all your questions, but first things first: I am a multiple personality construct and have been watching over this construct for close to three billion years."

Questions inundated him again, so jumbled that not a single one could be understood. The god figure sighed and transformed before their eyes into a human being made of gray matter without contour. It now resembled an unpainted wax replica.

"So. God obviously makes you very talkative. This brutish form is perhaps more fitting You are on the origin planet of those you call 'Elders.'"

"Are you an Elder?"

"Yes and no. I am many Elders. After our central star dimmed, we decided to preserve our greatest creation in the form of this construct. At this moment we are in a sphere two kilometers in diameter, moving at a constant speed away from the galactic center, in harmony with the positions of all other celestial bodies in the Milky Way. We are in orbit around our former home, which is now merely a cold rock in the interstellar medium. Our central stars belonged to the early suns of our galaxy, and according to all we know, we were the first and only intelligent species. No new ones came along later either, no matter how many probes we sent out to observe distant worlds. There were microorganisms and simple life everywhere, but no intelligent beings with which we could have interacted."

"So, you yourselves helped evolution along," James said, nodding slowly. "You created six solar systems yourselves."

"Yes, that was our masterpiece, I think." The construct looked pleased and rubbed its hands together, which was disconcerting since it still had no eyes, no lips, and no hair. It sat there like a mannequin come to life, which might have been creepy in a less weird setting. "From a certain point in time, we were able to simulate the exact creation of our system until we understood it perfectly, down to the smallest detail, at the nano level, as you say. Then we triggered this process six times at once because we had enough mass and energy to do so. Later, we sent the teleporters to see if it had worked and whether the same starting point led to the same result."

"Humans," Justus murmured. "You were humans like us."

"Oh, we still are. We're just not here anymore, because there's nothing here."

"Except you."

"Yes. I'm a coherent personality construct."

"An AI?"

"No. I am the digitized amalgamation of one hundred personalities who volunteered for the long watch. Before we exhausted all the energy of our central star, we ignited a new sun—a substitute sun, if you will. We encased it, too. Since it burns slower than our original sun, it will provide enough energy to keep the construct going until the end of time, many billions of years from now. There's not much going on in here, after all, except for this fine virtual environment."

"So, we're *trapped* in a program?" asked James.

"Trapped sounds so negative," the construct said. "Your personalities are in memory if that's what you mean. There's no room for bodies here, unfortunately, since the sphere consists only of a shell, energy, and a computer core. But don't worry, you're not dead."

"We have no more bodies." Meeks looked down at his body, his mouth hanging open, suddenly as white as a sheet. "Isn't that the definition of death?"

"I am still in communication with all the teleporters we left behind. So, it is easy for me to send you anywhere if that is your wish. Since the teleporters are working, you'll get healthy, fresh bodies exactly replicated according to your genetic information."

From the tangle of thoughts in his head, James tried to pick out individual questions he wanted most urgently to ask, but there were so many that he was barely able to formulate them. Mila beat him to it.

"You created us," she said, "six systems with six Earths and six civilizations. Why?"

"Isn't it always the same question that troubles us?"

"Where did we come from and why do we exist?"

The construct nodded. "Yes. The universe holds an incredible amount of mystery, all of which can be understood. Except for the origin. Yes, there was a big bang, and we know what it looked like, but there is always this curtain behind which we cannot look, which hides what was before time. The same is valid for the space into which the observable universe spreads. It arises only in the expansion itself. It is not as if there is a big emptiness that is filled by accelerated expansion. No, space exists only with the expansion of the space. What is there before that? Nothing, yes, but what is this nothing? Who created it?"

"You've never figured it out, have you?" James asked.

"No." The construct sounded almost sad. "But by creating six new worlds that followed the same blueprint we used to come into existence, we wanted to verify that this divine spark that allowed for the emergence of our conscious intelligence would also emerge in a real simulation. As it turns out, that is indeed the case."

"But it didn't bring you any closer to answering your question."

"No. We knew that a process from A to Z seems to happen the same way every time you take all factors into account—which was and will remain the greatest achievement of our species, if you ask us."

"But there were differences in the evolution of our species," Mila mused. "James told us about the evolution of the Al'Anter, which was very different from those of us on Earth."

"Yes," the construct admitted. "Minor coincidences kept

popping up that led to different developments. Tiny switch points that provided minimal bar deviations that naturally scaled up over time. In the end, six human civilizations emerged that possessed many commonalities and yet were fundamentally different."

"You received the data about your work from the Avatars?"

The construct turned its featureless face toward James and nodded. "Yes. We." It spread its arms. "The construct."

"What exactly are the Avatars?"

"They are artificial images of us; biomachines with some cybernetic components that were necessary to ensure their survival. They had their own consciousness and yet were equipped with clear programming to do their job: observe and report. Of course, we also had to rid them of some human shortcomings, such as the social interaction instinct, so they wouldn't become lonely and subject to psychological disorders. Thus, they are as human as they are inhuman. Nevertheless, their experience is close enough to ours to allow us to evaluate the transmitted data with all the senses at our disposal."

"How was the data transmitted? How did that work?"

"Ah, I know the game. I'll say 'something about quanta' now and then you'll respond 'aaah.' Let's just say that our kind has had many more millions of years for technological development, and a species that can create solar systems can also send data from A to B."

"Touché. So, you see everything they see, experience everything they experience?"

"Yes, with the appropriate time delay, of course."

"What delay?" James asked. "The teleporters worked without a time delay, didn't they?"

"That's because of the relative proximity between each

teleporter. There are merely thirty to ninety light years between them. From Al'Antis to the construct where we are now, it is one hundred forty thousand, far outside the habitable zone. That's why even the subspace transmission took fifteen years."

"Fifteen years?" they shouted at the same time, shocked and amazed.

"I'm afraid so."

"But..." Meeks stuttered in horror before James interrupted him. He didn't want to think about the implications, but at the same time, he needed to know more about the Elders before the chance was lost.

"Are your kind still around? You Elders, I mean?"

The construct shook its head. "No. We moved backward at some point after we reached the end of time and space. There were simply no more questions to ask, other than why, which could not be answered. We concluded that the universe is either the center of a singularity, the interior of a black hole, or a simulation. In any case, it is, by definition, impossible to escape from, to look beyond the event horizon, and we had to resign ourselves to that. Finally, only the question of the good life remained, and a large number of them decided that life itself was most worth living. At the end of our natural evolution, we had long since overcome death, if only apparently, because inevitably the universe itself will also end. Its energy is finite, and so everything is subject to the principle of birth and death. But how do we live in between? That was ultimately the question that became more important than anything else. We finally settled on a new world and did not take our technology with us. It had had its day, but it no longer aided us, at least not to live happily or come to terms with the fact that the only way to see behind the curtain was death itself, the great mystery that makes us all the same."

"You emigrated to a new planet?"

"Yes. To a place of peace and seclusion where no technology works. To make sure none can bite into that forbidden fruit, we simply stripped the tree of it," the construct explained. "It is a world where no high-voltage experiment will ever succeed, and an orbital ring with forty thousand pulse generators that creates a kind of EMP field ensures that."

"So, your descendants are like the Tokamaku?" Meeks asked, amazed.

"That's a good comparison. You don't know about any of this anymore; it's been millions of years since this process was initiated."

"Your advanced civilization is extinct then?"

"No!" The construct sounded almost indignant. "We have changed. Most of us would have said *evolved*. Even if you were president, you probably also enjoy retiring on a ranch with an orchard and lots of empty countryside all around."

"Why didn't you go along? A hundred personalities you say?" James looked at the construct curiously.

"Because we felt a responsibility to continue monitoring our creation and make sure that, if miracles did exist, the master teleporter, as you call it, could be accessed after all. We have a responsibility for what we have created. It's as simple as that. That's why we're going to stand guard here until the end of time."

"What about Nasaku? She sent a signal to an alien planet—from Earth," asked Mila.

"Yes, we received that information from the Avatar of Earth. The signal consisted of a complex malicious code that she sent to the Kazerun homeworld to destroy their civilization. A computer worm that should have infiltrated their systems throughout the home system by now."

"Revenge?"

"No," James answered for the construct and sighed. "She wanted to prevent a repeat of the Al'Antis disaster."

"So, it appears. We don't know why that Avatar, and in particular its decoupling, which should not have worked given its basic programming, developed such behavior. But we are not intervening."

"That's good. The Kazerun must be stopped."

"We don't believe that interfering with natural processes will change anything for the better. There are plenty of examples that confirm this."

"What are these objects that have been flying toward Earth from the direction of the Kazerun?"

"Their first, and so far, only interstellar fleet, which they sent off long ago after extracting Earth's coordinates from the Al'Anter archives. They are always looking for space to expand into and they fear competition in any form. That's why they will probably destroy you when their fleet arrives."

It took James a few moments to understand the implications of what the construct had said so casually.

"Excuse me? Destroy?"

"Yes." It raised a hand. "In the end, the timing is irrelevant. The journey always ends the same with the passing of all things living."

"When does it arrive? The fleet I mean?" Meeks asked, aghast.

"Twenty years from now."

"But if Nasaku's plan worked…"

"It will. Her malware was extremely sophisticated and

complex, far more sophisticated than anything the Kazerun could fight or even detect," the construct assured him.

"Will it destroy them?"

"The signal will arrive in their home system in seventeen years. According to our calculations, it will completely wipe out their civilization within four months by triggering the automatic firing of their weapons of mass destruction coupled with the subsequent shutdown of all electronic systems. A year after the fleet arrives, their warships will be all that's left of them."

"The planet where your descendants live: Where is it?" James asked.

"On the spiral arm of the Milky Way opposite yours," the construct replied. "Why do you ask?"

"Is there a teleport link there?"

"From here? Yes. Would you like to travel there?"

"Would you let us?"

"Of course. You are human beings, just as we are—or rather, *were*. We would have no right to refuse you. You should know, however, that life there is different from what you are used to on your planet. But you've gotten an idea of that from the Tokamaku. It is a simple, peaceful life."

"Would you let more of us go there, too?"

"What are you thinking?" Mila asked him.

"We have to get back to Earth and rescue as many as we can."

"Even if we get back and the teleporter is no longer underground, at least thirty years will have passed. Who knows what technologies they've found to fight the fleet," Meeks said. "We don't even know what it will look like there."

James shuddered at the sketchy memories of the Kazerun double agents who had replicated and taken the clones of the Al'Antic explorer expedition. He saw their irrepressible will to aggressively defend themselves against any imagined threat and their willingness to go to any extreme.

"We can't win this one, believe me."

"How would that even work? Only a maximum of six people can go through the teleporter at any one time. Which would be three hundred sixty per hour, eight thousand six hundred forty per day... In a year, you could evacuate something like three million people—and I don't even think we could do six a minute. Remember, the operation would have to run twenty-four hours a day, around the clock, and each group would have to be taken down the ramp while the next group was already coming in from below—and that's only if you could agree on criteria for selecting survivors and there were no riots." Meeks shook his head "Forget it."

"No," James said firmly. "We have to try."

4

James closed his eyes for a moment, moving his fingers carefully as if abrupt movement might burst the feeling of vitality in them like a soap bubble. Nothing had happened, except he had closed his eyes, and yet there was a vague fear that he had taken his last breath, his last look, his last thought.

Fifteen years, he thought and swallowed. He felt his esophagus contract and move saliva to his stomach—an abstract sensation so automatic that it seemed to have no meaning, and yet now it seemed extremely precious and significant. A proof of life. *And another fifteen years.*

He slowly opened his eyes and turned his head lazily to the right. He saw Mette on the neighboring seat, half sitting, half lying on the inclined seat. The circular arrangement of the inner seats prevented him from seeing the others, and he moved his gaze to the vacant outer seats and the honey-combed wall beyond. Mila was to his left, looking back at him and smiling. But the expression in her bright eyes was veiled, shadowed with the same concern that he felt.

Carefully, he got up from his seat and stretched the limbs

of his fresh clone body. It was still disconcerting to wake up in a brand-new, starkly naked form that looked exactly the same as it always had, except he knew it was an artificial copy that had not been born or grown like his original body, likely long dead by now. These hands had not done and made what he had done and made in his years of life. These eyes had not seen what he had seen, and the wrinkles in his face were the product of machine following an epigenetic blueprint, not the result of the injuries, sadness, or laughter of days gone by that had marked him. Everything was artificial and yet so familiar, as if nothing at all had changed. His "I" was still the same "I" that he had always been.

Only thirty years older, he thought and swallowed again. *No, thirty years later.*

Almost without thought, he stood, went to Mila, and hugged her tightly. The fact that they were both naked didn't even bother him anymore. He inhaled the smell of her hair and pressed her head against his chest.

"We're back," she murmured, pulling away from him. The others had stood as well and were hugging each other in turn, with relief.

"Hell, I have to confess I didn't think it would work," Meeks said.

"And I have to confess that part of me hoped it wouldn't work," Justus said, pursing his lips as he looked around the teleporter. There was nothing to indicate that they were actually on Earth. Nothing here was different from Al'Antis.

Except...

James paused and frowned.

"I know what you mean," he said to the German. He was also frightened by the prospect of seeing Earth thirty years in the future, where a great deal might be different, and which was about to be invaded by the Kazerun. Was anyone he had known still alive?

Joana? He swallowed.

"No cables. No cameras," Adrian stated what James had just noticed, and pointed around them. Indeed, the teleporter was conspicuously empty, just like the one on Al'Antis. Was it still buried under several dozen meters of concrete? What were they do if it was? Try knocking on the wall in Morse code and hope that someone had placed highly sensitive seismic sensors on the surface? But they wouldn't work anymore, not once the construct made the teleporter connection. The magnetic field that it generated would have destroyed any electronics on the surface.

Or have they managed to invent effective shielding? But not even the Al'Anters completely managed to do that.

"What if the construct sent us somewhere else?" Justus said. "We only know what it told us. How could we ever verify any of that?"

"I think we're about to find out," Adrian said tersely, gesturing to his right. James looked where he was pointing and saw the passageway had opened. A rectangle of pure, radiant light appeared where one of the walls had been a moment ago, dividing it in two with its glow.

It took less than two seconds for the first figures to appear, leaping through the light and then separating like a tide parting before an invisible obstacle, some taking the left side of the passage, others the right. They wore black full-body armor and carried short machine guns that looked like plastic toys.

James instinctively stepped back and raised his hands, bumping into his friends who were doing the same. All of them were now huddled close together, intimidated by the dark soldiers whose suits almost blended with the color of the teleporter wall.

"Identify yourself!" barked one of the men in a gruff voice amplified by an invisible microphone.

"James Hamilton," he said carefully. "Doctor Mila Shaparova, Doctor Mette Laudrup, Doctor Justus Falkenhagen, Doctor Adrian Smailov, and Doctor Vincent Meeks. We are members of the project—"

"Hands above your head, down on your knees!" a voice he couldn't match to any of the identical figures interrupted him. James swallowed, glanced at all the muzzles aimed at them, and reluctantly complied. He had rarely felt so helpless and naked, surrounded by weapons that could kill him with the twitch of a finger.

One by one, two men detached themselves from the semicircle of soldiers, bound their hands with cable ties, then pulled them to their feet, two at a time, and led them away. James was the first they dragged through the light.

He quickly found himself on a wide ramp in the middle of a gigantic cavern that looked like it had been cut from the rock. The walls were roughly hewn and littered with sensors that stood out like sparkling opals in the bright lights. Two guns were mounted at the base of the ramp and automatically followed his movements. About fifty meters away, a transparent panel the size of a movie theater screen was embedded in the rock wall, behind which he could somewhat make out men and women in black uniforms behind consoles.

He looked up at the ceiling and noticed several more autonomous guns that seemed to scrutinize his every move with their cold sensor eyes. Several spotlights illuminated the teleporter and the ramp.

So, they had found a way to make technical devices work

even near the machine. But how? Or had the scientists managed to stabilize the unstable magnetic field?

The floor was flat concrete and there were no visible openings like doors or windows in the walls. They had to be deep underground.

The men held him roughly by the arms and led him straight toward the panel, and just as he was wondering how they were ever going to get out of here, the concrete opened in front of them and descended with a hydraulic whir, forming a shallow, sloping ramp that led into an underground corridor.

"Things have obviously changed around here," he said, but none of the figures responded. Instead, they led him into the corridor, which was wide and high enough for ten people to walk side by side. There were arrows painted on the concrete walls pointing toward the teleporter, and cryptic numbers and sequences of numbers. He glanced over his shoulder and saw the others were close behind him, led by the other soldiers. He couldn't determine much from his quick glance, but they seemed as concerned and surprised by their treatment as he was.

After fifty meters, they turned left through an armored door into a much narrower hallway and then through another. After ten steps in the semi-darkness, one of the men opened a massive door and pushed him inside. One by one, Mila, Mette, Adrian, Justus, and Meeks, visibly enraged, followed. Meeks gave the two soldiers pushing him along an angry look.

"I'm still an American citizen, you fucking assholes!" he snarled, but it didn't impress the figures in their closed suits in the least. They turned on their heels and locked the door behind them.

James walked up to it and touched the cold metal as if he could melt it with his bare hands.

"Okay, what has just happened here?" he asked, turning and leaning his back against the door and looking at his friends.

"That went differently than expected, anyway," Adrian said. "But it could have been worse."

"Worse?" Justus asked.

"The teleporter could still have been embedded. Or the soldiers could have shot us as soon as we appeared. After all, we arrived unannounced. Possibly no one from the staff remembers us because no one from the original crew works here anymore," replied the cosmonaut. "A lot seems to have changed. Unless it's a completely different place."

"I think that's an understatement."

"It all went so fast," Mette said, visibly pale. "Before I knew what was happening, we're suddenly in a cell."

James looked around the cold room, which didn't even have a place to sit. It was only the walls, floor, and ceiling, where a single spotlight emitted white light that made them all look sickly and pale, and only added to their gloomy mood.

"Did they really just throw us into a cell?" Justus asked incredulously. "We're not their enemies."

"They don't know that, though," James said, trying to shore up his hope that their situation wasn't as bad as it could have been. "Maybe the teleporter hasn't been active for thirty years. Or it was active but had no incoming connection signal. Did you see the guns?"

"Mmm." Adrian crossed his arms. "And you don't install those if you're doing civilian research or don't expect any problems."

"That could also be because of Nasaku. That really scared some people."

"Rightly so."

"From their point of view, yes," he agreed with the Russian, taking a deep breath. "We should just stay quiet."

"What are we supposed to tell them when they question us?" Mette rubbed her hands uneasily. She looked like an intimidated child on the first day of school .

"The truth," he answered without hesitation. He was aware they might have been bugged—that thought reached him even through his excitement and dismay at their unexpected circumstances. He was simply used to always thinking about surveillance and never talking his way into trouble. When you made crooked deals for years with terrorists, warlords, and militiamen no one was supposed to know about, you acquired habits that became automatic. "We tell the truth because it's what they need to hear."

"The fleet—"

"That, too." He nodded and turned to Meeks. "Did you see those black suits?"

"I did."

"Do they look familiar to you in any way? You were a reservist in the National Guard, right?"

"Yes—and no, they don't look familiar. No insignia, no evidence of service arm or anything like that. Also, only the Navy uses black uniforms, and that's only as parade uniforms."

"Thirty years," Mila said, "that's a long time."

"They didn't change that much between 1990 and 2020," Meeks objected.

"It could just as easily be a different type of chemical protection suit that comes from another manufacturer or whatever."

"But those are usually white or yellow so it's easier to see colors should something spill on them," the engineer insisted.

"We have to remember that the Earth we left knew something was coming. Who knows how—or how fast—information like that might change everything?" James pointed his finger upward. "If they've found out about a fleet, then—my God, I don't have the vaguest idea what that information could have led to."

"I'm afraid we're about to find out." Adrian pointed to the door, which made a scraping sound before it swung open. Two soldiers entered, submachine guns drawn, and covered their prisoners. They instinctively raised their hands and backed a few steps until they were near the far wall. Two unarmed men came in, their faces hidden behind mirrored visors, and grabbed James by his cuffed hands.

"Hey!" Mila protested angrily, but he shook his head.

"It's all right. I'm sure this will all get cleared up soon."

Reluctantly, she took another step back, and the soldier who had been aiming the barrel of his gun at her did likewise. Again, James was struck by how odd the weapon looked. It was short, the shock pad almost as long as the weapon itself, and its stock seemed to be made of a clunky piece of plastic. The magazine gave off a bluish glow and had a rounded shape.

The men led him into the hallway, back to a larger corridor, where they pushed him to the right. Two soldiers remained outside the door to the cell.

"Where are we going?" he asked, an uneasy feeling in his stomach, but they didn't answer him. They were silent as they escorted him to another hallway where several figures in white suits milled around. They wore bracelets around their wrists and were making strange frantic gestures over them. They walked past them as if they were not even there. Two were waiting outside a door and seemed engrossed in conversation with each other, it was hard to tell since their visors were also mirrored. He might as well have been surrounded by robots. The thought made him shudder.

"Ah, finally," one of them said, sounding very human, even impatient.

The soldiers pushed him between the two white-clad figures into a room with a gurney, and after cutting his bonds, they pushed him roughly down onto it. As soon as his back touched the padding, they fastened him to it with cuffs on his wrists and ankles and left the room. Behind him was a ring with a wide rim. Robotic arms wrapped with white and gray plastic protruded from the walls and ended at several pedestals bearing various kinds of medical equipment. The sight made him break out in a sweat.

"Uh, guys?" he asked, tense, vigorously testing just how secure the restraints were for the first time. Unfortunately, the two soldiers had done an excellent job. "What's going on here?"

"Well, let's get it over with," said one of the two figures—a woman from the voice.

"Full spectrum, deep scan," the man said, his fingers literally flying over his wrist device.

"Could you talk to me?" James asked. "Please? What are you guys up to?"

Again, they ignored him as if he was not even there. The woman walked to the ring that looked like a very sleek CT scanner, flipped open a panel on the side, and made tapping motions on something James couldn't see because his head was tilted back. Her colleague looked at one of the robotic arms and pressed the index finger of his right hand to his wristband. The arm came to life. The ball joints began to rotate, and the long connectors performed multidirectional movements as if they were going through a test cycle. Then an attachment with numerous syringes approached his neck.

"Hey, wait a minute!" he protested, his voice shrill. He tugged at his restraints and arched his back, turned his head to the side, and yet the attachment followed his every move, smoothly and with extreme precision. "What are you people doing? I'm talking to you, aren't I? I can answer all your questions! Please, there's no need for this!"

The syringes came closer, and he broke out in a cold sweat everywhere at once.

"No, no, no! My name is James Hamilton, I live in New York at 22 Fifth Avenue A. My social security number is 234-99-3882. You... No!"

The first syringe penetrated his neck muscles just below the posterior arch of his jaw. There was a small, brief sting, and yet it felt like a severe act of abuse, a deep pain that made him furious. The helplessness he felt was as horrible as few things he had ever experienced. He was being tormented by those from whom he had hoped to gain protection—his compatriots and fellow Earthmen. Had they not spoken English to each other, he might have thought he had landed with the Kazerun. His struggling and rearing got him nowhere, except a second shot that was considerably more painful before the cold, unperturbed robotic arm retreated and settled against the wall like a menace of metal and plastic.

James warmed, as if hot syrup were spreading through his veins, and the cold, sweaty feeling was replaced by a dull calm that felt unnatural but at the same time seemed to constrain a part of him that wanted to scream and lash out. He was now a prisoner in his own body, unable to defend himself against the immobility of limbs that no longer obeyed him. He could only watch helplessly as the big ring slid toward him and engulfed his stretcher like a donut.

Again, he wanted to say something, to address the two doctors—or whatever they were—to provoke a human reaction that would show him he was dealing with sentient beings capable of empathy and not make him feel like some inconsequential object. Yet they continued to ignore him, walked around him as if he were an inanimate piece of flesh, busy with their bracelets while the ring began to hum and crack softly. He couldn't even move his lips anymore. The injections had completely paralyzed him. All he could do was watch as blood was not-so-gently drawn from him, and the ring traveled along his body several times until it finally finished its job and returned to the wall.

"He's ready for questioning," the man finally said. They removed medical instruments and attached new ones to the robotic arm.

The two soldiers—they might have been the ones who had brought him, but he couldn't tell because they all looked alike—came in and unstrapped him. Only now did James realize that he could move his fingers, but that didn't do him much good as the men handled like an inanimate object. They dragged him to his feet and half carried him out the door into the hallway. They had come from the left, but they turned to the right.

"Hey," he slurred weakly. "W-w-we c-came f-f-from over th-there."

They stubbornly continued to ignore him and carried him to another part of what appeared to be an underground wing, into a large room, and sat him on a lone chair under a bright spotlight that bathed him and a small circular area around him in white light. Across from him was a semicircular table behind which sat three men and three women in black suits and shirts. Thin tablets were lined up neatly in front of them, and they seemed to be paying no attention to him. He blinked a few times, and he was able to make out two extended gun turrets on the dark ceiling, their muzzles pointed at him.

Where in the hell am I?

5

"Your name is James Hamilton?" asked the woman who shared the center of the massive table with a balding man. Her stern, humorless expression only reinforced the impression of a tribunal he had felt since being led here. His wrists were cuffed to the chair behind his back and his feet to the chair legs so he could barely move. Not that he would have wanted to move at the sight of the two small guns.

"Yes," he answered quickly when she gave him an impatient look.

"Your social security number was 234-99-3882?"

James frowned at how oddly she emphasized the words "social security number," as if it were a very awkward, foreign term. She had also said *was*. Didn't his number exist anymore? That would mean he had been declared dead and no longer existed in the bureaucratic system. But should that really surprise him, after thirty years? Perhaps he finally had to admit to himself that much time had indeed passed. Part of him had not been able—or willing—to comprehend that such a thing could be real or was even possible, that it must have been a misunderstanding or an illusion, a dream. For him, a little more than half a year had passed, no more.

"That's... right," he confirmed. "Is there something wrong with that?"

No one answered as he looked up at them and blinked. They looked like unreal shadows across the five foot distance that separated them. Something shimmered in front of them, and the closer he looked, the more certain he was that they were separated by a gauzy, transparent wall.

"You said you were a resident of New York State, residing at 22 Fifth Avenue, New York City?" the man next to her asked.

"Yes, that's correct, too. Listen, I have rights! We're still in the United States, aren't we? You certainly don't speak with a Russian or European accent! Am I charged with a crime? If so, I'd like to talk to a lawyer! Make a phone call! You would have to read me my rights. How about that?"

Again, none of the six men and women seemed to hear what he was saying. Their reactions ranged from a raised eyebrow, which could have been mere coincidence, to complete disregard.

"Give us your resume from grade school through high school, then the last five years of your professional life before your alleged first use of the teleporter. Then fill in the gap between," the woman with the stern look said, and all eyes turned to him. James felt like a rabbit being stared at by six relentless birds of prey, ready to pounce any time the moment was right for them.

"Excuse me?" he asked, confused.

"Are you ceasing your cooperation?" the woman replied so impassively that he felt ice cold, even though he was freezing anyway. He was still naked, and there was nothing in this concrete room that radiated even a hint of warmth—certainly not the birds of prey in front of him. Something in her voice, perhaps it was indifference, startled him. Her question sounded like an unspoken threat, made more dangerous by its lack of emotion. What if "ceasing his cooperation" meant the guns would rip him to shreds? After everything he had experienced here so far, it would not surprise him in the least.

"No," he finally said, swallowing hard. "I'll cooperate."

"Then follow our instructions: Give us your resume from grade school through high school, then the last five years of your professional life before your alleged first use of the teleporter. After that, fill in the gap in between."

He took a moment to inhale, which he used to squeeze his legs together so he could somewhat hide his nakedness, he began talking. Stumblingly at first, but eventually he settled into his narrative. He told them about his childhood and his school days when he often got in trouble with the teachers for trying to distinguish himself as the class clown. He spoke openly about his graduation, which he had achieved with very good grades by clever cheating and even blackmailing one of his teachers. He left out no detail, nor did he hide anything, not his grief when he finally talked about Joana, and not about his work as a ransom negotiator for the State Department. They did not interrupt him, merely followed his recitation with emotionless expressions and an occasional gesture over their bracelets.

"Now tell us what happened when you unlawfully used the teleporter," the bald man prompted. James wondered what the other four people were here for. Aside from the one woman, they had not said a word.

"You mean the day the project was ended?"

"Yes."

James collected himself, then explained how they had arrived in the Death Zone on Prime, that Prime was Al'Antis, and how he and the team had found the wrecked spaceship with the weapons and the skeletons in their armor. He told of their confrontation with the monster, which had apparently survived their first encounter unharmed but had not killed them because they had not been Kazerun. He told of the gap in the wall, their contact with the Tokamaku and their tribe, their life there, and the things they had learned —until a door opened behind him and he was interrupted.

Everyone opposite him looked up as if on command and gazed at something behind him, then they all stood. Since he could barely turn his head, the sedative was still too strong, all he could do was wait.

"What did the medical tests show? DNA and scan results?" asked a commanding voice with the harshness of a grater. A figure in a black uniform walked past him. The man was tall and lean, and his silver hair was cropped short.

"Matches the database," replied the woman, who had stood, just like her colleagues, and saluted stiffly. "No implanted foreign bodies, no evidence of infectious pathogens. Polygraph negative."

"Good. Give us the room," the new arrival ordered and waited until, after a brief hesitation, the "tribunal" filed out from behind the desk and walked past James. The old man waved at two hooded soldiers, who brought in a simple aluminum chair and placed in front of James. The man sat and examined him closely. His eyes were bright and cool, but his gaze was alert and fiery. A trimmed full beard hid much of his face, but the skin above it was old and weathered.

"Norton?" James asked incredulously.

"How did we meet?"

He screwed up his face, surprised by the question, but quickly replied, "You ruined my attempt to explain to my ex-fiancée why I cheated on my job and your helicopter tossed a million dollars through the air of that luxury dining room when your men took me away like a felon. I'll never forget the look on Joana's face. Hated you for it."

"It's really you, isn't it?" Norton rubbed his mouth and shook his head. "James Hamilton. Missing for thirty years, presumed dead for ten. You still look the same as you did then."

James was about to say something, but then he looked around uneasily. The walls seemed to have ears here.

"It's okay," the old man assured him.

"Back when you had our backs so we could go to Al'Antis before the door slammed shut forever, Major."

"A decision that almost cost me my job." Norton pursed his lips, and although he no longer looked like a spry Golden Ager, more like a wiry grandfather fit for his age, his facial expressions were still exactly the same and extremely familiar. The officer tapped the four stars on his epaulets. "And it's general, now, not major."

"Congratulations."

"Don't be too relieved to see me. Times have changed since you left Earth."

"I've noticed," James replied sullenly. "We haven't even been given clothes. Nobody would talk to us, and then they did all these experiments on me. Aren't there any civil rights anymore?"

"No," Norton confirmed, to his horror. "At least not in that form. But you were classified as a potential enemy combatant before we could prove your identity and rule you out as a threat. I'm sure you understand why after the original failure of the project."

"You mean Nasaku."

"Yes. I've listened to your full report, and it seems to me that I can finally put aside the great doubt of my life and career."

"What kind of doubt?"

"Whether I made the right decision when I let you go." Norton straightened his midnight-black uniform. "We couldn't find any evidence you were lying when you told the supervisors what happened on Prime..."

"Al'Antis," James corrected him without thinking.

"Whatever—what happened on Al'Antis. What the Avatar showed you. It sounds too fantastic to even be classified as fact. But whatever happened there, *you* believe it."

"I'm telling you *it is* true."

"Do you have any proof of that?"

"No, the Avatar only showed it to me."

"And that's why you believe it without reservation? Because a supposed immortal being who appeared to you as a hologram and networked you to an alien computer system said so?" Norton raised a brow and shook his head.

"When you put it that way, it does sound crazy," James sighed dejectedly.

"You have to separate what you want to believe from what you *can* believe."

James wanted to say something that would assure the officer that none of it was imagined and that the Avatar was right; after all, James had experienced everything the Avatar had experienced. But how could he be sure? He believed he knew it for fact, but his brain had been connected to an alien computer interface, so what was there to provide any certainty about what was real and what was implanted? Was he merely the victim of clever manipulation?

No, he thought, determined. *I won't accept that.*

"I don't know how it is that you haven't aged a day since we last saw each other," Norton finally said, rubbing his beard thoughtfully. "But until just before we met, I also never believed that it might be possible to travel to alien worlds in an alien machine."

"I understand that it's hard to grasp. It's just as disturbing to us, believe me." James looked straight into the officer's eyes. "What about my friends? Are they being tortured somewhere right now?"

"No." There was a hint of disapproval in the general's voice. "The soldiers in this facility are very well trained and follow clear rules. They are prohibited from any verbal interaction with potential enemies until they receive clearance. They could be among the invaders—the Kazerun, as you called them in your verbal report. Any single contact could lead to disaster, and only under these strict conditions was it even possible to reuse the teleporter as a strategic tool."

"You said I was declared dead ten years ago. Does that date have anything to do with the fact that life support for my body was terminated at that time?"

"No. Your body didn't make it back to the infirmary, I'm afraid." Norton's wrinkled face was dismayed.

James felt as if the ceiling would fall on his head and crush him under its weight. So, he no longer existed. His original self, the body that his father and mother had conceived, the body his mother had carried and birthed, that had grown up slowly, naturally with all the good experiences and the painful ones. It had probably decomposed to nothing more than bones if it hadn't been cremated.

"I know this is difficult," the general continued, "but don't think about it now. There are more important things you need to know."

"And for *you*, I gather," James growled, angrier than he intended.

"Yes. Earth is not the one you left. We are facing an invasion that will begin in thirteen months. We have known about it for thirty years, now. For twenty-five years we've known with absolute certainty that it was not an asteroid swarm, but alien spacecraft on a direct course for Earth. This realization, which could not be contained or even controlled internationally, has changed every aspect of people's lives, and by that I mean *everyone*." Norton took a deep breath, in and out, and leaned back in his chair without losing any of the tension that lent him the air of natural authority that was always intimidating to James.

"When did you start using the teleporter again? Ten years ago, I would guess. When you declared us dead, you did so because the teleporter was active but there was no sign of us."

"That's right. The Military Council has voted to seek alternative solutions for defending near-Earth space and has also reopened exploration of Prime—under strict conditions. No one has returned from there, so Prime has been deemed unsafe and no one else has been sent through. With the help of some breakthroughs in nuclear fusion, we managed to raise the energy level of the teleporter enough to test the other connections. Two were apparently uninhabited, and on two others the teleporters could not be exited, so we assume that, like us, they were hidden underground and, therefore, there was no way to explore those planets."

"What about the uninhabited ones?"

"We've been deporting about forty thousand colonists there every week—for nine years now. Nearly twenty million people have already left Earth."

"Without equipment?" James asked, incredulous. "How are they going to establish a colony there?"

"They received brief training beforehand, and we were able to send some smaller tools like knives and lighters by implanting them in skin bags and similar procedures," Norton explained without particular interest.

"Wait a minute, you just said *deporting*. What do you mean by that? Aren't they going voluntarily?"

"No. Everyone who is a delinquent gets a deportation notice, and most of them are deserters who are avoiding conscription."

"What kind of conscription?"

"There is general conscription for men and women over the age of sixteen. I told you, things have changed. We're facing a massive threat, and the world community has had to find answers to what's coming." Norton's eyes twinkled. "You don't have the marble anymore, do you?"

"What?" James asked, irritated by the sudden change of subject. He was still busy trying to sort out what Norton had told him.

"That zero-D storage device," the officer repeated. "Where all the Avatar's data was supposedly stored."

"No. It's on Al'Antis in the control room of the experimental teleporter. We didn't have time to take it with us. Honestly, I didn't even think about it in that moment; every second counted."

"I understand." Norton nodded as if making a mental note. "Then we need to find the local Avatar."

"What do you mean by that?"

"If what you've reported is true—and so far we have no reason to believe you're lying—and each of the six planets has its own Avatar, immortal and endowed with a wealth of knowledge second to none, then we absolutely must track down ours to increase our chance of prevailing in battle. That being could be invaluable to us."

"But they do not interfere and are not biased. They are uninvolved observers, travelers in time."

"The one on Prime was different," objected the general.

"Sure, but—"

Norton leaned forward until only half an arm's length separated them. "Listen, Mr. Hamilton, this project I'm running here is held in high esteem by the Military Council because it's not only our Plan B, but it also lets us get rid of colonists who are unwilling to make any useful contribution and are just costing us money here. That's why I enjoy a certain degree of freedom in my means and methods. You may not know it, but those are two things that are anything but a given these days.

"I occupy this post because I'm willing to look in a different direction than the one I'm pointed in. Your story sounds crazy, but it coincides quite closely with what your colleagues are saying in their interrogations right now, so I'll give you the benefit of the doubt. We can't ignore anything, and if there's an omnipotent being living among us who knows things that could save our planet, we will find it. No one who looks like a human and doesn't die, doesn't even age, escapes the system these days."

"It hasn't been found yet," James said.

"No, but we haven't searched for it either. Imagine you were out for a walk and saw a bird flying backward. What would you think when you retunred home?" the general asked.

"I would think that I had merely imagined it, or that it was an optical illusion because I know birds cannot fly backward."

"Exactly. Your brain processes everything so it fits into

the framework of what is expected, makes it fit an established pattern. A person who doesn't age would probably change his residence frequently, and if someone does recognize him, he would probably say it was a case of mistaken identity, that he probably looked like someone else, and in their doubt others would believe it because they *want* to believe it."

"You'll never be able to find him. He has billions of years of experience in not being recognized."

"That may be true, Mr. Hamilton." Norton's face split into a winning smile. "But if what you've told us is true, then *you* have that experience, too. Who better to find someone who doesn't want to be found than someone who's been in their shoes? I won't let this strategic advantage pass unused. You're going to help me track it down, and then we'll see what information we can get out of your *Avatar* to save Earth from the invaders."

6

"He said *that*?" Meeks combed his fingers through hair he hadn't had in a long time.

James nodded gravely. "Yes."

"So now we're supposed to play sleuth for him. Why does that thought make me feel like a criminal? Like one of the bad guys?"

"Because it is a crime," Mila said somberly. "The Avatars don't interfere, after all, and there's a reason they don't want to be found. That's the way it is, isn't it? I don't even want to imagine what these people will do to one of them if they get their hands on it."

"Oh, yes," Mette agreed, snorting in contempt. "After all, they've already treated us like cattle without civil rights, and they didn't even expect us to give them any information on how to save Earth."

James puffed out his cheeks and laid his head back to take a short break from the conversation.

Their situation had visibly improved. After being examined and questioned by the extremely strict military personnel, they had finally been given underwear and gray, one-piece jumpsuits with a strange logo—a black-and-white Earth surrounded by a blue and red band. Once dressed, and thus restored to at least a semblance of dignity, they were ordered to wait in a lounge until the "next steps" were ready to be taken—whatever that meant.

The "lounge" was, in fact, more like an airport check-in hall. The ceiling was low, like everything else in the facility, but wide and so long that the lights at the far end twinkled like distant stars. Four rows of unadorned aluminum seats stretched side by side from the double entry doors to the room's far end. They sat and squatted here now, fenced off by a barrier of barbed-wire mesh and two security gates.

Everything about this brutalist structure—the confinement, the extremely rustic nature of the seating, and the lack of any color—was oppressively spartan. In the old facility, the missile silo at Francis E. Warren Air Force Base, there had been ornamental plants in every room, although he had never checked to see if they were even real. The absence of sunlight probably made it unlikely, but they had been an indication that it was a place where people lived and worked, a place where someone had considered how people would feel there. This chamber was the exact opposite, evidenced by the disinterest that accompanied its construction: functional, cold, and cramped.

Hopefully, this isn't a taste of what the earth has become, he thought, massaging his throbbing temples with his fingers.

Justus joined in the conversation that, distracted by his thoughts, James had momentarily lost track of. "I hate to spoil the general negative mood, but what if he's right."

"What are you saying?" Mila asked, upset.

"Let's put ourselves in Norton's shoes: A team of scientists disappears through the teleporter because you helped them do it, because you hope their trust in Nasaku is justified. Then you don't see them again for thirty years. When they show up out of nowhere with a completely insane story, you don't immediately reject it because, having already confronted a sophisticated alien machine and gone on a little side trip of your own to an alien hell planet, you've already looked the impossible in the face. Instead, you accept that they haven't aged a day, which alone says that you shouldn't dismiss anything out of hand just because it sounds insane. You take heed when they tell you about an immortal being who is not bound by time and has been watching Earth evolve for billions of years. To me, that would sound like an opportunity, an ace up my sleeve I didn't know about before, something that could possibly snatch victory from the jaws of defeat."

James gave Justus a long look, which the German returned more firmly than usual. Was there something else behind the astrophysicist's statement? A second message that was perhaps intended to address the open secret they were all aware of: that they were being bugged. Ranting about Norton and how he had treated them would do them no good, no matter what conclusions they might come to.

"He's got a point," James finally said, looking around the room. Meeks and Adrian squatted in front of him, Mila, Mette, and Justus were sitting on the floor, forming a rough circle. They all looked tired and worn, though their faces looked fresh, without dark circles or deep wrinkles. The teleporter had spit them out healthy and at their best, so it was the disappointment and fear in their eyes rather than their general appearance that told him how his friends were doing. After all, he sensed the same doubts in himself that he thought he saw in them. He had hoped that returning to Earth would provide them with a feeling of security, a sense of relief at no longer being cut off from home. Instead, he felt alien and mistreated in ways he had not been on Al'Antis. It was as if he had been hoping for a hug from his parents and had instead received a slap on the wrist and been banished to his bedroom. And yet Justus's argument possessed an undeniable logic. From the general's point of view, his request to try to find the Avatar made sense. After all, it was his job to protect the United States and Earth.

"It's just..." Meeks began to protest but James gently interrupted him.

"I think it's because the threat is not yet clear to us. We know a Kazerun fleet is heading for Earth, but that's purely abstract knowledge given to us by others. We haven't seen it with our own eyes and can't understand it until we've confronted it ourselves. If someone told you that a hurricane was coming in four weeks, you wouldn't panic. But if it was coming tomorrow, and you could see the dark clouds and cyclones on the horizon, you would be scared shitless and do everything you could to take precautions and protect yourself . Every board and nail you found could be the difference between a damaged house and one that was completely destroyed."

"Very encouraging," Meeks grumbled darkly, his eyebrows drawn together. "I don't like how that sounds at all, but damn, you're probably right."

The side door through which they had been brought in opened and two soldiers with angular faces and stony expressions entered. Norton came in behind them, and with a wave, commanded the soldiers to stop. He passed alone through one of the security gates and nodded briefly to them. It was strange for James to see the old officer like this. Partly because of everything they had been through together and partly because of the stark difference in age between the Norton he remembered and the Norton who now stood before him. He would never forget how he had carried the man's shattered body on his back to the Al'Antis teleporter, even though he had barely been able to keep himself on his feet. Nothing brought people closer together than sharing a look at death's ugly, grinning face. And yet there remained a distance between them that had never fully diminished—a distance that now seemed greater than ever, though there was also something artificial about it.

"I hope your clothing is satisfactory. It's temporary, but I'm afraid you'll all have to make do with it until all this is over," said Norton.

"Until what is over, exactly?" Adrian asked. "And has the Russian ambassador been informed?"

"Of course, right after your return."

The answer seemed to surprise the cosmonaut. James barely noticed the twitch around the corners of his friend's mouth that occurred on the rare occasions when he was rattled and wanted to hide it. Most people would have been fooled, but not him. Not only was it his job to pay attention to every nuance and read others, but he was also intimately familiar with his friends' every idiosyncrasy after the long time spent with the Tokamaku.

The Russians know about it and haven't intervened? Why hadn't Adrian and Mila been handed over immediately? Once again he got an uneasy feeling in his stomach that was growing into a dense knot of questions and grim fears.

"As soon as your hearings are over, I'm sure we can begin your mission," Norton said, nodding.

"Hearings?" James asked. "Haven't we already been through those?"

"Sorry. I'm afraid those were just the security checks that were necessary to let you out and get you in front of the committees."

"What committees?"

"You'll see. Now, if you'll follow me, please?" Norton extended an arm toward the security gate that suddenly looked very threatening.

"Are we under arrest or something?" Meeks asked cautiously.

The general looked serious as he eyed the engineer for a moment, then he smiled tightly and shook his head.

"No."

Flanked by the soldiers, who took positions ahead and behind them, their weapons holstered, they walked down a long hallway that eventually ended in a security door, which Norton unlocked by placing his palm on a scanner under the corresponding control panel. Behind the door, the confinement that had felt so oppressive since their return suddenly ended. A gigantic ramp, wide as a soccer field and at least as long, opened before them. It sloped steeply upward and ended in a rectangle of dim daylight. The rough concrete floor leading toward the light was covered with countless brown splotches of color. They broke through the drab gray and only upon closer inspection did James realize that they were dirty footprints, all pointing the direction they were going. On either side of that concrete monstrosity, which made him feel very small and insignificant, was a freight elevator with a simple platform of yellow steel tubing and a control panel on top.

Norton and the soldiers led them to the elevator on the right and waited until everyone had boarded before one of the men pushed some buttons. A crack and hiss issued from somewhere behind the wall and the platform began moving upward.

No one said anything as they approached the daylight. On the surface, they found themselves in the center of a huge field surrounded by high walls and barbed wire. Towers, mounted with searchlights, jutted upward at regular intervals and were silhouetted against the horizon. A sunny day was dawning, though it was still too early to provide any warmth. Behind them, where the ramp opened like the mouth of an oversized whale shark, was a wide three-story building with barred windows. In front of it were parked black Humvees adorned with the US flag as well as the logo of the black-and-white Earth with the blue and red ribbon. The entire area in front of the entrance to the underground teleporter complex was a single, vast field of mud and sludge that reminded James uncomfortably of the Death Zone on Al'Antis. There was not merely at spiky wall on which soldiers patrolled, but also a wide gate half a mile away.

He thought it had been opened, but before he could get a closer look, two powerful Navy helicopters with twin rotors thundered over their heads. Norton and his men were the only ones who didn't flinch in surprise. The machines traversed long circles and returned, losing altitude and landing in the mud fifty yards away. Drops of the whipped-up muck flew into James's face, but he didn't think to wipe them away.

The side doors flew open and two heavily armored figures, clad with full-face helmets and carrying angled assault rifles, leaped out. Their black boots left symmetrical fountains of mud in their wake. The rotors reduced their speed, and some of the noise abated. Norton began to move. James noticed that his neatly pressed trousers were tucked into his jump boots, while James and the others immediately got their trouser legs muddy as they followed him like a small herd of frightened sheep. The soldiers saluted sharply as the general approached and then divided them into two groups. James joined Norton in the rear helicopter, while the others were sent ahead in the first one.

"Don't worry," Norton bellowed over the roar of the rotors and the low hum of the engines as he lowered himself onto one of the six bucket seats and gestured for him to take the one next to his. "We're all flying to the same destination."

James swallowed hard but nodded and grabbed one of the soundproof headsets while the general took another from his headrest. All at once, the deafening noise ceased, replaced with some background noise that merely took some getting used to.

"I wanted to take advantage of the flight to have an undisturbed conversation with you," Norton said over the radio, sounding clear now except for a static crackle that followed each of his consonants. A message resonated in that simple sentence. James understood immediately, but he wasn't sure *what* he understood.

Does he mean he doesn't want the others to hear? Or those who might have been listening to us all along? If it's not just my paranoia and we are constantly bugged, then the confines of a helicopter cabin are certainly easier to control than a top-secret military facility, he thought.

It occurred to him that, if he were right, the implications did not make him feel particularly optimistic. If Norton had the pilots and the two soldiers accompanying them in his pocket and they had deactivated all the listening devices—if they existed—he would not have had to separate the team; there were enough seats in the helicopter. Which meant that each member of his team was subject to a personal listening device and Norton was unable to counter them all.

"I understand," he replied curtly.

The general eyed him appraisingly before waving to the

pilots through the open cockpit hatch. The helicopter lifted unsteadily from the ground.

Through the window, James watched as they rapidly spiraled into the air as if they were being pulled up on an invisible rope. The area below them was roughly circular and was located on a mesa in the middle of nowhere—a common sight in the West. Mountains loomed in the distance like indistinct shadows.

The machine headed east, and the large gate he had seen from the ramp came into view. Thousands upon thousands of people thronged together on an asphalt road that stretched into the distance, straight as an arrow. The people were surrounded by dark forms that stood on more than two legs and were clearly taller than the waiting figures. From time to time, he saw moving dots that could have been soldiers, but the helicopter was already too high for him to tell for sure.

"My God, what's going on?" he thought aloud. Norton's response reminded him that he had a headset on.

"The next wave of colonists. The gates open every day at six in the morning once the last trains have arrived."

Along the horizon to the north, James saw several rail cars lined up like a string of pearls. People were still streaming from them to join the waiting crowd. From that height, they seemed to move like some liquid forced through a narrow funnel.

"Every day?"

"Every day. Forty thousand. We need twenty-three hours to get them all through," Norton explained heavily.

"That looks like a lot of security personnel."

"A purely precautionary measure. The colonists behave, for the most part. The riot bots are deployed to protect them from themselves. The whole area is mined and the bots are there to make sure no one is blown sky-high over something as trivial as impatience."

"I see," James lied. "I would have expected it to be a privilege to be evacuated."

"You shouldn't underestimate how attached people are to their belongings—rich people in particular." Norton paused. "If you held a powerful office, or owned multiple properties, cars, prestige, expensive watches, were surrounded by pretty women—how would you feel about the prospect of starting over, naked and without any possessions on an alien planet?"

James's face twisted in displeasure.

"Exactly, they would rather put their hopes and money into defending what they wish to preserve at all costs."

"Do these people have reason to hope, then?" he asked. The waiting crowd was already disappearing from his field of vision, which was limited to an egg-shaped, double-glassed window.

"That's where the experts disagree," Norton said.

"And you?"

"We've known about the threat for thirty years, and I think we've made a lot of right decisions to prepare for it. Even with that much advance notice, it's not possible for us to reach the technological level of a civilization capable of building interstellar spacecraft, but physics is still physics, I've been told, and proper preparation can work to our advantage."

"You said 'a lot of' right decisions," James echoed. "Do you have any hope yourself?"

"That's not my job," Norton replied, unapologetic. "My job is to protect this nation and our planet as best I can. What the Military Council decides, unfortunately, is beyond my power."

He is unhappy with the decisions taken by this Military Council that he always talks about. But why?

"You're not a member?"

"No. Two years ago, I was supposed to be promoted the Military Council, but I declined."

"Why?"

Norton waved dismissively. "It's complicated. The Council is not what you could consider a legitimate successor to the US Senate or any other government body."

"Doesn't sound like it either. Let me guess: a military coup occurred shortly after it became public knowledge about what was approaching Earth." James said, looking somber.

"Well, it took two years for the Joint Chiefs of Staff to realize that the endless negotiations and debates were not leading to any decisive action. However, all the scientists and military leaders agreed that something had to be done immediately and that there was no more time for politics."

"So, they took over. How did it go down? Did they march into the Capital and the White House and arrest everyone?" Pure anger rose within him.

"Something like that. But that's not important. Since then, the Military Council has responded, and our allies have followed a similar path. The efforts we've made since then—the complete conversion of our industry to a military-planned, long-term transformation of our infrastructure and the training of millions of men and women who were suddenly subject to conscription—were unprecedented, and still are." Again, Norton paused, and James sensed that something he was not allowed—or willing—to express was troubling the man. "There's a price to pay, of course, and everyone has to ask themselves how much they're willing to pay."

Is he criticizing the Military Council?

The general turned to him and looked at him seriously before continuing.

"I want you to find the Avatar for me," he said seriously. "I'm not hoping for a magic bullet, but a way out. Some indication as to how we can do better without giving up on ourselves and everything we've been making these compromises to preserve. We accept them to protect our way of life, and as a result we have left our principles behind. There has to be another way."

7

Norton was silent for quite a while, probably concerned that he had said too much and was chiding himself to keep his mouth shut. James didn't believe the general was one of those people who often questioned what they did—he considered him far too focused for that. Yet James was also very aware that the general had taken a big risk expressing his concerns to him. Although he had not stated them directly, they were clear enough that his message resonated with James.

And so, he brooded as he watched the ever-changing landscape of green valleys and rolling hills and mountains flash past. At their low altitude, he was able to see individual towns and an interstate highway whose light gray asphalt resembled a barrier dividing the country like a ruler. What astonished him was the marked lack of passenger cars. Most of the vehicles moving leisurely along the east-west road were trucks, and most of the rest were military vehicles.

As soon as they reached the Appalachian Mountains, the traffic increased and flowed into a star-shaped structure near one of the peaks, their destination. Unless he was completely wrong, they were approaching Backbone Mountain, the highest point of the Appalachians in Maryland. The dense forest covered the peak, so even at over a thousand feet high it was hardly visible, especially since it was part of a long ridge and formed a cone at only one point. He had often hiked there with Joana.

Several asphalt roads that had not existed thirty years ago now led to the summit and were crowded with trucks and military convoys winding their way to the top.

As their helicopter raced over the highest point, James saw several massive concrete domes that he could only locate by narrowing his eyes and because the traffic betrayed their location. The trucks disappeared into the mountain below the facility as if swallowed.

"What is that?" he asked into his headset.

"The Washington PDC," Norton replied curtly.

"PDC?"

"Planetary Defense Center. We have four of them. This one is the largest and most advanced. There are also the Arkansas, Colorado, and California PDCs."

"And what exactly is that?"

"Heavy defense facilities with several dozen meters of protection constructed of reinforced concrete and carbin alloys. Each PDC has twelve latest-generation railguns and a large arsenal of hypersonic missiles."

"How many are there?" James craned his neck around until it hurt to keep his eyes on the mighty domes. Their camouflage paint kept trying to escape his gaze like snakes retreating into the undergrowth.

"Canada has one in Ontario, China has five, Russia has one, and Europe has five spread across the Pyrenees, the Alps, and the Carpathians. Then there's the ASEAN PDC in

Laos, the Hermon in Israel, and the ANZAC in the Blue Mountains in Australia."

"So, they're all in mountainous regions."

"Yes," Norton confirmed. "They are really elaborate facilities with a dense network of tunnels and bunkers dug deep into the mountains. Each one has its own dedicated fusion power plant and can provide power for fifty thousand soldiers for over ten years."

"That must have been pretty expensive."

"Four hundred billion per PDC."

James almost choked. "Four hundred? How is that even possible?"

"We're looking at the annihilation of our species, so many things became possible." The general's expression darkened, and he looked like he to want to say more before his features smoothed out again.

"Your list didn't include South America or Africa. And what about the Arabs?"

"They didn't build any." Again, it was obvious something was bothering Norton but he clearly didn't want to talk about the topic any further, so James didn't to press him. He had to proceed cautiously in this new situation.

"So, there are planetary defense centers spread all over Earth. That sounds like a global concept."

"It is. The UN has been coordinating closely to come up with the most general defense doctrine possible. We don't know exactly what the enemy fleet will do when it gets to us, so it's critical there is solidarity. If China cannot defend itself, then enemy units might land there and cause damage with unknown technologies that we don't even know about yet. Therefore, the current doctrine provides for a defense belt around the planet that focuses primarily on intercepting

UFOs. The PDCs and their underlying technology and logistics are identical in each country. They were developed jointly, as were the corresponding key technologies, without which they would not have been conceivable in their current form. The Russians have disclosed their research on hypersonic weapons and the Chinese their advances in autonomous robotic systems for life support. We have made our railguns technology available, which has continued to evolve since the prototypes were developed in 2018, and the Europeans have shared nuclear fusion from ITER in Cadarache. By focusing each country's economic power on research and armaments, and by sharing instantly across national borders, we have not only been able to provide technological balance to each participating country, we have also massively accelerated each process through knowledge transfer. The last time there was such a rate of progress was during World War II."

"That's amazing," James said. "I didn't think that was even possible since we were on the verge of a cold war with the Chinese before all this, and on the verge of a hot one with Russia."

"This threat concerns all of us, and everyone involved seems to have understood that."

Like the Kazerun, who always band together when they have a common enemy before lashing out at each other again because it's their aggressive nature, James thought, trying to shoo the thought away. They weren't like the people of LP-3445; they were better. After all, on Earth, they understood that war was a bad thing, and since the end of World War II there had never been such a long period of peace, so little hunger, and so few deaths from war and displacement. That was something worth considering.

"I'm not an expert on the military," James said finally, as their helicopter reduced altitude and headed toward Washington, DC, which stood out from the green landscape at the edge of his sight as a gray white mass, like underbrush infested with fungus, "Still I wonder if it's wise to spread all your defense capabilities across a dozen centers worldwide. What if the Kazerun use weapons from orbit that pulverize all the PDCs?"

"That's very unlikely," Norton said. "Our scientists have run many simulations and calculated the energy levels that would be required to destroy the upper armor of a PDC with just one hit. I don't know the numbers off the top of my head, but it was on an order of magnitude that our imaginations can't handle. Nevertheless, my colleagues on the Military Council made similar arguments, and so we and some of our allies went for a dual strategy: Defense on land with the PDCs and mobile defense on water with the Navy. By now, most frigates and destroyers are equipped with at least the latest generation of railguns that can also engage targets in orbit. This gives us the ability to react quickly to surprises. If the enemy is planning a ground invasion, we are well equipped with over one hundred and ten million active soldiers."

"Excuse me?" James said, blinking. "The world has armed itself to the point where over one hundred million men are under arms?"

Norton shook his head. "No, *we* have upgraded to the point where we have over one hundred and ten million men *and* women under arms. China and Europe have even more."

James thought he had misheard and searched the general's face for signs that he was joking, but could detect nothing of the sort—nor did he seriously expect it.

"But that means..."

"... That every resident of military age and acceptable

health wears a uniform and carries a weapon, or otherwise contributes to our defense." Norton nodded. "What did you expect?"

"I don't know," James admitted, sighing, "I really don't know. I just wish it hadn't come to this."

"A society with a clear common purpose that unites people across cultures and countries is not a bad thing if you ask me. What were we doing before that? People lived for a new TV with even more streaming services and let their time trickle away pointlessly searching for distraction. Another car on credit to adorn oneself with a status symbol. The rift that ran through our society was growing ever wider. Now, everyone is equal, working together toward a single goal—and a good, honorable goal at that. Every man and woman who got out of bed today knows exactly what they are living for and what they have to do. There are no more luxuries, hardly any free time, and no free choice of profession. These are the limitations we have to live with. But in return, there are no more drug-addicted young people who don't know what to do with their lives. There's significantly less sick leave, less obesity, hardly any depression or crime."

"And you approved of that?"

Norton's expression hardened. "I'm a soldier. I do what I'm ordered to do."

"But you have an opinion, don't you?"

"You always have them. Do I wish things were different? I certainly do, but on the whole, I think we're going in the right direction. The only problem I see is that with such strict organization and straight-line planning for the future, you lose sight of alternatives, of ways to get off the rail you're on. I'd rather be a car than a train."

"How does the economy even deal with all of it?" James

asked. The whole conversation sounded far too much like something he read in history books about a dark time a century ago.

"It's completely controlled from Washington. Everything is planned in detail, from food production to the textile industry to armaments. It was the only way to prepare for what we're going to face in thirteen months."

"The White House is handling *everything*? And people have accepted that?"

"No. The *Pentagon* handles everything," Norton corrected him, gesturing vaguely toward the window. "We're about to land."

James saw the huge pentagonal structure sitting on the banks of the Potomac River below Arlington National Cemetery, with its iconic white headstones marking the graves of fallen soldiers, and across from the Washington Memorial. From their altitude of about one hundred meters, it looked almost flat, and its broad dimensions made it hard to tell that it had five stories and was one of the ten largest buildings in the world.

They touched down in the center of the courtyard, which he remembered as a green park but appeared to have been completely paved over, creating half a dozen helipads. James looked up at the mighty gray facades that surrounded them as the rotors slowly spun down and the two soldiers, who had not exchanged a word during the entire several-hour flight, opened the door and hopped out. There was something desolate about the courtyard, an impression that was reinforced by the bad weather. Dense gray clouds were moving in from the east and would bring rain with them.

Norton motioned for him to take off the headset and they walked in a crouch out onto the landing pad, where they met up with the others, who seemed as relieved as he was. He deliberately avoided giving Mila an effusive hug, and from the look on her face, he could tell she understood and shared his reasons for doing so.

They were accompanied by soldiers and led to the south wing, where the main entrance to the building was located on the outermost ring of the building. The corridors through which they were led were extremely busy with black-uniformed people wearing bracelets like the ones they had seen in the teleporter facility and carrying tablets under their arms. They walked past, engaged in conversations with people James could not see. They all wore serious expressions and moved quickly but not frantically like precise, extremely disciplined, and well-oiled machines.

Everything here was built more compactly than he remembered from his last visit when he was a ransom negotiator, even if the marble floor with the large, stylized stars was the same. It gave the impression that Norton was deliberately leading them erratically through an opaque maze, where hardly anyone seemed to be interested in them even though they were wearing gray coveralls that made them stand out from the monotony of black.

Eventually, the general handed them over to a young officer with a crew cut, who saluted smartly and led them into a conference room divided into two parts: On one side was a simple metal table with ten nailed-down chairs that looked extremely uncomfortable. On the other side, separated by a glass wall, was the other half of the table, which had no chairs but instead four revolving displays that turned on the moment they were seated. The displays showed the black-and-white logo with the blue and red ribbon next to the US flag. James guessed that it was the new symbol of the UN.

"So, what now?" Meeks asked.

"I guess our debriefing isn't over yet," Adrian said, his expression glum.

"Hey, after all, I'm sure you're one of the first Russians to be let into the Pentagon in a long time."

"Great."

"Our situation is definitely better than it was a few hours ago," Mila said. "We might even get to eat eventually."

"Yeah, at least we don't have to sit here naked and freezing." Justus pointed to the displays. "James, did Norton tell you what this was all about?"

"No." He shook his head. "Only that some things have changed. It looks like the military has taken complete control. There are planetary defense centers with new technology that are also kind of like arks for worst-case scenarios, if I understand it correctly. Most of the world has come together to share technology and research. Thousands of people have been teleported to other planets. That's about all I've learned."

"That sounds like the most dystopian kind of science fiction I could have come up with," Meeks said.

"Well, let's wait and see."

"Good afternoon," a deep voice greeted them. James looked up, only now noticing that four people had appeared on the displays on the other side of the glass. All four wore black uniforms with lots of braid and five stars on each of their epaulets. Below them were their names, titles, and their branch of service. On the far left, a woman with short, ebony hair and a stern look underscored by full lips that resembled a compressed rosette eyed them: General Patricia Knowles, Chief of Staff of the Army, US Army. Beside her were two white men with gray hair, fastidiously shaved faces, and the twinkling eyes and confident look of people used to wielding power and getting their way: Admiral Bron

Jones, Chief of Naval Operations, Navy, and General John Booker, Chief of Staff of the Air Force, Air Force. The fourth general was a gaunt woman with sunken cheeks and crow eyes set deep in their sockets. She appeared to be the oldest. Beneath her name was written Chief of Space Operations, Space Force.

In the following three hours, the apparent highest commanders of this changed land asked so many questions that James's head was soon spinning. They wanted to know everything, from their arrival on Al'Antis and the circumstances that had led up to it to their first contact with the Tokamaku, the energy storage complex, and the experimental teleporter. They also asked about their detour to the homeworld of the Elders where only the construct remained.

As expected, they were mostly interested in the Kazerun, and they kept asking James about their homeworld, their nature, and the exact strategies they had used against the Al'Anter. He told them, as best he could, about the aggressive and devious nature of their enemies, their relentlessness, driven by fear of annihilation, that they directed at the external dangers they saw in everything and everyone. Time after time, the commanders wanted more details and asked cyclical questions, which he would have done himself in their place. But he knew the technique as a matter of course and did his best not to let on. He had nothing to hide from them, said openly what he remembered and what he didn't, but it hardly seemed to satisfy them. Even when Meeks and Mette in particular sprang to his defense and confirmed his stories with their experiences and memories, it didn't stop them from their relentless probing.

In the end, however, they had to accept the fact that he simply did not know more than he had told them and the people in the teleporter complex. He very much hoped they believed him and did not wrongly assume that he was withholding information from them. Eventually, their stern faces remained silent, and he was relieved.

Adrian then cautiously raised a hand. He and Mila had remained completely silent so far.

"Yes, Mr. Smailov?" General Knowles asked coolly.

"I'd like to speak with a Russian representative, ma'am."

"Of course. The Russian military ambassador is expecting you and Mrs. Shaparova outside the south gate in fifteen minutes. A couple of soldiers will escort you both to the exit in a moment and hand you over to your compatriots."

"Wait a minute," Mila interjected, "what exactly does that mean?"

The general raised a disapproving eyebrow before answering.

"You are being transferred back to Russia. Surely you are aware that your special visa for the teleporter project expired twenty-nine years ago?"

Mila paled, and James felt as if his veins would suddenly freeze so hard that the ice would constrict his throat.

"But you can't do that!" he blurted. "We're a team that only works well together! We—" *Norton's given us a mission,* he thought, and barely prevented himself from saying it aloud. What if Norton didn't have the Military Council's approval? After all, in the helicopter, he had acted very secretive for an officer conscious of duty.

"Out of respect for the fact that you are from another time," Admiral Jones said in a hard voice that sounded like someone grinding an iron bar, "we will let you get away with this one lapse. It will be the only one, the last. Do you understand?"

The sudden sharpness in the admiral's tone and his gaze froze James. This man wasn't joking, and he didn't want to imagine what would happen if he overdrew on the credit they were giving him—tiny though it obviously was. So, he merely looked helplessly at Mila. Her mouth quivered and her eyelids trembled as she looked him in the eye, and it almost broke his heart.

"It's okay," she said finally, with obvious effort. "We'll find a way, you hear?"

"Dr. Falkenhagen, Dr. Laudrup," General Knowles said, and her flashing white teeth looked like the jaws of a predator, "you will be transferred to the representatives of the European Defense Union, who are awaiting you in the west wing. That concludes this session."

The displays shut off and started rotating again.

The door opened and a handful of soldiers entered. James's heart sank.

8

James sat in front of his television, staring at the latest images of the approaching threat captured by the Heugens probe, which had been launched into orbit around Neptune ten years ago. A day ago its high-resolution cameras had captured the clearest, and therefore the most frightening, images yet of the invasion fleet.

"Due to the great distance to the solar system's outermost planet, Heugens's images took a little more than four hours to reach us," explained the newscaster in her black uniform. Behind her was the most prominent image released to the public by the Military Council. It showed thirty-four glaring stars against the black background of space. The sheer brightness of each of these brilliant suns was made even more impressive by the fact that it was not caused by any cross-fade effect, the cameras captured everything in sharp focus.

"Professor Ulyansky of the Stanford University Military Research Group," the dapper spokeswoman addressed a graying man also wearing a black uniform, but it looked incongruous on him, as if he had been pressured to wear it.

"We've been talking about nothing but these shots since this morning. Can you explain again to our comrades who have just joined us exactly what we're seeing here?"

"With pleasure, Sergeant." The professor pointed to the image covering the wall behind them. "In order to carry a spacecraft over a great distance—and in space, any distance is great—it must complete a flight that always consists of three phases. An acceleration phase that is maintained until it reaches its maximum speed. A drift phase where it continues at that maximum speed; since there is no air resistance in space, it does not consume any fuel during this phase, the engines can simply be switched off. This is also why we had such difficulty keeping track of the enemy fleet. Without drive flares, they are just dark objects against a dark background. Imagine searching for a deer in the woods on a cloudy, moonless night in total darkness. That's about as easy as tracking spaceships in the interstellar medium that aren't accelerating or braking because their hulls wouldn't reflect light either. After all, there is none out there.

"Now, I've just mentioned the third phase: The braking phase. The spaceship must now turn one hundred and eighty degrees so the drive nacelle is pointing toward the ship's destination. The engines fire again and begin to apply braking thrust. The acceleration it applied to reach its maximum speed must now be dissipated. That takes the same amount of time as the acceleration phase, just in the opposite direction, until the velocity is finally zero."

"So, in these latest images, we are seeing the invasion fleet decelerating?" the spokeswoman echoed.

"That's right. Their thrusters are reversed, and they are braking at high thrust. According to our preliminary calculations, the plasma flares we see here are between ninety thousand and one hundred thousand kilometers long."

"Excuse me?" the newscaster asked, blinking with surprise. For a split second, her controlled, professional expression wavered.

"In a vacuum, there is practically nothing to slow the emitted exhaust gases, to offer them resistance. It therefore does not fan out and remains very compact. So far, our models have shown that the enemy fleet is traveling at about thirty percent of the speed of light—that's the average of twenty-five as the minimum value and thirty-five as the maximum. So, if we assume thirty percent, then the plasma is coming out of the drive pod at about one-third the speed of light. That means these incredibly hot gas molecules have traveled over one hundred thousand kilometers in one second."

Professor Ulyansky awkwardly clasped his hands together as he looked from the picture to the sergeant.

"What can you and your team tell from all this?"

"A lot. First, roughly the size of the ships we'll be dealing with. Second, it confirms something we've assumed for a very long time: The drives are based on matter-antimatter annihilation."

"Can you explain this in a little more detail?" the spokeswoman asked.

Ulyansky nodded. "Of course. Even with our nuclear fusion, acceleration on the scale of the invasion fleet is unthinkable. We would be able to achieve perhaps two percent the speed of light with our latest-generation fusion reactors—a fraction of what we are seeing here. Only the annihilation of matter and antimatter is capable of such power because the energy released overshadows all other forms by far."

"So, these exhaust flares tens of thousands of kilometers long are the result of the annihilation of matter and antimatter?"

The professor shook his head. "No. The energy released during annihilation—presumably, there are only a few kilos of antimatter on each ship, and I put 'only' in quotation marks—is used to heat a so-called propellant, hydrogen, for example, and its exhaust provides the thrust that propels the actual spacecraft. This could be only about one hundred or two hundred meters long, so tiny that it could not even be seen in the glare of the exhaust tail. But from this we've also learned that there must be a lot of propellant mass on board. The energy mass tanks"—he pointed again to the image behind them—"will comprise over ninety percent of the entire ship's mass, which will be empty by the time they arrive. Half would have been used for the acceleration phase and the other half is being used now for the braking phase."

"But that's no reason to breathe a sigh of relief, though, is it?"

"No, no," the scientist hastened to assure. "We're still likely to be dealing with monstrous ships bristling with arms and, uh, lots of soldiers, I guess."

"Thank you, Professor Ulyansky, for these assessments." The image of the news anchor moved into center frame, and the image behind her changed to a stylized antenna sending small red emoji bombs toward an equally stylized Earth. "The firewalls are holding up" was written above it. "Now that the enemy's fleet is only two months away and will reach Neptune's orbit in as little as three weeks, our comrades in cybersecurity have again recorded a sharp increase in the frequency of signal attacks emanating from the invasion fleet. General Dimitrios Kavalos of the Space Force spoke of this during a report last night before the Pentagon and assured everyone that the firewalls had intercepted, jammed, or isolated all signals. Therefore, infiltration of our defense systems may be ruled out at this stage. Furthermore..."

Ding-dong!

James looked up as the door tone echoed through his apartment. He dropped his feet from the living room table and slid the tablet off his lap before standing with a groan and looking at his wristwatch. It wasn't easy to find it. With a few quick movements, he knocked the remnants of the dry cereal off his gray coveralls and walked across the hall to the apartment door.

Meeks was waiting in the unadorned hallway, holding a brown paper bag. He had lost a significant amount of weight and was now almost slimmer than James.

"Breakfast?"

"Hi, Vincent," he greeted his friend, stepping back so he could enter. Meeks walked past him into the living room and dropped onto the couch, sighing. James trotted after him and sat next to him before putting his feet back up on the table.

"Sound off," he said, and the TV muted. The report had switched to a live report from the Arkansas PDC. An Army camera crew was showing the rapid progress the rearming was supposedly making.

"Only two months to go," Meeks said, clicking his tongue. "And we don't have anything."

"Yes, we do. We have a war everyone seems to want."

"Don't you want it?"

James sighed, thinking back to Al'Antis—or what was left of it.

"No, but I understand that it has to be. I'm just worried about the general self-consciousness that seems prevalent. On the few occasions one of the outside uniforms talks to me, I always get the feeling that for them, there's only victory. Everyone is celebrating the PDC and the Navy's new super destroyers, which are really just upgraded old ships. They don't even think it's possible for us to lose. But I wonder what our ships—even hundreds of them—are supposed to do against starships powered by antimatter."

"Overconfident or not, at least someone is talking to you." Meeks tugged at his gray jumpsuit. "One nation, one world, one mission" was printed on the chest. "With me, it's like I'm a fucking leper."

James knew what he meant. In the America of now, there were exactly two kinds of people: those who served in the active armed forces and those who served in the civilian arm of the armed forces, that is, men and women like him and Meeks who contributed their skills as researchers, weapons engineers, or materials scientists, as farmers, roboticists, AI experts, or computer nerds. They were all military personnel, even the retirees, people over the age of seventy who provided nationwide childcare in gray coveralls. Everyone was assigned to one of these two branches of society by the time they turned sixteen so they could make their "contribution to the survival of humankind," as the saying went. Like any divided society, the division into black and gray uniforms led to mutual distrust. The former considered the latter to be timid quitters they had to risk their lives for, and the latter considered the former to be low-life stumblebums who could hold a gun straight but didn't have enough brains to make a more involved contribution. They were convinced that their work should be valued much more highly. As did Meeks, who had been drafted in as a production engineer after their post-assignment interview at the Pentagon. Despite his outdated technical expertise after thirty years of absence, he had been credited with leadership experience in project management, and his new boss used him primarily as a whip to get personnel on track. The problem was that as a civilian military man, you were also addressed as "comrade"—much to the chagrin of some in black uniform—but you hardly saw any of your peers. Most worked in the large inland war factories or research centers, while the soldiers virtually dominated all public life. They were everywhere, maintaining law and order by their presence, standing on every street corner, and patrolling every residential neighborhood.

James had met this new life with mixed feelings. On the one hand, it was frightening for him. He was a man who'd been brought up as a liberal pluralist and he found the sight of armed soldiers everywhere oppressive. On the other hand, there was virtually no visible crime anymore, and the rampant poverty that was once typical had disappeared. Everyone had food and housing, enjoyed uniform health care with identical benefits, and there was a sense of community that he had never experienced before. Everyone knew why and what they were working for and what they had to protect. No one had to fight for jobs or go begging. But New York was quite a bit gloomier. It had lost its happy, hectic atmosphere, its colorful, loud, and, yes, rebellious character that had once made it the city it was.

"Have you heard anything?" Meeks asked earnestly, looking at him with a mixture of compassion and pain.

"No." James shook his head and swallowed to fight the lump in his throat that he'd been carrying around for eleven months from growing even bigger. Vincent visited him almost every day—since no one had private cars anymore, it was an advantage that they lived in the same apartment complex in Manhattan. Norton, at James's insistence, had arranged for them to be housed near each other with the understanding, of course, that they were looking for the Avatar together. Exactly how the general envisioned they would accomplish this was another matter entirely. The internet no longer existed in a form they recognized. There were three networks. A public news and education network, to which everyone had access and where all information was approved by the Military Council and not subject to any "secrecy." There was a network for research and development, where all participating countries worldwide shared their research data in real time in order to maintain their high rate of technological progress. The third was the military network, which was for communication and coordination of the world's fighting forces. This meant that the days when over a third of the world's data communications were occupied with pornography and cat videos were well and truly over. James had to rely on the public news and education network for his searches, which was colloquially called the "civilian network," even though there was no such thing as civilian anymore. With no journalism left to live up to the name, little unpartisan information existed, and he spent every evening brooding with Vincent in his apartment. If they had no way to retrace the Avatar's footsteps in the data stream or look for anomalies like reports of people who didn't age, people who just disappeared and supposedly showed up somewhere else, then they needed another way to find it. They just couldn't figure out how.

In addition, they were suffering greatly from their separation from their friends. Justus and Mette had been flown to Europe and were supposedly working for the PDC Western Alps. Except for emails, which they were entitled to send once a month, there was no contact—no phone calls, no video calls, nothing. With Adrian and Mila, it was even worse. There was not a single sign of life from them, and

James was consumed with longing for Mila. He didn't eat much and worried constantly. His anxiety level diminished somewhat when Norton had noticed his deteriorating condition two months ago and had pulled some strings. So, he'd finally learned that they had been inducted into the active military and were stationed near Moscow. Or maybe Norton's assistance was some kind of bribe; after all, there was a second job that James fervently hated, even though he was very good at it. Shortly after their reintegration, Norton had made him an offer on behalf of the Military Council that he couldn't refuse, simply because one did not refuse requests in the new order—not unless you wanted to end up hanging for insubordination.

He was to make public appearances and report on his experiences with the teleporter. Certain "facts," however, were supplied to him, like the one that he would never mention any aliens. While they didn't want to lie openly and claim that humans had built the machine, they still wanted to give that impression, so it became a widely whispered and accepted fact. He was also told not to make too much of the involvement of the non-American members of his team, supposedly for diplomatic reasons, which he didn't really believe.

So, he was repeatedly flown and driven around the country for public appearances, speaking to thousands of workers at a munitions factory in Colorado, to a sea of soldiers at a missile test site in Nevada, to the workforce at a foundry, at a former football stadium, and at the West Point Military Academy—to name just a few. He was always surrounded by the Army Press Corps, which edited the videos of his appearances to include lots of pomp, waving eagles, and pathetic, onlooking soldiers of both sexes. The only reason he had agreed to it in the first place was that they had agreed not to put scripts in front of him and allow him tell the truth—except for the aforementioned restriction of certain facts. At first, he had thought they would never agree to his demand, but in the end, it had struck him that he was still doing, in effect, exactly what they had probably hoped he would do: warn people about the deviousness of the Kazerun, their violence and persistence, the endless war the various factions of their civilization fought incessantly, that only expansion and common, external enemies ensured their cooperation. His hatred for the first children of the Elders drove him to an eloquence more than he thought himself capable of, and they inspired a veritable storm of rage against the invaders, who had been faceless until now. Now the Americans had a story about the aliens, the story of another world that had been annihilated by the Kazerun once before, and the press officers regularly assured him that troop morale and comrade production work performance had never been so high. Determination was spreading, which was just what the Military Council needed.

"A shame," Meeks sighed sadly, opening the paper bag before holding the open end out to him. "Cereal?"

James waved it away and reemerged from his musings. "Already had some, thanks."

"Aren't you bored out of your mind here? I can barely concentrate at work because I feel like someone chopped off my arms and legs. But you... you don't do anything but sit here, watch the news, and brood. How long has it been since your last gig? A month? That can't be healthy."

James rubbed at the stubble on his chin and turned off the television. In the dark mirrored surface, he saw himself sitting next to his friend, his cheeks sunken, his eyes recessed in deep, dark sockets. Vincent was right, of course.

Teleport 3

He was wallowing in self-pity and a suppressed rage that made him restless. He hadn't felt so helpless since his breakup with Joana, which he had thought was worse than dying. It had been a shock, imagining that he'd never kiss and hold Joana again, and it had nearly killed him. But he had still been able to act. He had distracted himself with a new job, turned to sports, met up with friends to make his inner hell a little more bearable. Should he look for her? No. She was an old woman now, if she was still alive. Who knew what that would do to him?

Besides, he wouldn't have been able to visit her anyway. There was no more commercial air travel. Globalization had basically come to a halt and only extended to the military. So not only could he not visit anyone who didn't live nearby, he couldn't distract himself. There were no gyms, except for the military fitness centers where every citizen was required to work out several times a week. Cafés and restaurants no longer existed, as they merely distracted people from their mission.

He had plenty of time to grasp his predicament, that he was not only separated from the friends with whom he had spent virtually every minute of his life before their return, but also from the woman he loved. Not because she no longer wanted him, as Joana had, but despite the fact that she wanted to be with him too. It was simply not possible to get together.

The worst thing, however, was that part of why he had been so motivated and committed in his speeches for the Military Council during the past year was because he had hoped for special privileges in return. For example, a flight to Russia to see Mila again. But all his requests had been dismissed with "maybe later" or "we'll see what we can do, but first..." But for the last month they had not needed him, because he had nothing new to tell, and now he found himself here, empty-handed. Sure, his apartment was luxuriously furnished by current standards, and he got the best rations and thousands of electronic fan letters. The troops revered him as someone who spoke plainly and had walked among the stars, but he took no joy in it.

"You sure you wouldn't like a bite?" Meeks asked, and something about his only remaining friend's voice made him refrain from an almost automatic refusal. Instead, he frowned and peered into the dark interior of the bag. His friend acknowledged his look with an encouraging nod, and he reached inside. At first, he only felt the angular outlines of the cereal pieces between his fingers, but then he touched something larger and cooler than the cereal.

He didn't let on as Meeks looked serious. He pulled the item out of the bag along with a handful of cereal.

"Thanks," he said, selecting a few pieces to pop into his mouth. Out of the corner of his eye, he realized the object was a thin black wristband, an e-pal, one like every American used as a replacement for a computer and cell phone. A device far more powerful than anything he remembered from his former time on Earth.

"Friends share rations with friends, don't they?" the engineer said, and James understood. "Don't worry, I'm not passing on anything that isn't important or good."

James stuffed some more of the cereal between his lips and let the bracelet disappear into his pants pocket, making his movements look like he was rubbing his hand on his pants and brushing off crumbs.

"I'm going to the bathroom for a minute." James stood and stretched. "Thanks, really."

"No problem. Take your time, I'll just watch the extremely exciting television program, if you don't mind."

"You practically live here anyway."

James went through the kitchen and across the short hall to the bathroom, the only place where he thought he was not under surveillance. True, comprehensive surveillance did not officially exist, but he didn't believe for a moment that a state that could control everything and did not tolerate deviants would not extensively monitor its citizens—and the Military Council hadn't even bothered to deny that, as far as he knew.

Once in the bathroom, he locked the door, pulled the e-pal out of his pocket, and thoroughly inspected it. The bracelet was dull and black as night with a single button no bigger than his thumbnail below the small display.

"Why did Meeks bring *you* to me, huh?" he whispered, turning it over again so he could look at it from all sides before reluctantly slipping it over his left wrist and fastening it. "He knows I hate these things. My own has been sitting in a drawer for months."

The little device didn't give a damn about what he wanted and came to life unapologetically after he pressed his thumb to the button.

9

A small hologram appeared above the bracelet, showing an extremely vivid image of a young man who appeared to be sitting in a wooden hut surrounded by laptops old enough for James to feel a twinge of nostalgia. He was wearing only a stained tank top and yet seemed to be sweating, so either it was very hot in his hut, or it was located in a jungle.

"All right, people," the man said and pointed directly into the camera. "The dictatorship goes merrily on, keeping quiet about anything that happens outside the blinders they've put on you. In the last week alone, two entire communities were forcibly deported for refusing to send their conscripted members to the nearest armed forces training camp. They were only two hours overdue when military police also arrived at their homes. Can you imagine that? Of course, not only the conscientious objectors were deported, but their families as well. You have to meet the targets to keep the teleporter busy. Such an expensive technological development has to be profitable."

James frowned while the young man continued, almost feverish.

"But what if it's not Pentagon technology at all? If we were able to build something like that, surely we could create more of than just one for all UN member nations? Every week over two hundred thousand foreign forced deportees arrive in the US to be 'evacuated.' Why not build one hundred teleporters to get rid of even more forcibly criminalized citizens? Surely there's no better way to tackle the problem of overpopulation." The speaker leaned forward, bent over, his arms folded in front of him, resting on the tabletop. "Oh, so there's no overpopulation? That's interesting."

He turned one of the laptops around to reveal a graphic with an arrow pointing downward.

"In fact, the population in our country has been decreasing for twenty-nine years, ever since the threat of an alien fleet became known. And this low birth rate is called defeatism! Hardly anyone wants to bring children into the world anymore when we don't even know if this world will still exist by the time they grow up."

The man's eyes widened, taking on an expression that would have suggested madness to many. But James, from experience, saw it as a total conviction that, while close to insanity, was somewhere in between.

"So, they just want to get rid of those who question the system, the so-called 'disruptive elements.' People like me who are dedicated to the truth and therefore have to hide in a no-man's land outside the UN, cut off from progress, from international support, and from the global data stream. But my voice is being heard and yours must be, too. They will also try to deport you as soon as you deviate from the ever-stricter limits of tolerated behavior and thinking—and believe me, it will get stricter. Even for us free broadcasters. If you're watching this, you've merely found yourself at the edge of a whole network of free thinkers passing memory blocks under the table, risking their lives. When the current ebbs, you have to become active and no longer leave it to others. Become a free transmitter yourself! Or make your way to the last free regions of Earth, to South America or Africa. Life is hard, but it is free."

The young man turned the laptop away and closed it.

"Even though this recording is for new viewers and doesn't include the latest dark chapters of our dictatorship, I want to leave you with one more thing. One of us, a free thinker from Bolivia, has made a big breakthrough. You know about it from the controlled news. The evil aliens have once again tried to send us a computer virus to sabotage our infrastructure and destroy our resistance even before the battle has begun. We hear this about once a week, along with self-congratulations about how well the UN's cyberdefenses are working and how great the training center support programs are.

"But have we considered that it could be something other than a computer virus that the ships are sending us? Are we so entrenched in our thinking that we can only see in one direction? That of absolute war and danger? Is it really true that there can only be one motivation for these ships to send us such a signal? Namely, sabotage? I'll tell you what"—the man leaned forward again, and his lips narrowed to thin lines—"only someone who thinks only of war and deviousness himself can think so narrowly.

"This fleet has been around for many decades. What if it's changed its mind? What if they aren't invasion ships at all and have no living beings on board? They could be machines or even just structures, an automated colony bringing equipment and resources, similar to our first mission to Mars, to set the stage for settlers to follow in a few more decades. What kind of opportunity would that be? How much could we learn from these artifacts? What if the signals contain no code at all, but were merely samples? What if they are repeatedly sampling the nature of the planet and our atmosphere? I don't want to say that we're not in danger—I consider it my duty to think freely and not to be forced into a track, so I won't pretend that the possibility doesn't exist that Earth is in danger and that the Military Council is right. But we must not allow ourselves to be blinded. In the next issue, I hope to be able to tell you what our friend in Bolivia has found out. If it's true that he's decoded one of their signals, then we'll be anxious to learn what the content is. Unless we never hear from him again, in which case the Military Council was probably right."

A wry grin appeared on the man's face. "But when has that ever been the case, huh?"

The transmission ended and was immediately followed by a knock on the door.

"Did you fall into the toilet?" Meeks asked.

"I'm just washing my hands. Come on in," James replied.

A moment later, the engineer, who showed no signs of his once-large belly even more than a year after their return, joined him. In a low voice, he asked, "Well?"

James motioned for him to close the door all the way and whispered, "Where did you get it?"

"Even though you've shut yourself up in your apartment this whole time, you've heard about the on-call alarms that are held once a week on random days across the country?"

"They simulate an unforeseen alien attack, evacuating everything, arming the workforce as quickly as possible, and rehearsing distribution among the respective National Guard brigades."

"Yes, something like that. Anyway, the alarm is loud enough that you can talk undisturbed while you're still in the building." Meeks cleared his throat and lowered his voice once more, so James had to strain to even understand him. "One of my coworkers got upset with our boss and called him *Obersturmbannführer*—that's a Nazi designation for an officer—so I took notice. When I tapped him, I thought he was going to have a heart attack. But he quickly relaxed when I said he was lucky I didn't belong to the Gestapo like those damned colleagues of ours, those humorless robots who volunteer for standby drills on weekends."

James nodded as he unfastened the bracelet from his wrist and stared at it, his brow furrowed.

"Well, anyway, my joke seemed to have broken a dam with him and he blew off a lot of steam as we walked down the stairwell. He talked about the Pentagon's Nazi ways, about how he'd been beaten two days earlier after being picked up by an MP patrol half a mile from his apartment ten minutes after curfew—and a bunch of other stuff. I told him that I didn't even know anything like that was happening. He said that none of us knew enough because our media was controlled by the Pentagon and the only thing one could rely on were the pirate stations. When I revealed that I wouldn't know what he was talking about he hesitated, but then told me to volunteer for the cleanup crew after work. Not only would that give me four points per hour on the Army's scorecard to get more rations, but I'd also learn more about the truth."

"The guy told you all that?" James asked incredulously.

"Yes. Why?"

"You could have been a spy for the Military Council. After all, that's course 101 of any repressive system, whether it's a supposedly necessary one or a truly evil one: spies who covertly fish out those who deviate. Your associate had no way of knowing if you were one of them."

"Hmm, sure," Meeks admitted. "But I think people like him—free thinkers, as they apparently call themselves—have to take risks if they want to spread alternative information. After all, they never have any certainty that they won't stumble on the wrong people."

"True again." James waved impatiently and whispered, "And then what? What was that about a cleanup crew? I've never heard of that."

"The whole country is nothing but bunkers and ammunition dumps. Besides the central underground ones in the barracks, there are lots of smaller, decentralized depots all over the country. Explosive stuff likes to blow up, and since all this country sees is nails, hammers are running all over the place."

"Get to the point, Vincent!"

"Mistakes happen. Every once in a while, one of the depots blows up or there's a fire. But firefighters don't just go out to combat major incidents like that, they also get called out for domestic fires. Just about every living space in the country houses at least one weapon and some ammunition, and accidents happen all the time. Then the fire department puts out the fire, but since it's not exactly overfunded, the Military Council relies on its Army scoring system. You can build up your score, not only by taking part in field exercises and earning extra qualifications, but also for taking part in cleanups that the fire department needs because it doesn't cost them anything."

"There are no cameras or microphones in a burned-out house," James mused aloud. "I see."

"All right, so we went to Queens after work. There had been a shooting on a bus, which went off the roadway and crashed into an apartment building. Half the complex burned down and was put out that night. So, the next night we went and started clearing everything out, including the bodies." Meeks screwed up his face as if he'd bitten into a lemon. "We made sure worked in the same room, and then he told me about the pirate radio stations. He said that in the free zones, as they call themselves, there are still functioning democratic governments where there are less strict laws. Pirate radio stations have formed and are broadcasting their signals worldwide via hacked satellite networks. However, they can hardly be received in our country because the Military Council has set up broad jamming programs. Therefore, their messages only reach us in the form of memory blocks that are passed hand to hand."

"Free zones? You mean South America and Africa?"

"Yes, the only two continents that no longer participate in the UN and its common defense."

"Well, they can afford to celebrate their democracy," James grumbled. "They probably don't spend anything on Earth defense because they have the UN spending *everything* on it."

"Possibly, yes." Meeks raised his hands placatingly. "Hey, I know you hate the Kazerun and you're worried about our planet. But at least hear me out."

James nodded and suppressed a sigh.

"Countries like Bolivia, where this new hacker is said to be based, who claim to have intercepted and decoded one of the signals from the Kazerun fleet, are at an impasse. They are free but technologically and economically far behind, isolated from the major industrialized nations and without global supply chains. They are impoverished and virtually unable to defend themselves if, for example, our country decides it's had enough of the pirate broadcasts and sends in a few missiles or even invading troops. That's why they work against the broadcasts, and thta makes it harder and harder to receive free news."

"That's why the memory blocks, got it."

"Anyway, he gave me this one and told me to look at it. So, I did, and then I brought it right over to you."

"I understand, but what does that have to do with our job of finding the Avatar? You don't think it's one of those whacked-out pirate radio guys, do you? That seems pretty far-fetched to me. From a billion-year-old being with no agenda of its own to a dedicated rebel sitting somewhere in the jungle between ancient laptops, spewing his enthusiasm while some sweaty teenagers film him and smuggle these blocks into the US?" James put his head down. "Come on."

"Yeah, yeah," Meeks frowned. "I get what you're saying. But look at it this way: If someone really claims to have managed to decode the signals of extraterrestrial people who are thousands of years ahead of us in their development, then it must be someone who knows far more or is far more intelligent than we are."

"There are so many unverifiable assumptions in your statement that I don't even know where to start picking it apart." His friend looked offended and he put a hand on his arm. "Listen, I think it's good that you're trying to broaden our horizons and investigating paths where fools fear to tread. That's good, we should keep that up. But we shouldn't get desperate either."

"We're not *getting* desperate! We *are* desperate, James! There's a big difference. My *snooping* has come too early? It's too late if you ask me! There's a fleet of Kazerun ships out there racing toward us and they've just crossed Neptune's orbit. That's on the edge of our planetary system, not somewhere in the interstellar medium, far, far away!"

"Shh, not so loud!"

"We have not found a single indication of an Earth Avatar in almost a year. *None*. We now have to find a solution in twenty percent of the time that we have been unsuccessful so far. How is that going to work? And twenty percent only if we count until the day they arrive in orbit. There are enough experts in the military who predict a bombardment could start from Mars orbit. Then we'll have no success at all, even with the latest hypersonic missiles that can easily reach high orbit." Meeks snorted like an enraged bull. "So don't tell me not to despair. It's high time, man!"

"It's all right," James hissed, clenching his jaws until his cheeks ached. "What are we supposed to do? Call Norton and say we want to book a trip to Bolivia?"

"He's the most powerful officer in the country outside of the Military Council. If anyone can do it, he can."

"That may be, but the Military Council is so high above the rest of the leadership that it makes no difference. In the end, they decide."

"Maybe. But he certainly has a lot of operational freedom. As you know, my son is a major with the Washington PDC, and he told me before I came here that the Military Council has been considering neutralizing these pirate radio stations for some time. Now that the invasion is approaching, they seem more afraid than ever of rampant defeatism within society. They have to keep morale high at all costs before things go boom, you know?"

"Wait," James said with a scowl. "You told your son about this? On the phone?"

"No, no," Meeks hastened to assure him. "I was on the phone with him and just asked if there would be any foreign missions. That's when he said, on his own, that there would be virtually none left and, yes, most of the overseas bases have been disbanded. The only exception he talked about was that the pirate radio stations might still be taken out, but then only with smaller special forces. I swear to you, he said that without me bringing it up."

"I don't know, Vincent—"

"Do you have a better idea?"

"No, but—"

"Then there are no buts, James! If you have discovered a solid lead up until now, you have to follow the first one that comes along, don't you? That's what you've always said!"

"I've never said that!"

"But it would suit you."

"What's that supposed to mean? This is—"

"You can continue to hole yourself up in your apartment as an aspiring depressive, look sadly out the window and say how bleak and cold our world has become, and how horrible the Kazerun are—not to mention your fears for Mila and your broken heart. Or you can pull yourself together, call Norton, and tell him you finally have a lead. I'm sure he'll come right over."

"Even if I did, what would I tell him? 'Oh, by the way, I got ahold of an illegal broadcast—from whom I don't know, but you probably can't imagine it's because I meet so many people. Some conspiracy theorist wants to decode the alien signal, please fly us there, it could be the Avatar. No, I don't know what we'll find, but it's better to do that than not follow a lead.'" James snorted peevishly. "Is *that* what I should say?"

"I admit it sounds a little nuts, but you could try a little harder. You were the ransom negotiator who managed to make fools of the good guys and the bad guys for years, right? You'll be able to talk Norton into it. Now that the invasion is imminent, he'll be desperate enough to try anything. After all, he probably went pretty far out on a limb when he started searching for the Avatar in the first place. Even if there's only a tiny chance of success, he'll take it. I don't even have to be a ransom negotiator to believe that."

10

James sat in the back seat of the uncomfortable Humvee, getting tossed back and forth with every pothole. Since the ancient military cross-country vehicles had been designed for use in combat zones, the seat usually held armored soldiers wearing helmets who, for one thing, were tightly packed and, for another, didn't have to worry about lacerating their foreheads with every bump. There were no seat belts, and the bench was so low that he couldn't even bend his legs all the way, which meant he couldn't use his feet to steady himself.

Over the past eleven months, he had gathered enough information from the civilian network to fill in many of his knowledge gaps. Knowing that all the information was sanctioned by the NSA, he had ignored that fact because he could fill in most of the gaps himself.

For example, the encyclopedia entry on the Humvee stated that the High Mobility Multipurpose Wheeled Vehicle was an extremely reliable, all-terrain, four-wheel drive vehicle. AM General, the manufacturer, officially began production in 1985. Knowing that thirty years ago the world was about to make a rapid switch to electric motors, James had at first been at a loss to explain why the military was still operating almost entirely on diesel vehicles and why an entire industry of innovation had died out. But it soon become clear to him that climate change had taken a back seat because a more immediate threat to the continued existence of Earth was just around the corner. In addition, vehicle modernization would have been very expensive, and all available funds were going to other projects: Research and Development for new weapons systems, construction of the PDCs, restructuring society, and mass production of war goods. This reprioritization was probably why he was being subjected to countless potholes and bumps on the way to McGuire Air Force Base.

The badly maintained roads were annoying but not serious for military trucks and jeeps, though it would have been devastating for private traffic. But that was pretty much non-existent now, as long-distance civilian traffic had ceased completely, and local traffic was regulated by the Army. A convenient circumstance, since renovating the road network would have also been costly and so ranked pretty low on the Pentagon's list of priorities. In any case, the leadership always wondered which investments would be important if Earth were destroyed or occupied by aliens in the foreseeable future.

Whenever James looked out the window, he saw desolate, empty streets. Tufts of grass grew wherever the asphalt had cracked and never patched. He felt like the protagonist in a post-apocalyptic zombie movie. Everything looked like decay and smelled like decay, making it a fitting metaphor for what was actually going on. Achievements, such as universal human rights and social participation through co-determination had perished faster than he would have thought possible. Out of necessity, which he could understand, and at the same time out of an alleged lack of alternatives, which he did not understand. At a time when there was supposed to be only one possible solution, one had to be particularly alert. He agreed with the feverish, young man from the pirate show. Absolutism in any form was alarming, and the sadness he saw through the window, the lifeless order, reminded him of that once again.

It took them just over an hour of travel on Interstate 95 to reach McGuire Air Force Base. During the drive, they had encountered other vehicles only once: a convoy of twenty trucks with US Army markings that they overtook on their way southwest.

At the air base, which turned out to be a joint Air Force, Army, and Navy base, he and his two drivers were given a quick security check and then driven along the northern barracks to the main building where the staff offices were located. Driving along rain-flooded tar roads that were in much better shape than those outside the heavily guarded gates, they passed several platoons of jogging soldiers, despite the inclement weather, their eyes sternly straight ahead. Not even the splash of Humvee tires seemed to bother them.

He finally met Norton in a small conference room on the second floor, where one of the two drivers delivered James with a crisp salute until the general dismissed him with a careless wave.

"Hello, Mr. Hamilton."

The aged officer made a few final entries on a tablet, then set it aside and put his signature on some documents.

James waited for several silent minutes after he muttered "Sir" and remained standing in front of the desk, the erratic scratching of the ballpoint pen on the pressed fiber became a dismissive sound that seemed to compete with the ticking of the clock above the door to see which sound could make the wait more uncomfortable.

At some point, Norton looked up, the bags under his eyes wobbling slightly as he did so. He gave James a brief, appraising look, then gestured toward one of the chairs.

"Have a seat, please."

James settled into one of the two simple chairs that seemed to exemplify the new United States as the general pushed aside the stack of papers and sighed.

"You would think that the armed forces would no longer be occupied with shoveling paper nowadays. Digitization and all that sort of thing. But apparently some things can't be avoided in any future." A sigh escaped the aging soldier's mouth. "So, what brings you to me today, Mr. Hamilton, that couldn't be discussed over our e-pal?"

"I may have information on the whereabouts of someone we're looking for," James said freely, and Norton's eyes widened a bit, which he noticed immediately. His counterpart raised a finger, pulled open one of the drawers on his desk, and his right hand disappeared inside it. A brief murmur flooded James's ears, which became a high-pitched whine that was steady enough not to be too unpleasant.

"You found the Avatar?"

"No, but I may have a lead," he replied, suddenly unsettled by the barely suppressed impatience of a man he knew to be rather level-headed. What if Vincent's idea was too abstruse after all? What if he was just making a fool of himself here, and would never again be allowed access to Norton, even with a simple phone call? Then what would they do when it really mattered, when they had a real lead?

"I'm listening."

"I'm going to have to ask that you don't ask for my source when I give you the information that I've... researched."

Norton waved impatiently.

"Dr. Meeks and I suspect that the Avatar may be in Bolivia," he said finally.

"In South America?"

"Yes. There are some..." James paused and cleared his throat to dispel the uncomfortable feeling that was spreading through him. Then he steadied himself and continued in a firm voice: "There are some pirate radio stations in the region that claim a secluded hacker living in Bolivia has decoded one of the signals from the Kazerun ships."

When the general merely raised an eyebrow, James calmly interlaced his fingers and nodded.

"You see, if it's true, then I can tell you that it must be the Avatar," he lied. "I've learned enough about the Kazerun and their technological level to know that no human hacker, especially in a country at least as technologically backward as Bolivia and equipped only with ancient laptops, would be capable of deciphering something as complex as a signal from a civilization that is centuries, if not millennia, ahead of us—and that was before they set out to pay us a visit."

Norton didn't respond, but James could see the doubt in his eyes. He had expected this. After all, his argument was obviously flawed and weak. Just because a civilization was more advanced didn't have to mean its signal was complex. It could be—as unlikely as it was—a simple message saying "hello" or "surrender." In addition, there was the possibility that they *wanted* the people of Earth to understand their message and had accordingly kept it simple, perhaps even unencrypted. For the military, the risk of finding out was simply too great, and he would have acted similarly in their place. If they were wrong and it was a computer virus, which would be smart if it was an invasion, then that one mistake would be enough to completely destroy the already slim hope of defending their planet.

"We should check it out," he continued, putting a hint of eagerness in his voice. "You see, even if it's not the Avatar, there are only benefits for our nation and the UN if we check on the ground there. If it's true and this hacker *has* decoded the signal, we'd finally have clarity—whether it *is* the Avatar or not. If it's not true, we'll at least take down a pirate transmitter, and if it is the Avatar, we'll have achieved our biggest goal. Even the minimum bottom line is something we could use justify it to the Military Council."

"When did you come across this information?"

"Recently," James said, keeping it vague.

"Interesting."

"Why?"

"Sergeant Ruben 'Ruby' Ohamu," Norton replied, leaning back in his chair.

"What about him?"

"Sergeant Ruby was a cook on the teleportation project when we were still in the silo in Wyoming. He was still a private then. A nice, rotund guy, always in a good mood with the sunny disposition of a Hawaiian. He was the only soldier in the installation you talked to from time to time—except for me—and the only American you've made contact with since returning." The general looked him straight in the eye. James shrugged and tried hard to look unconcerned.

When he had discussed his plan with Meeks, it had not been particularly easy to put it into action. It had taken him several days to reach Ruby. At first, he'd thought his calls were being blocked, but apparently that was not the case. As it turned out, the friendly Hawaiian, by now a sergeant and chef on a Navy transport, had been at sea. His ship shuttled between Lisbon and New York as part of military logistical exchanges between the United States and the European Defense Union. The gray-haired man he had seen in the e-pal had looked cheerful, despite his many wrinkles, and he had been overjoyed to see James again, though not necessarily because they had become friends, after all, their conversations had been limited to pleasant small talk even back then, and James had been surprised that the man had recognized him at all. But his fascination with the fact that James had not aged had been enough to get his interest. Then, when James had learned that Ruby would be stationed at McGuire Air Force Base in ten days for a week of emergency training, the idea had occurred to him to contact Norton and see if he could take advantage of coincidence.

"Don't tell me you made all this up so you could see Sergeant Ruby in person," Norton said blandly. "That that was why you said you'd like to see me the next time I was around. You knew that my position requires me to do a lot of commuting between the various bases, and here in McGuire is where the international colonists arrive. Now I hear that Ruby is undergoing some advanced training here."

"You are eminently knowledgeable about who I am in contact with," James countered coolly.

"Don't play games with me, Mr. Hamilton. I have too little time for that. The Kazerun fleet is less than five weeks away, and the pessimists in JSOC think we can expect fire from the fleet in as little as one, a full three and a half weeks before we can fire back. And all of that could be wrong, just like everything else we've calculated so far because we lack a sufficient database for just about any assumption. So, what do you want?"

"I want to go with Vincent on a mission to Bolivia and track down the hacker."

"Do you know where he is, then?"

"No, but I'm sure the Pentagon can easily find out. There can't be that many facilities able to pick up the fleet's signal, can there? And since our AIs are likely to be considerably more advanced than anything floating around on the South American internet, I don't expect it will take any effort or time to draw some sound conclusions from there," James said.

Norton smiled faintly. "And what if the Pentagon decides to send a hypersonic missile there rather than go to elaborate lengths to activate Special Forces? That's significantly more expensive and involves more risks."

"In that case, I guess we'll have to count on the fact that you actually have as much power and influence as they say you do, and that the Military Council won't want to miss the chance to grab the Avatar." He paused for a moment. "That's your job. Oh, and I have a request."

Norton raised an eyebrow.

"I need my team. Mila and Adrian and Mette and Justus."

"You *need* your team? What for?"

James knew this would be the hardest part but couldn't give it up easily until he tried to fight for it.

"We work best when we're together." One look at Norton's face clearly showed him how weak that sounded, so he quickly continued before the general could respond. "We've been through a great deal together, and they've all had contact with the Avatar and the Elders in the Construct. That knowledge and experience will be invaluable if we are really dealing with the Avatar here."

"I don't think you're quite clear on how the new UN

works. It is an association of just twenty states—if you count the European Defense Union as a bloc. While these include many long-term allies, they also number some former rivals with whom relations have improved but who are not yet regarded as close partners in the same sense as Germany, England, or Canada."

"The Military Council wants the Avatar for itself," James said bitterly.

"You have to understand, the teleporter project was extremely costly and difficult and came with a high diplomatic toll that caused us some real headaches. We couldn't change that because the EU and Russia had drilled in Lake Maracaibo and now knew. Would the US government have preferred to get things going on its own? Of course! Many cooks spoil the broth, as we all know. Cooperation is laudable but always costs valuable time in reaching consensus," the general explained, unusually eloquently. "It's best to forget about reuniting your team right now."

James sighed. "It was worth a shot."

"I understand your frustration." Norton stood and smoothed his already immaculate uniform. "I have to get back to the Pentagon now."

"To the Pentagon? Are you no longer commander of the teleporter facility?"

"Yes, I am, but I'm hardly ever on site. These days I'm busier talking my colleagues at Arlington out of stupid ideas." The officer opened the same drawer as before. He paused as he started to slide his hand inside. "I'll be honest with you, Mr. Hamilton. Your idea sounds desperate, but I'll take any excuse, no matter how outlandish, to distract the Military Council from doing something stupid."

"That sounds like you're worried about something," James said with rising concern.

"Yes. They want to put the teleporter in a heavy-lift rocket filled with a nuclear weapons and send it toward the fleet."

"Excuse me?"

"The Council listened well when you told them about antimatter technology and the devastating effects of a containment chamber failure on Al'Antis. If there is anywhere near the amount of antimatter dormant in the teleporter's reactor, as our scientists assume, then we'd have in our hands a weapon that surpasses anything we have in our arsenal."

"But we don't even know if a nuclear warhead could overcome the reactor's protection."

"No, but we would find out."

"And gamble away our only way to the stars!" James protested.

"I told you I have to talk them out of some bad ideas." Norton reached into the drawer and the latent beeping in James's ears disappeared so abruptly that he only now realized it had been there at all. "Meet your friend, for my sake. He's at the Delta Training Center right now and he'll be on break in half an hour. I'll get you an escort to take you there. The driver of your Humvee will be ordered to wait another hour."

"Thank you, General." In his mind, he added, *"Really."*

Norton nodded curtly, grabbed one of the tablets, and headed for the door. He spoke briefly to one of the waiting aides, who came in and grabbed the stacks of papers and remaining computers.

Once their footsteps faded, James slowly stood. He was startled to see a young, uniformed man behind him, leaning casually against the door jamb, his arms folded in front of his chest.

Teleport 3

"Are you ready, sir?"

"Uh, yes," he said. "I'd like to see Private Ruby now. *Sergeant* Ruby, I mean."

"Follow me." James followed the soldier down the hall to the stairwell, which was bustling with activity. Outside, they got into a Humvee. This time he sat in the vacant passenger seat, which was considerably more comfortable than the back seat.

"You know the Sarge?" the private asked as he steered onto one of the barracks' ring roads, practically leaning over the steering wheel as he tried to see through the thick veils of rain despite the windshield wipers.

"We met a long time ago. Sounds like you know him?"

"Yep. I was gunner's mate on the *Roosevelt*, where he still pounds the schnitzels," explained the young sailor with the soft-spoken R of someone who grew up in Philadelphia or Baltimore. "He's a good guy."

"That's him. Do you have much to do with the colonists here? On this base I mean?"

"With the FDs?"

"FDs?"

"Forcibly Deported."

"Ah. Clearly, the euphemisms 'colonists' or 'chosen' aren't as widespread around here as the Military Council would like," James said over the loud patter of rain on the vehicle.

"Things should be called what they are. We're all glad to see these wimps, deserters, and criminals go," the sailor grumbled. "I have no desire to fight for my country and our planet next to someone who'll turn tail and abandon me at the first opportunity to run for the hills or someone who'll steal some of my ration as soon as I'm not paying attention."

"I thought the threat of deportation existed for even the smallest offense," he objected cautiously.

"Could be, I don't know, but it's the same thing. If you lie once, you won't be believed, and if you steal once, you're sure to do it again. People like that should be weeded out even more rigorously, but this NASA machine probably doesn't have enough room for us to get rid of them all." The soldier shook his head and snorted. "Should have put more of our deadbeats in there rather than play Salvation Army for the whole world again and let Europeans, Russians, and the damned bamboo benders from China and Japan dump their human waste on us, too."

"Um, I see." James decided to remain silent for the rest of the ride before his self-control failed him and made him say or do something stupid.

The Delta Training Center was a functional one-story building with an elongated roof. Lights burned behind all the windows, refracted by the masses of water running off the dark corrugated metal and tumbling into pool-sized puddles in front of a paved path protected by the overhanging roof. Isolated groups of smoking soldiers stood close together, eyeing them as they stopped in front of one of the entrances.

"The Sarge should be out here soon," the sailor announced, casually pointing his thumb out the rain-streaked window to the double door on the other side. "You have thirty minutes. The general instructed me to deliver you to the west gate on time, so I'll be very grateful if you don't get me into trouble."

"I won't," James assured him, pulling the hood of his rain jacket over his head and stepping out, only to sink in water up to his ankles. With a hissed curse on his lips, he looked down at his completely submerged sneakers and hunched his shoulders as he hustled around the hood of the vehicle. Under the cover of the roof, he pulled the hood back down and shook himself like a wet dog to drive the chill from his limbs. He was completely soaked, even though he had only been exposed to the downpour for a few seconds.

"Shit, damn it!" he cursed and furrowed his brow in frustration. He was almost tempted to ask for a cigarette from one of the soldiers leaning between the windows a few meters away. They were talking at a normal volume, but the rain swallowed their voices with its pounding intensity and made it easy for him to focus on trying to warm his hands instead.

He recognized Sergeant Ruben Ohamu immediately when a portly yet burly dark man with a bald head and huge paws came out the door and put a little blue garrison cap on his head.

"Aloha, Ruby!" he greeted the Navy cook, who was about to put on his huge poncho and paused in a contorted pose when he heard James's voice. Slowly, he disengaged his large arms from the rustling plastic and his jaw dropped open.

"My goodness, James Hamilton," Ruby said incredulously, and his face lit up. "Mahalo! It really is you."

"Yep, looks like it."

"Man!" The sergeant waddled up and embraced him as if they were best friends. He felt irritated at first, but he eventually patted the gentle giant on the back.

"I'm glad, too."

"Whew, it's been so long, and I thought you were all dead. Really good to see you, man!"

"Likewise!"

"Even though we only saw each other a few times a day for a chat back then, I haven't forgotten any of it."

"Guess it was the intensity of the project. I mean, an alien artifact that opens a gateway to the stars?" James snorted. "How are you supposed to do normal duty on that?"

"Shh!" Ruby looked around uneasily, but the rain covered even the roar of passing military transports and a few turboprops taking off from a nearby runway. "The Pentagon doesn't like people saying that."

"I've heard that. They don't like a lot of things since the last time I was on Earth."

"You can say that again."

And there it was. James scanned the cook's expression closely as he spoke and decided his gamble had paid off— probably, at least most likely. If his people skills failed him now, it would be his first and last mistake, he had no illusions about that. But he couldn't gain anything without risk, that much was certain. In which case, it wouldn't matter if they executed him or deported him through the teleporter.

"I hear you've been shuttling back and forth between New York and Europe," James said cheerfully, changing the subject.

"That's right. My class ended today, so we're leaving tomorrow. Really lucky this worked out so spontaneously!"

"You call a week spontaneous?"

"In these times?" Ruby chortled. "You can say that again."

"Do you at least get some shore leave over there? Surely Lisbon is a culinary highlight for a chef?" James winked at him.

"Are you kidding? Yes, we have two days of shore leave while the war equipment is unloaded and new equipment is loaded. But things have changed since you left. Europe still has restaurants and a rudimentary public life, but it's not the same. And Portugal has never been known for particularly good cuisine. They have some disgusting fish pickled in salt that makes you shudder, but that's about it." Ruby shook his head. "Why am I even talking about dining in Portugal? Let's talk about you, buddy! Thirty years and you haven't aged a day. I want to know everything! I mean, everything!"

James sighed. "We've only got half an hour, I'm afraid, but I'll do my best. What do you say we walk through the rain? It's so nice and loud."

The chef eyed him before nodding in understanding and gesturing for him to lead the way.

"Sure, why not?"

11

"This is a risky game you've been playing." Preston Lacey, leader of SR Team 5, was squatting with James and Meeks in the cramped cabin of the futuristic stealth helicopter as they raced low over the jungles of Bolivia bathed in the sparse green cabin light. SR stood for Special Reconnaissance, as he had learned. It was something like the Special Forces of the Air Force trained for particularly difficult reconnaissance missions behind enemy lines. However, since this kind of force was on the verge of extinction in the face of the alien invasion, which, one suspected, would be fought with heavy military equipment and not with the help of military intelligence, there were only three such teams left.

The five other team members were hand-picked Norton loyalists, he had learned. On the trip to French Guiana, where they transferred from the transport plane to the helicopter that had been brough with them, folded and lashed down inside the plane, he and Meeks had had plenty of time to talk to the soldiers. They were four tough-looking men and one even tougher-looking woman who had turned out to be surprisingly humble and affable. Smart with alert eyes and no rough edges, they seemed focused and easy-going. Lieutenant Lacey was in his mid-forties and looked more like a particularly edgy elementary school teacher, with his matchstick-length hair that seemed almost an affront to Air Force guidelines. Early on in their flight, James realized how close he was to Norton. He only ever talked about "Tim" when he spoke of the general, and his eyes always took on a slight gleam, the kind he knew from many sons who idolized their fathers.

"What do you mean?" he asked, careful to maintain an innocent expression. "The general agreed with my assessment and now we're going to see if it's accurate."

Lacey smiled, amused.

"Yeah, right. Because of you, we've touched down five miles from the target and have too many civilians on our hands. To us, that's kind of like asking the team to go shopping with a St. Bernard strapped to their chest."

"But you have competent support for that, and you're not on your own." James returned the smile. His mood could not be spoiled since Norton had called him two days ago and he and Vincent were picked up by a convoy three hours later. After nearly ten days, during which he had heard nothing from the general, his hopes had all but vanished, and Vincent's mood, half depressed and half possessed with rage, must have suffered greatly.

Then, however, it had happened, the mission had begun after all. The fact that Norton had not been angry, but rather tightlipped during their brief telephone conversation, was due—he suspected—to the fact that it had been James who had caused the change in thinking at the Pentagon. There was no other way he could explain how the general had not had any success until it was suddenly announced that they

Teleport 3

would be allowed to use the European Defense Union's military base in French Guiana.

"Tim described to me exactly what happened," the lieutenant explained. "You handed over an e-pal recording to a guy named Sergeant Ruby, who smuggled it to Europe for you, and handed it over to someone there who made contact with the pirate radio stations inside the Defense Union. What did you say, huh?"

James considered lying but decided against it. He would have to trust this man and his people with his life before long, besides, he was tired of living in a world of secrets.

"I was merely told Ruby about a conversation between myself and Vincent, about how we were the first teleporter researchers to find a clue about a new weapon that could turn the war in our favor." He shrugged. "That's all."

"Of course, you knew that would be enough to make our allies in Europe sit up and take notice. You knew the leadership in Brussels would see it and draw the right conclusions. After all, they know all about you and your team of researchers."

"Yes. I wanted my team with me, and I knew Europe would inform Russia and send my old team, along with some Special Forces soldiers, because only my team would be able to judge if my statement were true. After all, they were the only ones who had ever seen an Avatar."

"Simple logic, huh?"

"Exactly."

"Sounds to me like someone who risked everything and was pretty lucky nothing went wrong," Lacey said. "I'd be completely obliged if you didn't use that kind of strategy on this mission. Believe it or not, you and your friends are not our mission priority."

"Is that a threat?" James asked conversationally.

"Of course!" the lieutenant replied. His grin didn't quite match his serious tone, but it was enough to make him realize who he was dealing with. This soldier and his team had very clear instructions and would not hesitate to sacrifice him and his friends if it was necessary to accomplish their mission objectives, but they would try to prevent such a situation if possible. "If I'm going to have civilians with me, I'd like to have some with balls. What you pulled off there, with your little pirate show disguised as a leak... that took balls. But it was also stupid and reckless. Don't you ever do that around me, you understand?"

James looked into the lieutenant's eyes, which were no longer smiling, and nodded.

"Wonderful. I'm sure we'll become good friends." Lacey leaned forward and patted him on the shoulder as if they were longtime buddies. He looked at his team, who were crouched on the floor of the cabin, weapons in front of their chests, faces made up, and helmets with their flat night-vision goggles flipped up, and made a circling gesture with his hand. "One hour to rendezvous, people."

James looked at Vincent, who was next to him tugging at his camouflage uniform like a teenager who had been forced into a scratchy wool sweater by his mother for a special occasion.

"You okay, big man?" he asked.

"I don't know, I'm kind of nervous."

"We've got these Special Forces guys with us and two more teams coming soon. I don't think we have to worry about getting overpowered by some Bolivian hacker."

"That's not what I mean!" growled Meeks. "I mean our team, for crying out loud!"

"Why does that make you nervous?"

"I... it's been so long, and the world has gotten so crazy.

Man, we've been apart longer than we were together on Al'Antis. Longer, even, than when we knew them before we were transported." The engineer let out a long sigh and looked like a sad reptile in the green cabin light. "The world has gone crazy and I just worry what it might have done to them."

"It hasn't changed us!" James assured him.

"Is that so?"

He didn't answer his friend. Instead he thought about those three words, reflexively wanting to deny them. He was himself, unchanged and constant, just as he always was, but could he be sure of that? If there was one thing he had learned from his teleportation travels, it was that there were different constants in life, a spiritual, mental, and physical constant.

The spiritual was the "I" feeling, a constant feeling of being "James," the way he sensed the world while reflecting on it, the "I am." The mental constant was something he could not yet fathom, a mystical energy, perhaps, that enabled him to be *him* even though he had changed bodies. But perhaps that didn't exist at all.

The physical constant, on the other hand, was not really one, except for the fact that it also amounted to a "feeling," though not in psychological terms, of inhabiting one's own body, which formed a sensory "home." It was interchangeable, he had learned, albeit within narrow limits. The physical body he now lived in was, after all, an artificial product and yet so identical to his original that he didn't notice any difference. But what was it about these constants that changed? Was it his sense of self, his "I" feeling? The impression that he was pitiful because he had felt increasingly worse over the course of the past year? He had to admit to himself that he had felt desperate and only now, when he was full of anticipation at seeing his friends again, especially Mila, did he understand what he had lost in the last twelve months. It was the close bond with other people that only came from confronting danger together. But it was also the intensity of life, the constant newness, the exploration, the wonder, the fear, the relief, the adrenaline—all of it had been so pervasive that he hadn't had time to worry about little things at all, like here on Earth. When you were confronted with new things every day, learning new things every day, life became simple, like it was with the Tokamaku, or even when running from the monster. Everything was focused on the present moment. There was simply no room for a luxury like worry.

In New York, the opposite had been true. He spent a lot of time alone, with no occupation, and a new world that he hardly recognized. It was so tame and disciplined that he could hardly breathe in it.

Then there was the constant news about the end of the world threatening them from space. The many analyses about what would probably happen. For the last two weeks, since his meeting with Norton at McGuire Air Force Base, things had only gotten worse. The Kazerun fleet had passed Saturn, piercing one of its rings in the process, resulting in spectacular images from the orbiting telescopes. They were burned into James's memory like glowing lava: three dozen twinkling stars amid a spreading cloud of dust and ice, blowing apart like a blizzard. With the brown gas giant in the left frame, the sight gave an intimidating impression of larger-than-life violence that had given him, and certainly the entire Earth population, a massive fright.

The problem was getting closer, made more "real" by its imminence. What was almost worse was that the Pentagon's top scientists disagreed about why the fleet had passed through one of Saturn's rings, of all places. Although Saturn was a massive planet against which Earth was about as formidable as a marble next to a medicine ball, the probability of passing so close to the planet by chance was virtually nil. In terms of celestial bodies, the solar system consisted of virtually nothing in its vast expanse, and the system's planets were extremely far apart—even the distance between Earth and the Moon, which was widely considered close, was more than thirty times Earth's circumference.

So other explanations had to be found, ranging from creating fear in the defenders—if so, it had worked—to acquiring mass for ammunition and water, which seemed implausible to the physicists, but it was agreed that the aliens were likely far more advanced, so the possibility could not be excluded. Then, in recent days, the UN space agencies attached to their respective militaries had unanimously confirmed that the fleet had slowed enough that individual ships could be identified in some of the clearer photographs. They were gray, cone-shaped monstrosities, three to four hundred meters long with smooth outer hulls that sported a huge disk on their back, which was actually the front and only pointed backward because the thrusters were pointed forward for braking, what scientists thought was a protective shield. Because of their unimaginably high flight speed, the Kazerun needed protection against interstellar dust. Even hitting a speck of dust or a gas molecule at one-third the speed of light could produce bursts of energy that would make an atomic bomb on Earth seem harmless, as well as produce hard gamma rays. If one believed the experts on television, the shields had probably been larger still when the fleet had left its home system and set course for Earth. In any case, the images had the effect of silencing the last doubters, and a tense heaviness had settled over the member states. It was the weight of expectation and fear because nobody knew what would happen next.

Nobody doubted that it would come to battle. After all, human society had been sworn to the coming conflict for thirty years and knew no other future, no other purpose in life than to prepare for the Battle for Earth. But what exactly would happen? Who would fire the first shots? And how long would it last? Days? Weeks? Or would it turn out to be a months-long battle? Maybe one of just a few days? Brutal and so one-sided that the PDCs would be left in smoking ruins within minutes and the vast number of Navy ships on the seas would explode before they could even fire on the invaders?

No one could say anything for sure, and for the first time in human history, there was no basis for strategies, tactics, expected casualties, and courses of battle prior to an armed confrontation.

"Nearing landing zone," the pilot announced in a hushed voice through the speakers. "Touchdown in T-minus five."

"All right, people," Lacey called out, loading his assault rifle before checking the safety and double-checking his gear. His soldiers did the same. "We're about to go! I want to see one last check!"

James and Meeks did what had been drilled into them on the trip to French Guiana; they checked the fit of their camouflage uniforms, the surprisingly light armored vests, their helmets, and the rest of their gear, which included a backpack with a water supply and drinking tube, a combat knife, a small first aid kit, and a variety of emergency medications. The soldiers would lug everything else with them in their oversized backpacks. When they were finished with their own gear, they set about checking each other's, which included the fit of all straps and buckles. James and Meeks were not armed—the lieutenant had forbidden it. That decision had been a relief to James, while it annoyed Meeks.

The helicopter banked right in a sharp turn, so silent that even without headphones in the cabin they heard no more than a hiss. Once again, James wondered how he could have doubted that the Pentagon, or Norton's people, could track down the hacker and his hideout in no time if they wanted to. Whether they had done it with the help of satellites, spy planes, or their own hackers, he didn't know, but they had. That, in turn, had made him wonder why they hadn't cracked down on the pirate radio stations in the past. In any case, it couldn't have been out of consideration for the democratic states of South America and Africa, since they were globally isolated and would have hardly been able to defend themselves against any measures the global alliance might take. So, they had either decided to tolerate the deviant elements because they didn't want to waste resources on them, or they were somehow useful to their cause. The latter thought worried him.

The feeling didn't last long as they approached a clearing behind a wall of tall trees draped with vines, where two other helicopters had already landed. In the early dawn, he couldn't make out much except for one dark, somewhat dashing, silhouette and another that resembled a rather gray pockmarked structure. But more important to him were the waiting figures gathered in front of it. Not the brawny ones with guns in their hands, but the four who ducked away from the storm of rotors and held their arms in front of their faces.

As soon as they set down, James jumped up and tore the door aside.

"Hey!" Lacey shouted and tried to grab him, but he was faster and driven by an irrepressible impatience so he escaped the soldier's grasp. Outside, the wind from the rotors whipped at him and he instinctively pulled in his shoulders to protect himself from the circling blades, even though they were more than a meter above him, a shimmering disk separating him from the dark blue sky that was losing its last remnants of black, like an ink painting on which too much water had run.

He recognized Mila first by her figure and body language, even before she broke away from the group and ran toward him. Her blonde hair blew around her head, longer than he had ever seen it and unruly.

They met halfway and he embraced her, nearly falling from the impact of their bodies. He began to sob uncontrollably. The smell of her skin and hair rose to his nostrils and kindled a feeling of home in him, as if he had fallen onto his sofa after a very long day at work, somewhere he felt safe and secure and could finally switch off.

"You're really here!" he whispered in her ear, and kissed her unabashedly. She returned his affections, and for a moment they forgot the entire world around them. The wind from the rotor, the voices, the footsteps, the sultry heat, the presence of the others.

"Yes," she breathed, "it's been so long…"

"I know, I know." He laughed and sobbed at the same time.

"You fucking clever bastard!" Mila laughed, her eyes moist as she detached his face from hers and cupped it with her hands, as if memorizing every detail of his face. "What you did there was completely crazy and stupid, but I'm indescribably glad it worked!"

"I had to do something." James looked into her large bright eyes, enjoying the indescribable feeling of something he'd been imagining for months, envisioning in his dreams, only to wake full of sadness that it hadn't been real. "I *had to*."

"I know. I'm sorry I—"

"Shh. You couldn't. None of us could."

"Hey, we're here, too, Mr. Hamilton!" he heard a familiar voice and reluctantly turned away from Mila. It was Justus, who had appeared beside him with Adrian and Mette in tow, all grinning broadly. He hugged them all at once, as if he wanted to sweep them off their feet like a football player. None of them had changed much, except Mette, who had put on a little weight again, but the slight curves suited her much better than the gaunt figure she had become after their time with the Tokamaku, which had always made her look a little sickly and haggard.

Not an eye remained dry during their reunion and, thankfully, the soldiers from Russia and Europe stood to one side exchanging pleasantries, leaving them undisturbed.

12

"I kind of imagined our reunion being more glamorous," Meeks grumbled, pulling a blood-engorged leech from his lower leg. The animal looked like a miniature inflated balloon. The engineer had slung his leg, wet from his sweaty jump boot, over his knee while the group rested in a clearing created by a row of fallen trees. He, James, Mila, and Justus sat on one, gathering their strength after an hours-long forced march that took them little more than three or four kilometers. The thicket was so impenetrable and the terrain so mountainous that they had to fight for every meter. In addition, the eternally damp ground of fresh leaves and shrubs growing between old rotting ones ensured they had to be careful with every step they took, not least because of the many snakes and other venomous animals.

"You can say that again," Justus agreed as he removed his shoes, which wasn't easy since he was wearing gaiters over his pants as protection against the bloodsuckers and each was tied tightly below the ankle and the knee.

James had already removed three leeches from his right

ankle and was holding the fourth and final one between his fingers. Mouth agape, he held the bulging worm in front of his face and flinched as it burst, splattering his own blood across his nose and forehead.

"Yuck!"

"Gets better all the time." Meeks snorted and crushed his specimen with his left foot, which was still in his boot. Then he looked up and pointed to the soldiers, fifteen strong and wearing slightly different forest camouflage patterns, standing a little apart and talking to each other in small groups. "They seem to be getting along pretty well."

"Why wouldn't they?" James asked. "They're all trained for this sort of thing, and I'm sure they're joking about us because we look so pitiful."

"We don't just look pitiful," Justus admitted.

"I don't care where we are, the main thing is that we have found each other again."

"Amen." Mila paused in her attempt to straighten her gaiters and smiled at him. She still looked melancholy, and he thought he knew what was feeding it: The worry that their time would be short-lived and only make the next goodbye worse. "How have you been this past year, anyway?"

"Not well," he admitted freely, shaking his head and sighing. "Norton put me in charge of finding the Avatar, but I didn't even know where to start looking. I can't get a job because my skills aren't needed in the civilian manufacturing industry, and the general only saved me from conscription by giving me this assignment, even though I would have been a borderline case anyway because the invasion is so close. I was therefore exploited as a promotional figure for the Military Council because they knew I could talk reasonably straight, and they needed someone from the civilian section of society whom they could make into a hero. Of course, that was all so the non-combatant herd would continue to be motivated to manufacture their ammunition and missile parts. I was a damned mascot and I was supposed to get everyone fired up and convince them how dangerous the Kazerun are."

"Adrian and I were questioned for weeks about what happened on the other side of the teleporter and exactly how the project went in Wyoming," Mila said. "After that, we were moved to Voronezh to strategic planning. We had to write manuals about the Kazerun, even though we knew very little about them, and what little we did know came from your stories—hardly enough to fill manuals with. It was all very strange. Adrian didn't even know anyone back home anymore. All his friends, and even the last of his relatives, are dead now."

"Sometimes that's better than the alternative," Justus said, sighing heavily. James had noticed that the astrophysicist looked considerably worse than the last time he had seen him. Bags had formed under his eyes and his tan had not returned. Instead, he looked almost as pale as Adrian.

"Your family..." Mila suddenly looked as if someone had hit her, and the look she gave Justus was full of sympathy. He nodded.

"Sarah, she... is an aged grandmother. Her second husband died of cancer two years ago, and our children, they—" He broke off and sniffled. "They're both in the military, stationed at the PDC Western Alps as rocket engineers, and they're my age."

"Oh, Justus," James said in a pained voice. "I can't even imagine what that must feel like. I'm so sorry."

"It could have been worse, you know." His friend nodded, his lips pressed together, as if trying hard to believe his own words. "They're still alive and they somehow got over my disappearance, moved on. Even though it hurts, it's what I always hoped for in my prayers on Al'Antis. I wanted them to be okay and get over it. I was even comfortable with the idea of Sarah finding a new husband to take care of her and the boys. That's exactly what happened. Frederick and Michel live and work in a defense center deep under the Alps. There is no safer place in Europe, and I know how few have been chosen for that location. I should be grateful, and I am."

"You haven't contacted them, have you?" Mila asked.

Justus shook his head. "No. That wouldn't have been fair to them. They moved on, and if I showed up now, same as the last time they saw me… I don't know what that would do to them. They'd probably feel guilty for moving on and putting me behind them. In a few weeks, it's going to be raining fire from the sky and they certainly don't need a ghost from the past tearing their whole world apart with his mere presence."

"I understand."

The German waved dismissively and forced a tired smile. "Doesn't matter. I'm staying strong for them now, and I've got something else to do again besides making orbital mechanical calculations for the use of hypersonic weapons."

"You're working on hypersonic missiles?" Meeks asked, apparently glad for the change of subject, away from the oppressive melancholy.

"No, not directly. I am an astrophysicist and quite good at calculating orbital mechanical relationships. Those fundamentals don't change, even after thirty years. I calculate the exact flight vectors and corresponding acceleration phases."

"And what do you think? Are we armed against what's in store for us?"

"Who knows? The hypersonic rockets are impressive. They fly at up to twenty times the speed of sound and can reach orbit, which is something. But cosmically… for a flight to Mars, that would be way too slow. Just because something is crazy fast on Earth doesn't make it so in space. Railguns are exciting because they fire many projectiles without requiring their own propulsion and have an extremely high muzzle velocity. Firing at objects in orbit is very, and you can't intercept the tungsten cones because they are small and create no propulsion signature. But we would need a lot more of them to have an effective defensive shield." Justus shrugged. "We'll see how we do. I wouldn't get my hopes up, though, to be honest." He nodded toward the soldiers at the edge of the clearing. Some of them were talking to Adrian and Mette. "They all believe in it, but it's no wonder, they've grown up in a world that has only known one goal. This one huge, desperate battle and the progress in military technologies has been amazing, after all. Necessity is the mother of invention, but it's deceptive because it's no match against a civilization like the Kazerun, who have been engaged in wars with each other for millennia and can build starships like the ones they've sent against us. Believe me, if they come to the party with machine guns, we'll shoot back with water pistols, at best."

"Great," Meeks grumbled.

"He's right," Mila agreed with Justus. "You're an engineer yourself, and you know it, too, if you're honest with yourself."

"So, we have three more weeks before the sky literally falls on our heads. I refuse to think in such defeatist terms."

"It's not like everyone's going to die," Mila said. "The

PDCs are already impressively protected, and material is material no matter what weapons you fire at it. Unless they burn everything so aggressively that the whole Earth ends up irradiated, but that would be pretty stupid. A fleet like that one up there"—she pointed in the direction of the leafy canopy—"has as much fuel as it needs to get there, but it doesn't just fly away. They've come to stay, that much is certain, even if we don't know much else."

Meeks sighed and wrung out his socks before pulling them over the bleeding bites inflicted by the leeches he had pulled off, and they wouldn't stop bleeding for the next few hours because of the anticoagulants in the worms' saliva.

"I know, I know. Then all we can do is hope that our defenses work better than expected, or a miracle happens, and we really do meet the Avatar out here—even though that seems a pretty absurd idea to me."

"We'll find it. Somehow."

"You don't actually believe that, do you?" Justus asked, eyeing him. When James didn't answer, he nodded. "I figured as much."

"It's not that I don't believe it, but the Avatar on Al'Antis was anything but reclusive. It always lived where there was the most to observe and comprehend. It was always jumping back and forth, never staying in one place for long, and certainly not in some jungle where nothing was happening that could move the world."

"But if this hacker really did decode the signal," Meeks said, "then the focus of Earth's fate would be right here, at least for a short time. What bigger message could there be?"

"It might not be a message at all if the signal simply infected all the hacker's computers with a virus, then the whole matter would have no meaning at all," James insisted. "My hope rests more on the fact that we can use the hacker's findings to draw out the Avatar and then identify it when the time comes."

"We should, after all. The Kazerun will have reached Mars orbit in a week, and then we'll see if they can actually knock us out from there."

"All right, people!" Lieutenant Lacey shouted suddenly, making a circular motion with the outstretched index finger of his right hand. "Here we go. Put on your shoes, strap on your packs, and let's go!"

"On through leech country," Meeks grumbled, nodding gratefully when James helped him to his feet. He kissed Mila and they continued northwest, climbing ever steeper hills through the green hell of the South American rainforest.

After a couple more hours, during which the column of soldiers and civilians stretched for nearly a hundred meters and shifted ever so slightly in composition, he found himself near the lieutenant just as he finished a conversation with his German colleague, commander of the European team.

"Fifteen heavily armed Special Forces personnel to grab a hacker," James said, breathing heavily, and Lacey gave him a sidelong glance as if he only now noticed him. "Seems kind of overkill to me."

"I would have preferred a single team, too. But thanks to your little e-pal show, the Russians and Europeans are dying to get in on the action."

"I hope you're not too offended by that?"

"I'm a soldier. It's not my job to judge the actions of others. I do what I'm told to do, and I've been told to protect some civilians and take down a hacker's hideout if they fail in questioning the criminal." Lacey shrugged and rested his assault rifle across his shoulders like a yoke and draped his hands over the ends. "More reinforcements can hardly hurt, no matter what might come our way."

"I've been meaning to ask; how did you find the guy?"

"The hacker?"

"Yes." James pointed around them and stepped over a gnarled root, shiny with moisture, as a handful of insects detached themselves and flew away with protesting chirps. He continued to fend off swarms of buzzing mosquitoes by waving his hand all around his head. "I mean, how do you find someone who doesn't want to be found, is probably a paranoid hacker, and probably knows how to stay hidden? And so quickly, too."

"The general has his ways," Lacey said vaguely.

"You think he tracked down our target himself?"

"No, not himself!" The lieutenant chortled, amused, as if they were on a simple hiking trip. "But he's extremely well connected with all branches of the armed forces, enjoys prestige in all of them, even at the highest levels. He was himself considered the most promising successor for the Military Council should Fleet Admiral Jones pass away, but the old scoundrel seems to be as tough as he looks. So, the general will have to settle for number five in the pecking order."

"Whereas ranks one through four hold just about all the power," James said.

"Yes. That's just the way it is. But if we win the war, it's only a matter of a few years, I think." The lieutenant winked.

"But how did he do it? Or had it done?"

"I don't know. I'm not an expert on that sort of thing. He probably called the NSA chief, told him who and what he was looking for, and had him push some buttons."

"Satellites?"

"No. We hardly have any satellites over South America and Africa. Especially no spy satellites, which is what it would take. What we do have, we focus on our own country, so the sheep stream in the right direction." His grin was more a half smile, half smirk. "But the remnants of the internet that these people still use are not entirely overlooked by our computer guys at the NSA. They still have access to it. The Military Council doesn't like to leave things to chance, and certainly not to other forces."

"If Norton is so well connected, he could have looked for the Avatar himself," James muttered.

"He's a busy man," Lacey said. "And with the deportation program, he exercises a pivotal influence on our future. The responsibility is great, and I think the Military Council's view is also very... exact, if you know what I mean."

"I understand."

"Doesn't have to bother us. Norton is an outstanding string-puller and does nothing impulsively. If he sent us here, he has a clear strategy, you can be sure of that."

"Norton not impulsive and a string puller?" James snorted. "He's taken a different turn in the last thirty years than we thought he would."

"He's gotten old. You're supposed to get wiser and calmer in your old age." The lieutenant eyed him appraisingly. "What's he got on you, anyway?"

"I carried him with a shattered spine into the teleporter on Prime, and I wasn't in great shape myself. Until then I always thought he didn't like anyone and just growled all the time, but since then he seems to respect me."

"Hmm. That only happens in combat. A soldier never forgets you when risk your own skin to bail him out. I've never heard of the general protecting anyone. He's a chess player, no Mr. Nice Guy. You're the first exception, but now I know why." Lacey nudged him with his elbow. "And I also know now that you're not so bad for a civilian."

"No Mr. Nice Guy is probably the understatement of the century. At the time, I thought he was a typical robot officer, with no feelings and no will of his own. But he's had outbursts that always challenged that image."

"He's been promoted from major to general in a very short time and then marched through the general ranks like a marathon runner. That's pretty unusual for someone his age who hadn't made it to the senior ranks by then. I've been told that he was often passed over because of his unbending nature. I guess you misjudged him there."

"How did he manage that?" James wanted to know.

"Don't know. When I joined the military, he was already a brigadier general." The lieutenant shrugged. "I suspect he's gotten his impulsive streak under control. Also, the teleporter project probably earned him a lot of important contacts in Russia and the EU. In any case, I know he's one of the best connected international leaders we have in the Pentagon. That should also explain his great value to the Military Council and why he moved up so quickly. During the restructuring of the UN, there were years of negotiations that were not exactly easy and Norton played an important role. However, he is not the most popular with the troops."

"No?" James asked, surprised. "Why not?"

"Because his coldly analytical manner comes across as rather callous, and the majority of the men and women in black thrive on the fire that is constantly stoked within them, be it with pep talks like yours or the constant propaganda on the networks and on TV. Most of them are just looking forward to kicking some alien ass. They're like teenagers racing down a street in their parents' Porsche.

They want to see other sports cars, not an immovable wall before them and ending the fun."

"I understand."

Lacey narrowed his eyes and appeared to be watching something through the trees that James couldn't see. Then he looked down at the display on his forearm that was protected by a protective plastic cover from the ever-present moisture and dirt of the rainforest, and his permanent smile disappeared.

"What's going on?"

"We're approaching the target point."

13

Dakhra was lying under the flattened console and wiped her hands on her ruthenium-reinforced ship's overalls before picking up the separator again and connecting the spectral circuits, which looked like plucked stalks of a particularly ugly weed. That the ship was still flying at all was nothing short of a miracle, after all the decades it had been subjected to cosmic rays, bombardment by microasteroids, and a general lack of attention from energy. Everything the fusion reactors did had gone into the antimatter reactor, specifically the magnetic confinement chambers to keep the positrons away from the surrounding protons. The magnetic coils and energy pattern cells had also always been flooded, but without giving off too strong a signature that might have allowed them to be detected early.

Now that they were on final approach to the target it no longer mattered because the final phase of their plan had been initiated. All that was left was to make up for the lost decades of cold sleep before deploying the full force of their fleet. This required engineers like Dakhra, who understood war and the need not to make any mistakes when time was of the essence.

"After nearly sixty years of inaction"—she groaned as she turned the separator, her tongue between her teeth, and quickly squinted as lubricant splashed her face—"we're suddenly in a hurry."

"Dakhra!"

"Bloody moon!" she cursed as she winced, startled, and bumped her head on the underside of the console. She frowned and slid back until she was looking into her father's face. Captain Ultrak was a tall man with the stocky figure of a much shorter one. Genetic adaptations to a life in space had made his muscles knobby and his face rounded, his hands and feet were larger than they would have been on Kazerun if he had never left the ground. His eyes were large and his forehead long and receding. For his one hundred and twenty years, he still had surprisingly little gray hair and the body tension of a much younger man.

"Father! You could announce yourself when you come down here."

"Am I not allowed to talk to my daughter?"

"I have a communicator for that." She tapped the chest of her ship's overalls. "What is it? I thought we were in a hurry. Or would you rather let the bots get to work?"

"No!" he replied firmly, his eyebrows drawn together darkly. "No bots."

"See?" Dakhra spread her arms. "Then you shouldn't distract me, otherwise our own field emitters will roast us when we open fire."

"We have a very short window of opportunity."

"And how is that going to help me now?"

"I don't mean for the repairs!" Ultrak paced, back and forth, something not particularly easy in the small maintenance room, which was normally designed for the dwarf-like, eight-armed bots, and was accordingly low and squat.

"You want to talk to me alone." She sighed and set the separator aside before sitting up and wrapping her arms around her knees. "So? What's on your mind?"

"You know very well."

"You want me to agree with you that our attack is necessary because our attack codes have had no effect. You want me to say 'Yes, fire all guns. If they don't die, we will. Besides, they're not Kazerun and they're not even human.'"

"Something like that, yes."

Dakhra sighed. In her data consciousness she went over the latest analysis messages the ship's core had processed for her. Numbers and graphs settled over her field of vision and she went through them intently and systematically with her mind.

"You didn't have to bother coming here," she finally said. "I know you're afraid morale will suffer if our passengers realize we might blow up if we fire, but we won't. Reduce the number of field emitters used to one-third and the reactor shouldn't overload. I'll indicate the corresponding guns that have flawless leads, then we should be safe."

"Good." He nodded thoughtfully and smoothed his dark red uniform, which no longer showed any insignia. There was no need for that, either. "We'll try the attack code one last time. Malak said we could try minimizing the scatter and increasing the signal strength to maybe get through."

"Their firewalls are too strong. Or they've been blocking all incoming signals since the state of emergency broke out. This system will shortly be in flames, remember? Nobody's going to open the mail voluntarily anymore."

"I still want to try. It would be a waste if we were forced to—"

"Father," she interrupted him. "They are not human beings. They are in the way and must be destroyed so we can be free. It's as simple as that."

Ultrak eyed her for an endless moment, then nodded and turned on his heel. Dakhra watched him go, staring at the door that had formed after his departure before she held the separator to the magnetic belt on her hip and stood. Quickly, she patted her jumpsuit off and, via data consciousness, ordered the bots to continue their work.

The traces of decades of sabotage to the ship's weapons systems—and her nearly three dozen companion ships were no different—were not obviously visible, but with her data awareness, which could make the walls transparent to her and reveal the superconductors and spectral cables beneath, the damage almost jumped out at her.

They had done a good job, a deviant potential amid order of violence that was equated with progress. And yet it seemed to her that it was just more of the same: devious and calculating. At least they could boast of having been relatively prescient, if not prescient enough, for now they had the problem of having too few field emitters available to take out the entire defense with the first volley. Not that it would have made much difference because they were in no real danger. They would have fired the second volley long before they could expect a response and ensured that nothing but smoking ruins remained. The only question was what would happen then, how would the conflict develop? Would they have a chance to start over so far away from home and everything they knew? Or were they merely destroying their future livelihood for generations to suffer the consequences?

The coming battle would tell, and it was closer now than ever before.

Dakhra left the maintenance bay and walked through the corridors in the heart of the ship, which she had christened *Ashzarun* even before it was stolen, in memory of the legendary admiral. It was the flagship of her fleet, but that was only due to its internal fleet codes, which were only relevant in the shared data sphere. Apart from that, the *Ashzarun* was identical in construction to her sister ships: a battlecruiser, several generations old and long out of date.

At the heart of the titanium structure of spiderweb-like struts was the crew toroid, a carbin cylinder two hundred meters long and forty meters wide, heavily armored and rotating along its longitudinal axis. The front ended in the gigantic shield of sixty-meter-thick alloys they had built in the shadow of the destroyed moon Kulptra to survive their species' first interstellar voyage. At the rear, in front of the fifty-meter diameter drive nacelle, was the antimatter reactor, which, unlike the fusion reactor, was decoupled from the crew toroid and had even heavier armor. The titanium struts surrounding everything encased both and their tops were crammed with propellant tanks that contained a significant portion of Kulptra's former ice mass, considering the volume of tanks in their entire fleet. That their operation had gone undetected for so many decades bordered on nothing less than a miracle and was probably due solely to the fact that Kulptra had already been stripped of all its rare earths and precious metals two centuries ago when the Kas'Ashtra mining ships had arrived to plunder the larger moons of the asteroid belt. No one was interested in the ice of a plundered rocky moon, which was just an oversized asteroid, because if there was one thing in abundance in space it was ice.

Time and again, she was amazed that her civilization had never managed to send spaceships into the interstellar void and pursue their urge to expand in this way. In the end, however, she had naturally understood why none of the ever-shifting power blocs wanted to risk spending so much of their resources and time to facilitate a mission that brought them no benefits in their home system. Because of the great distances involved, any interstellar journey meant that extremely long periods of time would pass and there would be no return—at least not within several generations. In addition, the competing factions simply could not do it. Since the Kazerun were always at war, hot or cold, there was always only one way to avoid being subjugated or wiped out by their enemies, and that was: show no weakness. So, every bit of money was put into armament and military research, even during the war against the Al'Anter, the only major threat from outside they had faced so far, and an indication that humans had not only appeared on Kazerun.

But that war was a very long time ago, and for all they knew, Al'Antis had been destroyed. All the more reason for the leaders to emphasize how important it was to always be alert and ready, and not be caught off guard. Every investment was evaluated only in terms of its short-term usefulness for the survival of their power bloc. This thinking had, paradoxically, not only ensured that war and hostility remained a permanent condition—after all, one had to be able to justify one's policies—but had also led to long-term projects such as interstellar exploration being seen as unpatriotic, risky, and dangerous. It was a notion that had been burned into the collective consciousness over the centuries and millennia, not least because of controlled schooling that was ultimately aimed at producing more motivated soldiers.

In the crew toroids, along with five hundred cryostasis chambers, there were accommodations for the two hundred-man crews, located just like the mess halls and sickbays in the outer part of a ship's rotating tube, where the centrifugal force was strongest, creating a comfortable half-G.

In the corridors, she encountered several crew members, some of whom were still saluting reflexively. They either hadn't been around long or had been woken up early, so for them, only a few minutes had passed, while for the rest of them nearly a century had passed. But all that would soon come to an end, and then they would all have to readjust as a new life awaited them.

But first, they had to clear the last great obstacle that still held them back from their common future, the next step in the progress of Kazerun civilization as it should have been taken long ago, without all the baggage and destruction that had disrupted their home system over the millennia. A final departure to a new world, a new shore, unsullied and possibly very much like their homeland, if the few astro-mathematicians could be believed. Soon they would know more.

Very soon.

14

The hacker's hideout lay in a densely vegetated basin in the middle of the northeastern foothills of the Andes, which walled off Bolivia's west. From the maps, James knew that in only a few kilometers the landscape would radically change and become arid. The vegetation line was only a few hundred meters altitude away. Above the line, conditions were very different, including lower oxygen levels, which were already making themselves felt.

The three teams were moving along a ridge running to the east, where a storm had cleared it of trees. The trunks, already rotting and eaten by vermin, lay crisscrossed on the forest floor as if a giant had gone berserk with a scythe. But the logs offered them the perfect cover, and when Lacey handed him the binoculars, it only took him a few minutes to find the hideout. It was a ruin left by miners who had apparently dispersed into the wilderness after the gold rush ended instead of returning to La Paz. The foundation walls were still standing, but the windows and roof had been improvised, patched, or replaced without much care. Rusty, corrugated metal sheeting, composed of several roughly connected segments, were overgrown with grass and creepers and protected them from the rain. The building itself was only one story, but large enough to provide shelter for several families. Its full dimensions were not readily apparent, as much of it was obscured by trees and brush to the south. Several satellite dishes were mounted in the surrounding trees, and a larger facility stood on the ridge behind the building, several hundred feet higher than the relative ground level. Thick cables, visible even from their elevation without electronic magnification, looked like white silk threads running along tree bark and slopes connecting the house and dishes like telltale fuses.

"No access path," James whispered without setting down the binoculars.

"Uh-huh. I couldn't detect one either," the lieutenant replied at a normal volume. The hideout was a good half kilometer away, and James now felt stupid for whispering. He felt like a civilian who had to be babysat by the soldiers —something he had resolved not to allow. "It doesn't necessarily mean anything."

"Not necessarily?"

"It *could* mean that there's a bunker under that ruin with an underground entrance where supplies are delivered. I've seen this setup before. It's a favorite of terrorists who are constantly expecting to be raided at some point. In most cases, the above-ground decoy gets attacked, while in the *actual* hideout below, they have time enough to disappear through tunnels." Lacey shrugged and took his field glasses back from James. The other soldiers and his friends had all taken positions more or less in a straight line behind fallen logs, sticking out their fingers to point at something from time to time, or talk quietly enough to each other so he couldn't make out what they were saying even from a few feet away. "But it could also be that the guy just doesn't have any cash and stocked up on supplies for after the invasion before he moved out here."

"So, what do you think?"

The officer seemed surprised by the question and eyed James as if searching his face for signs that he was joking.

"Well, go in with everything, of course."

"I see. Professional ethics, probably."

"Exactly."

"So, we have a half hour, right?"

"Mmm, right," Lacey confirmed. "I'll time you once you and your team are down there. Then you'll have thirty minutes before we come in and take care of everything."

"What's your order, anyway? Or is it classified?"

"Oh no, it's not secret. Not only do we have orders to film the whole operation—and you"—the soldier tapped the uniform buttons of his two breast pockets on his flak jacket—"but to arrest the hacker."

He was about to express his relief that there was no apparent kill order for the hacker, James suddenly blinked and stared at the buttons in turn.

"You're filming all this?" he asked, irritated.

"Of course. Standard procedure for special operations forces. Besides, Norton wants to know exactly what's going on."

"That means you've recorded every conversation?"

"Sure. But don't worry. The recordings go to the general, not directly to the Military Council." Lacey winked as if he'd made a good joke.

"Well, then I'm even happier that we'll have some peace and quiet when we go in there... without your nosy little spies," he grumbled.

"Enjoy it if you can. For the record, I would like to note

that I still think it's a stupid idea to let six civilians, without backup and without any prior intelligence on the target and how dangerous he is, to show up at a criminal's hideout without protection. Anyone who's hunkered down out here is not going to be the kind, next-door neighbor type who takes out your trash and pets your dog. You should really think about at least taking along pistols. The offer stands."

James shook his head. "No. The thing about guns is that if you have them, you use them. With a hammer in your hand, everything becomes a nail, and with a gun, everything becomes a threat to be eliminated. Besides, the Avatar is not a killer."

"If you say so." Lacey sounded unconvinced but shrugged and strapped a military e-pal around James's wrist. "In case you do want to call us."

He gestured forward as if extending an invitation. "Good luck."

15

"I'm not so sure this is such a good idea anymore," Meeks said as they made their way down the slope through the undergrowth. Again and again, they had to stop and support each other to avoid slipping on the wet ground, which was rocky and slippery in numerous places. Now it was clear to all of them why they had not come here with the helicopters. Even with the new stealth technology and the very quiet rotors, there was still the problem of the rugged landscape and narrow little valleys that were so overgrown that you couldn't even rappel down into them. Not to mention that they probably would have broken their backs in the process because none of them had any training for it.

"No matter what happens here, it was worth it," Mette stated. "Seeing you guys again, I mean. Sneaking into a hacker's creepy lair somewhere in the Bolivian jungle isn't exactly what I had in mind."

"It's no worse than stumbling through the storage complex on Al'Antis plagued by radiation sickness and surrounded by thorny brush. Or the death zone with the monster," Justus said. "Just a reminder."

"I don't think any of us have forgotten."

They reached a large boulder that had been halted by two mighty trees as it crashed into the valley. Dense bushes to the right and left blocked the way and teemed with snakes, so they climbed over it. James and Adrian posted themselves at the top and, one by one, helped the others so no one sprained their foot or suffered any serious scrapes the last few meters to their goal. They remembered they were very far from their respective homes, and the nearest outpost with halfway decent medical care was the EU exclave in French Guiana, three thousand kilometers away as the crow flies. Even with their modern aircraft, the flight had taken over six hours.

"What are we actually hoping to find?" Mila asked, curious rather than critical, reaching her hand up to James to climb off the boulder after Adrian.

"I don't know," he admitted. "If I'm being completely honest, I let Vincent talk me into it because I saw an opportunity to get us back together."

"I don't blame you," Adrian said, patting him on the back. "None of us do. On the contrary."

"Thank you. Now that we're here, though, I have a feeling we're right. Hard to say."

"The Avatar isn't hidden here, anyway."

"No," James agreed, shaking his head. "This is the last place a being whose primary job is to witness and see and store as much as possible would be."

"But Norton must have been aware of that, too," Mila objected.

Meeks snorted. "He always has his own agenda, doesn't he? He's not stupid. He has to know that something doesn't add up."

"He did," James agreed, pushing vines out of his way.

Raindrops filled with dirt fell from the small leaves and joined the mixture of rotting branches and mud on the ground. "And he'll know that I was aware that he knew."

"So, there's another reason," Mila said.

"There could be quite a few. He might think that tracking down the hacker will give us a clue about the Avatar."

"You mean that the hacker got help from the Avatar to decode the signal?"

"For example. That would be fairly easy to do without leaving much evidence," he mused. "An anonymous tip on an internet forum, a chat with an anonymous hacker who gives our man on the ground here the crucial tip, contact through a mutual friend or an internet acquaintance with a cryptography tutorial—the possibilities on the internet are endless and wouldn't expose the Avatar, but at least we'd have a clue, and even if it only enables us to contact this anonymous tipster from the 'net, that would be a big win in itself."

"And how are we going to get it to respond to us at all if worst comes to worst?" Meeks wanted to know.

"Easy, by giving it information that obviously proves that we are aware of it and know what it is and why it's doing what it's doing. The prime directive of an Avatar is not to be recognized because it is vital that the observed are unaware of being observed."

"Because then the observed don't behave normally."

James nodded at his friend. "Exactly. The public doesn't know about the Avatar yet."

"Didn't you refer to it in any of your speeches?" Mila asked.

"No. I talked about my experiences on Al'Antis, but not

about the fact that presumably each of the six planets has or had one of its own."

"There must be more to it than that," she said. "Norton wouldn't expend so many resources to send us out here if he didn't hope to get much out of it."

"What could he possibly hope for?" As if to punctuate his question, Meeks snapped off a half-rotted branch and tossed it away. "The Kazerun fleet is probably nearing Martian orbit right now and will blast us into nirvana soon —or today—and then the matter will be settled. What would he gain by sending us out here? We have seen what the Kazerun are capable of. Al'Antis is the best proof of their aggression and cruelty."

"If the Al'Anters had visited Earth during World War II, I'm sure we would have tried to destroy them as well. The whole planet was at war," Justus said.

"What I'm saying is that he can't consider a last-minute trip like this to be very useful."

"Unless he knows something we don't," Mette said. "And I'd *wager* he knows things we don't."

"But then he didn't have to send us."

"Maybe he just wants to know what the signal really is," James thought aloud. "The UN is refusing to provide even a single hard drive for this, and I understand that. A computer virus would be the biggest disaster for our defense; the fight would be over before it started."

"We're going in circles," Adrian said. "We don't know what Norton hopes to get out of this. That's just the way it is. We're here and he's not, so we have to make the best of it."

"He's right," Mila agreed. "We've all spent the last year coming to terms with the idea that we're next on the Kazerun hit list. I haven't had a quiet night since."

She was silent for a few moments, and only the cracking

and smacking of their footsteps through the dense undergrowth broke the silence as they clumsily made their way toward the valley floor.

"I keep wondering what it will be like. Sometimes the whole sky is on fire, sometimes it lights up only briefly, and other times everything around me explodes. Invariably, I'm standing on a street at night, and I see the battle burst out in light and flame. Monstrous ships swoop down on us with long tails of fire, incinerating the entire landscape. I see PDCs firing whole volleys of hypersonic missiles and long streaks of railgun fire. Sometimes it's a savage battle, sometimes it's a massacre, and, always, our planet burns in the end, and only a few, buried deep within the PDCs, survive." Mila sighed and the silence was uncomfortable. "I'm sorry if that sounds grim, but it's gotten worse since the fleet crossed Neptune's orbit. It's kind of become real and not just some abstract problem NASA has suggested. They're here and they're close, and now we're in the final weeks—maybe even days—before my nightmares become reality."

"It's okay," James said, putting a hand on her shoulder. "I think I speak for all of us when I say we're all terrified. Even more scared than most people because we've seen with our own eyes what a world looks like when the Kazerun are done with it."

"It could be that the time has already arrived, James," she replied firmly. "If they've reached Mars orbit and the pessimists are right, they could start firing at any moment, and by the time we get out of the jungle, the world as we know it won't be there anymore."

"It's still speculation," Adrian said. "I feel that inner tension too, like we're going through the last days of Earth, but we can't let it get us down. We have to do what we can do, and that's to *keep going*! We shouldn't become obsessed with things we can't influence."

"Amen," Mette agreed.

"There's the building!"

James stopped and ducked behind the cracked root of a tree uprooted decades ago, its overgrown trunk long since part of the jungle floor. The others followed his lead, taking cover to his right and left and raising their eyes just above the edge to see the house through the leaves.

It was late afternoon and already darker than it had been an hour ago, but even with the heavy rain clouds overhead, it was still bright enough to clearly make everything out. The windows, which he had thought would be empty, had simple panes of glass like those used two hundred years ago. Most of the varnish had peeled off their rotted wood frames. Tufts of grass and weeds grew in the joints of the ancient masonry, which had reclaimed the old gold mine structure over the decades. Only the patched, corrugated iron roof—though rusted—seemed to have remained somewhat untouched by nature, if one disregarded all the dirt and smaller branches lying atop it.

"There's the entrance!" Adrian hissed beside him, pointing to a dented metal door on the right side, set in a T-shaped structure that ran like a spur into the forest. Through the dark shadow cast by the trees, James hadn't recognized it at all.

"How should we proceed?" Justus whispered, licking his lips tensely.

"We're going in," James decided. He felt the surprised looks his friends gave him and he raised his hands. "What? We're not trained Special Forces soldiers like our companions up on the hill. Imitating them would not only be ridiculous, but fruitless. Adrian is the only one of us who has served in the military, but not in the jungle."

"But we're wearing camouflage clothing," Mette said. "How would the hacker know we're not a threat?"

"For one thing, we're unarmed. For another, I'm sure they could tell we're civilians from ten miles away. So, let's not pretend. We'll do what we do best: remain analytical, be friendly, and look for a solution without any bang-bang."

After no one objected, he left his cover and walked in a relatively straight line toward the door. There was rustling behind him as the others followed him.

Hope you're not mistaken, he thought to himself as he stepped onto a weed-covered sidewalk originally made of rough-hewn cobblestones that followed the half-crumbled wall of the house and continued to the left. There was more rustling in the bushes and he winced as some sort of lemur darted from one bush to another.

"Man." He exhaled slowly, long and drawn out to release the tension in his body. He reached the door and noticed several spider webs overlapping in the upper corners. In one of them sat a palm-sized specimen with long, yellow legs. The sight made his guts tighten.

"They're just spiders," Adrian said, from beside him and used a small stick to remove the webs. The arthropod quickly moved to safety and disappeared into a crack between two of the natural stones that formed the door frame. James reached out, intending to knock, before stopping and pressing down on the handle, which promptly snapped off and fell clattering onto the pitted stone slab at his feet.

The sudden noise broke the silence and made him cringe. He froze for a moment, listening for some reaction, but he heard only the sounds of the jungle that he had not even noticed before: monkeys chattering in the distance, the twitter of birds, and the chirp of insects fighting in the undergrowth.

"You could have knocked, you know," Adrian said breaking the tension. James screwed up his face. He looked closer and realized the door wasn't locked at all. A fine shadow on the frame showed it was open about an inch. He hesitated only a moment before slipping his fingers into the gap and slowly pulling the door open.

The door protested with screeching hinges that had not been oiled for at least a hundred years. The smell of must and rotten paper hit him, mixed with the acrid stench of black mold and fungus. As soon as he opened his narrowed eyes, he saw a long room where a mold-eaten wooden table stood with one leg rotting away. Chairs lay crisscrossed on a floor full of old leaves and rampant with red and yellow mushrooms. Cobwebs hung in gray veils from the ceiling. Crumbling shelves and open dressers held picture frames and tools covered in a patina so thick they could only be recognized as such by their outline.

"It's all ancient," Mila said.

They slowly formed a semicircle just inside the ramshackle room. The ceiling was made of old wood planks, but were so decayed and hung so low that James expected them to collapse on him at any moment. Just then the room was filled with what sounded like hail on a car roof.

"What's that?" he asked, startled.

"Rain!" Mette grumbled, who had come in last. She had to raise her voice to be heard at all. "A downpour, to be exact. This corrugated metal makes it pretty loud."

"Whoever used to live here," Meeks said, "certainly doesn't now."

"This place has been abandoned for decades, maybe

even longer." Mila picked up one of the picture frames, blew most of the dust and dirt off it, then rubbed the patina away with her sleeve. James stepped up beside her and looked at the faded black-and-white photo of three men with long beards and suspenders over plaid shirts. They wore leather hats and looked at the camera with serious expressions. "Just men. No wonder the place is so messy."

He snorted at her jest and moved further into the room, lifting an old hammer that lay between a knot of mushrooms and a newspaper that was now only a pulpy brown mass, soaked with moisture and largely rotten. An arched doorway led into what had once been a kitchen with two wood-burning ovens with cast-iron stove tops that could be removed. Some wall shelves were broken and beneath them lay the shards of canning jars whose contents had produced a pile of wild growth. They cautiously continued their exploration, walking gingerly over the rough floor littered with the remains of ruined furniture, glass shards, and mushrooms.

As if they had agreed beforehand, they stayed together, not speaking a word to each other. The house was like a maze with many rooms arranged in no logical pattern. There were bedrooms with wooden bunk beds, one of which still stood upright with a black-stained mattress riddled with fist-sized holes that showed the work of rats that had gnawed on anything organic. In the living room, half of which had been cut into the rock that formed the northern end of the building, they found two skeletons with tarnished bones sitting on the remains of a sofa that was barely recognizable as such. One of them was holding a rusty old revolver, and both skulls had holes near the temples.

"Great," Mette muttered, and gulped. "I guess it couldn't get any creepier."

"I don't think anything like hackers were around when these two killed themselves," Adrian said, squatting in front of the stained bones and inspecting them closely.

James turned in a circle, searching the walls and ceilings. "But we saw the antennae. They definitely don't date from the time these men were alive. Someone had to be here to put them up, and use them, too."

"Yeah." The cosmonaut looked up at him. "There's only one thing wrong with your assumption. Someone has been here and installed them to use it, sure. But maybe they installed the hardware and is sitting in La Paz right now, five hundred kilometers away in a high-rise, their laptop open and their eyes on a feed from a surveillance camera hidden around here somewhere."

"No, he separated the signal source from the transmission site of his signal. We were aware of that possibility beforehand." James shook his head. "There's a reason Norton discovered this location and sent us here."

"He may have wanted to get rid of us," Meeks said.

"But why?"

"What do I know? After all, he doesn't let us in on anything."

"The authorities in La Paz certainly won't allow a hacker to turn the UN against them. Far too dangerous," Mila said. "After all, there's a good reason all those pirate radio stations are operating in huts somewhere in the jungle, in remote territory far from civilization, with a sufficient cache of supplies and independent carrier signals. Also, now that we've seen the hideout, two things seem to be nudging us in the same direction. We are afraid and would prefer to turn back immediately. This is the effect on our reptilian brain.

Our logical mind is telling us we've been tricked, and this location is just a front. The obvious conclusion is that we're just looking in the wrong place. Right?"

Adrian nodded. "That sounds about right."

"So, our hacker must be *here*." She sounded certain. "If I were him or her, I'd do the same."

"But there's no one here."

"No, not here."

Mila's eyes glanced downward then she looked at the group. James understood and retrieved some branches from the fire pit in the kitchen. After he spread them out, they began systematically tapping the floor covered in biomass and debris until a hollow sound rang out from Mette's direction in a corner of the living room.

"I think I've got something!"

16

Dakhra arrived at the bridge a few minutes before they reached effective combat range. It was a heavily armored globe in the center of the crew toroid. At its center was the commander's gimbaled seat, which could be rotated in three dimensions. The consoles of the ship's supervisors were arranged on the walls like little rungs inside a ball. Their seats could be adjusted depending on the direction of acceleration, and the consoles were mounted on sturdy poles as back-ups for the data consciousness the bridge crew used to make all inputs. Since the bridge was at the center of the longitudinal axis of the rotating crew module, weightlessness prevailed there and Dakhra had to use the handholds on the right and left of the access bulkhead as she floated in.

All the seats were occupied and the typical whispers of a crew operating in data consciousness filled the interior of the darkened globe. The wall of the globe glowed a faint dark blue, just bright enough for her to get her bearings—which wasn't particularly easy when there was no up or down. Dakhra remembered exactly how she had felt her first time on the battle cruiser. Back then, it had still been mothballed in one of the deep crevices on Kulptra, waiting for them to repair it during years of painstaking work, using just enough energy so they would not be noticed and gain the interest of one of the power blocs. Just one passing mining ship would have been enough to jeopardize their daring mission, and with it everything they believed in.

Her father, Ultrak, provided the best position for her to orient herself. He sat in the central commander's seat. His head was laid back and he didn't seem to notice her. The eight long struts that held his seat in the center of the sphere looked like spears impaling him. During their time on the ruined moon Kulptra, a thoroughly exploited wreck orbiting in the asteroid belt, they had not become as close as she had hoped. Their respective pasts had been too different for that. She was sure she was treating him unfairly by insisting she had always been part of the movement, while he was a "convert" whose hands were dipped in blood. Some things just could not be set aside, and they had to live with it.

Now they were on the verge of unleashing an angry chaos of violence in the hope that it would create a new opportunity for realizing their goals and their future. A future far from their enemies who had held their entire home in their iron grip for as long as she could remember.

"Father," she said as she reached his seat and caught herself on one of the circular bars that held his gimbal. Ultrak opened his half-closed eyes, which had been twitching erratically back and forth under the lids. He seemed surprised.

"Dakhra! You shouldn't be here. We're on combat alert!" he declared. She heard suppressed anger in his voice, felt it almost physically as a kind of subliminal vibration. "If we have to fly a maneuver, then—"

"But we don't have to," she interrupted him. "I know how it will go. We fire a salvo and hope it takes out all their defenses. That will achieve the breakout we're hoping for. If not, it will get more complicated."

"It usually gets more complicated," Ultrak sighed, and at that moment she saw how old he was now. It wasn't the crow's feet at the corners of his eyes, nor the deep nasolabial folds that made his mouth protrude. No, it was his eyes, which had grown small and watery, as if they were furtively trying to shut out the world. He waved at her. "Here we go."

Dakhra turned away from him and swallowed. She did not want to risk him seeing she was worried something would go wrong. They had every advantage in hand, were close to their goal. The defenders could not even scan them yet. By the time they could, it would be too late. Her eyes fell on some of the bridge crew seats, arranged around her in a star shape, their backs turned toward her. White hoses extended from the wall to the headboards, where the red marker bands showed the system was offline and disconnected, formed a dense forest that confused her eyes. Every ship from every Kazerun power bloc was equipped with them, direct injection access points to the crew's neural stratum. They were not used merely to administer blood thinners and anticoagulants, it was an open secret that if a ship's captain detected disobedience, or even a hint of opposition on the part of a crew member, he merely had to push a few virtual buttons in his data mind to kill him on the spot. Since its introduction, there had been virtually no mutinies or opposition from soldiers of ranks lower than captain.

"Make it work, Father," she said softly. He did not

respond. Whether he had not heard her or did not want to be distracted, she could not tell.

"Full charge to the energy pattern cells!" one of the bridge officers called out. It wasn't Dakhra's first battle aboard a starship, the Kazerun spent most of their time in space, and there was not a single one who had never experienced combat in a vacuum after their thirtieth year. Still, this was different because they were aboard a battlecruiser. These ships formed the heart of any military battle in the endless expanse between Kazerun and Lampak, the blue gas giant at the edge of their system. And of the many thousands of battlecruisers that remained, they possessed almost three dozen to deploy against defenses that had never been made to withstand such force.

"Energize primary weapons!" Ultrak ordered with the imperious tone of a commander with several decades of service on ships similar to this one. Of course, him speaking the orders aloud was irrelevant since it all played out in the much faster and more efficient data consciousness into which they were all networked. But it seemed to give the situation the seriousness and grounding it demanded.

"Command executed!" came the obedient reply, and Dakhra shuddered at the cold precision with which work was done here, as if they were poring over a complicated mathematical puzzle.

It's not them anymore, she told herself in her mind. *If they were the same as before, they would not have joined this mission.*

"Fire!" came Ultrak's instruction, cool and sharp.

The forward field emitters—which became the rear ones in a normal engagement because the ship was usually oriented with the propulsion nacelle forward—fired. Positrons joined protons in a dance of annihilation within the heart of six smaller antimatter reactors in the center of a magnetic chamber. With the entire amount of their energy released in their mutual destruction, the field emitters came to life, projecting their focused magnetic fields onto the planet's deep defenses far ahead.

Dakhra imagined how the few orbital installations, which should have been protected by their own fleet and were intended only as support, were destroyed in less than the duration of a blink of an eye, forming clouds of dense debris. On the ground, the magnetic fields burrowed hundreds of meters into the ground, creating gigantic fireballs of and plunging the world into a scene of death.

"Report!" Ultrak demanded.

"All field emitters have hit their designated targets!" came the response.

"Any reaction?"

"Negative. All defensive capabilities have been knocked out." A collective sigh of relief went through the bridge like a ghostly whisper. Dakhra exhaled deeply, careful not to make a sound.

"Bring us to maximum acceleration. We can't lose any valuable time."

"Did we make it?" she asked.

He did not answer right away, and that made her nervous, even though confirmation from one of the bridge crew could not mean anything other than there nothing was standing in their way. Her father's eyes moved back and forth for a few moments, then they flicked open, and he looked at her. His mouth twisted into a serious smile.

"Their resistance has been destroyed before it was of any danger to us," he said. "We are unhindered. Now we determine what happens next."

"That sounds good," she sighed. "After over a hundred years of preparation and waiting, frozen in cryostasis chambers and time itself, it's time we set our feet on a green world with no one to confront us."

"We require only a little more patience, then I don't see any anything that could possibly stop us. No weapons, in any case. It's been a long road to this point, Dakhra. You should rest, maybe you should be the first one to go the chambers."

"A new time is dawning, Father. We are the first to leave the home system and set a Kazerun foot on a new world. History is changing right now and we are in the middle of that change. Isn't it ironic that we of all people are those Kazerun?"

"It all still feels normal, like my job so far. I just led a battlecruiser into combat and swept away the enemy defenses. They were puny and had no chance. It wasn't an even fight; a battle of materiel."

"What are you saying?"

"I would have liked a different outcome." Then he waved his misgivings aside.

"A more glorious one?" she asked, narrowing her eyes.

"No," Ultrak assured her, "one without all that."

17

James nodded to Adrian. The cosmonaut rested one hand on the handle of the hatch, which had been cleverly camouflaged under a layer of old newspapers and dirt. Someone had gone to quite a lot of trouble because what had looked like a pile of garbage had been neatly formed into a solid layer that appeared loose and yet didn't move a millimeter when you ran your hands over it.

Adrian pulled slowly, and after a loud crunch, a square section detached itself from the floor. Dust and newspaper debris crumbled from the edges, and James almost coughed. Faint yellow light poured from the widening opening and his gaze fell on a ladder. At the same moment, he was met by a gust of cool but stale air that smelled of circuits and circuit boards—a mixture of electrically charged dust and silicon.

"I'm going in," he said quietly, trying to ignore the worried look on Mila's face. It had been his idea to bring them all here, so he would be the one to take the first risk. Thinking about it, he couldn't shake the impression that this situation had repeated itself throughout the time he had spent with his friends. He always came up with an idea and got the others to join in, only to realize how risky it was and that he had to go ahead to maintain his credibility. Besides, something like genuine conviction had set in at some point. He didn't *want* Mila to confront dangers he could take on himself to spare her. Not only Mila, but also Justus, Mette, Vincent, and Adrian. A strange change, since until a year and a half ago he would have thought it impossible to ever develop even the beginnings of an altruistic mindset. Even then, he would have done anything for Joana, even sacrificed himself, but in retrospect, the whole thing smacked of self-pity and emotional dependence rather than a healthy protective instinct toward close friends.

Carefully, he descended the ladder and found himself in a small room that was about the size of a large storage closet. Two bare light bulbs hung from the ceiling and illuminated the dusty concrete walls and a wood-panel floor. There were two doors leading left and right. He raised his head to tell the others it was safe, and his gaze fell directly on the lens of a camera stuck to the ceiling like an upturned coffee cup.

"It's safe," he whispered, without taking his eyes off the small electronic eye that was focused on him. A bundle of black insulated cables protruded from the back of it, tethered to the concrete with retaining clips.

One by one they joined him, first Justus, then Mette, Vincent, and Mila. Adrian came last and closed the hatch behind him. James went through the door directly in front of him since there was hardly any room left in the now-crowded space. The door was cold, gray metal and didn't squeak when he pushed it inward. As soon as a small gap opened, he slowly pushed his head in and looked around.

The room was considerably larger, almost like his bedroom in Manhattan, with an extremely low ceiling. Two air conditioners rattled away, battling the thick humidity that seemed to haunt every corner of the jungle. Judging from their plaintive moans, they were working at the limit of their capacity. Their undersides were yellow and the water supply behind the plastic cladding gurgled, a sound that mingled with the whirr of three server cabinets located along the left-hand wall behind bluish glass doors. The cabinets were equipped with their own waste heat hoses that disappeared into the concrete below the air conditioners.

Straight ahead was a wide desk squeezed between a server cabinet on one side and desks piled high with electronics and cable clutter on the other. On a single office chair, a figure sat in front of a half-dozen monitors, half of which were mounted on the wall and tilted downward. Some showed the solar system with the approach vectors of the Kazerun fleet as he knew them from the news broadcasts, only in false colors. Another displayed a CNN news feed showing that the fleet had apparently crossed the orbit of Mars. The news ticker was running reports about some disaster. He couldn't read anything from where he stood except for that word. The rest of the displays showed complicated hacker stuff—at least that's what he thought—that were incomprehensible to him, especially from several meters.

The seated figure had was wearing VR goggles pointed toward the ceiling, his head craned back.

"Excuse me," James said, feeling immensely stupid, but he couldn't think of anything better to say. "Mister?"

There was response. He frowned ad looked over his shoulder. Justus was waiting to enter, and kept trying to look past him. His friend merely shrugged his shoulders, puzzled.

"We're coming in now. Don't be frightened. We mean you no harm, we only seek answers." To emphasize his point, James raised his hands after opening the door all the way and walked into the room. The closer he got to the figure, the more he was able make out. It had stringy, dark blond hair that looked like it was combed back from the VR glasses. The hands wore dark gloves from which cables hung to the floor and ran over to one of the many computers under the desk. The fingers moved restlessly, back and forth, and a whisper reached his ears that he hadn't heard a moment ago, possibly because of the constant noise of servers and air conditioners. The air was almost cool.

"Hello, mister? Can you hear me?" He considered walking over to the motionless figure. James felt like the protagonist of a horror movie who had arrived at the creepy lair of some evil being. In the movies, the figure would jump up when he shook it by the shoulder, causing his heart to leap out of his chest.

"I'm going to take a look," Justus said, walking toward the monitors. Mila and Mette followed Vincent to the hacker, whose lips were moving at breathtaking speed, as if he were trying to set a world record for rapid whispering, but it was so fast that nothing came out intelligibly. Everything overlapped and did not resolve into a proper flow of speech.

"Well, he's not dead, that's certain," Mette noted.

"No, fortunately not," Mila agreed. "But why does he seem unaware of our presence?"

"He's wearing headphones and completely sealed VR goggles. His hands are in something like feedback gloves. How would he be able to sense us? At most by our breath on his skin, but I wonder if he still has the capacity to perceive that." The Dane shrugged. "To me, he looks pretty absorbed in whatever it is he's doing."

"The cameras," Meeks said. "He should be seeing the pictures."

"Maybe he's not looking right now."

"There's probably some software that alerts him to movement where there shouldn't be any," he insisted.

"Then we should make our presence known," James said.

"Is that a good idea?"

"Probably not, but I can't think of a better one right now. Besides, the man is unarmed, unless you count his stained undershirt as an offensive weapon. And whatever Justus is doing, I don't think he'll be able to hack the hacker's system and get us the answers we need."

Meeks nodded slowly but with obvious discomfort.

James braced himself and put a hand on the shoulder of the man in the reclined office chair. He squeezed it lightly.

"FUCK!" the hacker screeched, folding forward like a jackknife. His feet sprang off the floor and hit the underside of the table with a *thump!* His upper body literally popped up and, in a burst of activity, he ripped the wired device from his head. He looked around in panic, the whites of his eyes as prominent as a skittish horse. "FUCK!"

"Calm down, calm down." James did his best to look as harmless and non-threatening as possible, but didn't know exactly how to go about it. He held out his hands in a placating manner. "You're not in any danger!"

"Who are you? Fuck me! Where did you come from? How did you find me?" The startled man sat back in the seat, swallowing and wiping sweat from his brow. He moved as gingerly as if he was sitting on a board of nails and he expected them to shove him down onto it. His glanced restlessly back and forth between them.

"You decoded the Kazerun's signal," James said flatly.

"W-what?"

"You're still alive, and your computer systems are still working, too. So, I'm wondering what exactly the enemy could have that you were able to decode. And most importantly, we're very interested in how you decoded it. What's your name?"

"Gabriel—" The hacker fell silent after the reflexive response, and his face darkened.

"All right, Gabriel. We're not military and we've arranged for some time alone with you. We don't want to kill you or arrest you. All we care about is finding out who you had help from and what the signal is all about. Any advantage is useful at this moment!" James tried hard not to stare at the CNN images flickering across one of the displays to his left. The Kazerun had passed the Martian orbit and that alarmed him. Perhaps it was already too late.

"I'll tell," Gabriel said, rubbing a hand over his sweaty auburn face with its three-day beard. James noted with astonishment that he looked to be about in his mid-twenties.

"What?" Mila asked, completely flabbergasted.

"You *must* see it!" The young man seemed to have shed his initial shock and panic after looking them over, and pointed to the VR set lying on the floor beside him. "If what you say is true and you're not from the UN, then you may represent the last and only chance to save human lives."

"So, you found out something that will help us?" James could barely contain his relief. "Can we still save ourselves?"

Gabriel shook his head vigorously and pointed upward.

"Not we. You."

18

Dakhra swung her legs over the edge of the cryostasis chamber and looked over the rim at Zelva, her childhood friend who ran the ship's infirmary. Her tight-fitting white jumpsuit was stained like almost all the crew's clothing, which had been repeatedly patched over the last century. The recyclers and assemblers on board were old enough to pass for museum pieces and had degraded noticeably from constant use, as evidenced by the increasingly poor performance they'd had to live with for about ten years.

"I recognize that expression," Zelva said. Her face cleared as she withdrew her mind from the data consciousness and warmed as she looked at Dakhra and placed a hand on her chest. With gentle pressure, she slid it onto the cold pad beneath her back.

"I hate cryostasis."

"Because of the dreams?"

Dakhra nodded.

"They're just dreams."

She shook her head. "No, they're memories. I haven't

dreamed since... since *then*. The memories play out in front of me. The longer I sleep, the longer they are."

"And they hurt?" Zelva asked sympathetically.

"They're not like nightmares, but they are painful, and because I realize it's something real that I've experienced, even in that dream state, I want to get out, come out of it, not relive it. But I can't. I'm trapped in my own head. When I sleep normally, I often wake up and have a drink to calm myself down, but I can't do that in cryostasis. It's like a prison."

"Don't worry about it. Just before we get there, you'll wake up and it'll all be over. Then you'll set your oversized feet on a new planet untouched by everything we left behind."

Dakhra sighed. "I wish it were that simple."

"It's always as easy or as difficult as we make it." Zelva stroked her forehead and smiled. "Sleep well, old friend. I'll see you in a bit."

Cryostasis started as a tickle in her feet after the lid closed and the glass turned milky. Through the injection ports, her system was flooded with a cocktail of highly potent drugs that spread through her veins like hot lava. Then she became very tired and, without knowing it, dozed off before she could even think about it.

Dakhra spent the first days of her childhood in the Kashtraz Habitat in orbit around the gas giant Taak, the second largest celestial body in the system after the central star. Its gigantic cloud bands moved in rings around its transverse axis. From her habitat, of course, she could not see Taak, since life took place inside the twenty-kilometer-long tube that rotated around its long axis at an almost leisurely place, producing a pleasant G of gravitational acceleration. The interior of the habitat, its technology hidden beneath the relative ground, was filled with endless green meadows and hills, crisscrossed by smaller rivers and streams that ended at the large reservoirs at the terminating caps. Smaller towns and villages could be seen along the curving surface and would have been visible above her head had it not been for the fluorescent tube running through the weightless center of the habitat, mimicking the warm yellow light of the central star.

Her early years were kind and peaceful, except for a few minor altercations with other children whenever someone pulled another's hair in an outburst of emotion or a game got out of hand, but it was nothing serious.

One particular memory stuck with her. She was playing with her friend Zelva at one of the rivers with the springfish they loved so much. The little blue things were extremely slippery and hard to catch, but almost every day after school they went there and stood in the water up to their knees to grab one. They had never succeeded before, but on this one day they would. Laughing and cheering, they splashed through the small river, snapping their hands forward again and again to catch a jumper. Zelva fell several times and was soaking wet, causing them both to burst into a storm of hilarious laughter. Tears of amusement and splashes of water mingled on her face as she caught a soft shimmer beneath the surface. The fish grew larger, as if she were staring through one of the magnifying glasses from school, and then it shot out of the river with a great splash. Dakhra didn't think, but instinctively clapped her hands together and could hardly believe it when she felt the slippery creature between her fingers.

"Ooooh!" She was wide-eyed and Zelva rushed toward her.

"You got one!"

"Yes!" Dakhra clamped her tongue between her teeth and tried hard not to let the fish escape as it wriggled frantically between her hands. It slipped back and forth, but each time she was just able to hold onto it.

"I want to touch it too!" Zelva whined, disappointed, as the struggle continued. The fish's mouth opened and closed again, looking very funny.

"If I give it to you, you'll let it get away."

"Then throw it on the grass!"

"Okay." Dakhra turned and threw her prey in a high arc onto the shore. Even before it disappeared behind the small grassy bank, they were already tumbling after it, sending up huge fountains of spray. Laughing and cackling, they climbed up the grass and bounded over to the water dweller. Its eyes bulged large like marbles and its scales glistened royal blue, reflecting the artificial sun above their heads that warmed their wet bodies.

"Whoa!" Fascinated, Zelva stroked the scales with an outstretched index finger and Dakhra did the same. They were slippery and rough at the same time, and she could feel the increasing warmth of the small body underneath her hand. The animal's twitching increased, causing them both to squeal in delight. "That's funny!"

"Yeah, it's like a bouncy ball smeared with soap. Mommy said that most Kazerun eat those."

"Eww!" Her friend screwed up her face in disgust. "They eat things like that?"

"Yeah."

"Oh, look!" Zelva slapped a hand over her mouth and

pointed at the fish, which was no longer wriggling but lying motionless with its mouth agape.

"Is it...?"

"Dead," said a familiar voice, and Dakhra was startled to see her mother coming toward them, past the tree where their wet cardigans hung, puffed up to three times their normal size.

"But—"

"You killed the poor fish." Her mother sighed and knelt in the grass beside them. She had braided her hair into matted pigtails, as was customary in the habitat. Her eyes always had a kind expression and her wide mouth a warm drawl. "It can't breathe outside the water."

"But I didn't want to kill it!" Dakhra said, staring in horror at the lifeless animal that had so fascinated her. Zelva also looked dismayed and just stood there with her mouth open, as if wishing she were in another place. "Mommy, we just wanted to play with him."

"We can't mistreat other creatures just because we enjoy it or are curious."

"But it's just a fish," Zelva objected.

"*Just* a fish? Is it worth less than you because it can't solve math problems? This one is a female; it may have had young that now have to survive in the river without her. How would you like it if a giant pulled me out of the habitat and played around with me until I froze to death in a vacuum?"

Zelva's shoulders slumped , and Dakhra felt miserable. She imagined little blue jumping fish searching for their mother under the surface of the water and never daring to jump again.

"But there are also fish that eat each other. Teacher Ishla

said there is a food chain, and the stronger animals eat the weaker animals."

"That's right." Her mother nodded. "They follow the struggle for survival. But we are capable of rising above that. We always like to think of ourselves as the top of evolution, more evolved than the rest of creation, but at the same time, we claim to be part of that food chain and deal with others as we please."

"Is this what the evil humans are like?" Dakhra asked, shuddering as she looked at the reservoir lake of the northern termination cap in the distance. Beyond it was only dark space, full of warships stalking each other—if she were to believe her father.

"Yes. They think that way not only toward animals but also toward their fellow human beings. They think constantly only of their short-term advantage, forgetting that they only harm themselves if they always seek revenge." Her mother stood and held out her hands to them. "What do you say we bury the fish and then go home?"

"All right," Dakhra said gloomily. She had to master her squeamishness when she was told to pick up the springfish. Now that it was cold and dead, she was plagued by a guilty conscience, and she just wanted to run away without ever coming back here so she wouldn't have to see it again.

Dakhra remembered the dinner outside on the veranda that her father had prepared. At that time, Ultrak still had braided nut-brown hair and looked young. He had been in his early thirties then, a former starship captain of long freighters. Only many years later had she understood what he had given up to live in orbit around Taak, in a habitat cut off from all sources of supply.

As a child, she had not been able to comprehend what was happening around her. The Kashtraz Habitat was one of six space stations built before the Battle of Taak to house Coalition settlers because available living space back on Kashtraz had dwindled. Overpopulation and vast landscapes torn apart by constant warfare ensured that pressure to deport more citizens continued to mount. As was so often the case with their species, the Coalition had not been able to hold its territorial gains around the gas giant for long, and so many men and women had died in that infamous orbital battle that a demilitarized zone had inevitably been agreed upon with the hostile Alliance. All settlers and soldiers from the four largest moons were withdrawn and the newly completed habitats were never settled.

Until the "One Kazerun" movement was finally able to get past both Coalition and Alliance military stations with a fleet of stolen colonist transports on the night of the Black Moon. Two hundred ships from both power blocs had managed to coordinate without rousing the attention of intelligence surveillance systems and made history on that unprecedented day. Several ships were intercepted and destroyed, along with several hundred families, but the rest were not deterred from their goal of making a difference where seemingly nothing could be changed.

The two fleets met over the Kashtraz Habitat, unarmed and without pursuers, because no armed ships were allowed within the demilitarized zone. A violation by either party would have led to an immediate resumption of war, which neither side was ready for after the heavy losses they had already suffered.

The ships docked and the crews gathered on the meadows of this marvel of ancient technology, which could go without resupply for over fifty years. The habitat had automated helium divers—small swarms of robots that could collect helium-3 from Taak's gaseous atmosphere to feed the fusion reactor tanks. She was only two years old that day, yet she would never forget how thousands of adults had thrown themselves into each other's arms—people, she had later found out, who were actually from opposing blocs, and had never met except through their outlawed One Kazerun network.

The small pacifist movement was mercilessly persecuted then and later for the crimes of sedition and subversion of combat morale, but until the Night of the Black Moon, the movement had never been taken seriously enough to devote many resources to its suppression. Their life in the Demarcation Zone was to serve as an example to all other Kazerun of how to live together without weapons, in the eye of the storm over Taak, surrounded by two well-armed armed fleets that stalked each other beyond the demilitarized zone.

The situation remained that way until Dakhra was twenty-two. By then, she was working as a trained maintenance engineer in the dark tunnels between the inner wall of the habitat and the outer hull, maintaining the fusion reactors and superconductors and making sure life went on, even without supplies and maintenance bots. The Coalition had secretly devised a plan to secure the space around Taak and its four valuable moons in a lightning advance, and it needed the living space available in the six habitats to house soldiers and supplies.

It was a warm day, as usual, when she sat down on the terrace of her wooden house after a long night in the tunnels and knotted the sleeves of her overalls around her waist. In several places, the grass between the hills had been blown apart and black-armored soldiers with red-visored eyes were spilling out of their holes like insects. The cries of peaceful settlers harvesting crops in the fields was something she would never forget. It was the plaintive sound of people facing the inevitable, something they had secretly feared since their arrival. Those who fled were shot on the spot, the few who resisted were brutally beaten and arrested. The rest were rounded up like cattle. Among those were Dakhra and her parents.

Hundreds of them squatted close together, guarded by armed men near the river where she and Zelva had caught the springfish while the soldiers repeatedly separated small groups from out of the throng and took them away. At some point, they came for her family, as well.

"Ultrak, second-class shipmaster," one of the men said in a cold, hard voice and a small hologram formed over his right hand, which was covered with a scary-looking gauntlet. It showed an old image of her father in the uniform of a cargo pilot.

"That's not him!" Dakhra shouted, which earned her a violent jab from the butt of a rifle. Her nose broke with a sickening *crack*, and blood splattered across her mouth and chin.

"Don't! Not my daughter!" Ultrak pleaded, shoving himself protectively in front of her as if she were still a child. He tried to shield her and her mother with his outstretched arms. It was a pathetic attempt to stand up against a superior force.

"Doesn't even fight back, the cowardly piece of shit!" one of the gunmen snarled.

"And this is the kind of filth we're supposed to conscript?" another asked.

"Orders are orders. We need pilots on the front lines."

"He can't go to the front!" said Dakhra's mother in horror. "We are peaceful people! We won't get involved in your killing machine or in your damn lies!"

"We stick our necks out for you damned freeloaders and

this is how you repay us, huh?" one of the soldiers snarled and raised his rifle.

"Don't." The apparent leader put a hand on the barrel and pushed the gun down. Addressing Ultrak, he asked, "Do you refuse?"

"I have sworn off killing. Someone has to break the cycle," he replied in a firm voice. "Kill me if you must, but I won't kill anyone else."

"Daddy, no!" Dakhra cried in horror.

"It's okay, little one," he replied calmly. "We all die sometime, and while I'm sorry you have to see it, never forget that it's not so much how we die that matters, but how we live."

"Oh, what a brave good-for-nothing..." sneered the soldier as his commander drew his pistol and pressed the muzzle to her mother's forehead. "We need you because you are a pilot, and we need experienced pilots for our coming offensives, but we don't need your wife. So, think again."

Dakhra's mother shook her head. "Don't do it, Ultrak. Stay strong. I am, too."

What happened next was something she had never forgotten. Every single detail, down to the individual pores on her mom's face, had been burned into her brain.

"Amazing," the commander said and pulled the trigger. The gun made no noise as the short-lived x-ray laser ate through her mother's head. Her face lost all expression from one moment to the next, her eyes went blank, her eyelids became rigid. Then, as if in slow motion, she tipped to the ground. Her killer was pointing the muzzle at Dakhra before her mother hit the grass.

"NO!" Ultrak shrieked in horror. "Not her!"

"Daddy!"

"Not her! I'll come with you, but let her live!"

Many emotions fought for dominance in her heart at

that moment. Anger at what he was saying, since it meant her mother had died for nothing, consolation in the knowledge that he was doing everything he could to protect her, but above all, a firm belief that she had to stay true to her cause, as she had been taught by her mother—so that all of this would retain meaning and her fabric of the world would not become unhinged.

"No, Dad! You can't do that! It's not right!"

"Take him with you. She's an engineer, put her with the other Category Two prisoners and assign her to the appropriate work squads," the commander ordered in an almost bored tone that angered Dakhra deeply. He had murdered her mother as if it were a mere trifle. She had to force herself to restrain her urge to violence and give vent to anger and despair.

They grabbed her father and dragged him away. She stared after him until he was out of sight and she was eventually led away from her village with a large group of engineers. It meant that she was separated from Zelva, who had nearly completed her medical training so was assigned to a different group. She wanted to cry but could form no tears nor gather enough strength inside her to grieve.

She was horrified, and this horror expressed itself as an oppressive emptiness that she could not get past, as if her personality were being displaced by it beyond the edges of her consciousness.

Over the next few days, she and two dozen other young men and women from her village were locked in the barn on the western edge, where they were tossed meager rations while individuals were slowly taken away. When it was her turn, they beat her for several hours until she lay whimpering on the floor of a damp cellar, ready to die. But instead of killing or torturing her, she was given work. First simple repairs to food assemblers or power lines, then, after several weeks of what was supposed to be fierce fighting in space around her, she moved on to the station's maintenance shafts. It was a terrible life spent working virtually around the clock, always under the eyes of spying maintenance bots or Coalition soldiers who acted like prison guards.

The One Kazerun movement was history before they even had a chance to show the entire system that there was an alternative to the endless conflicts between the Coalition and the Alliance. Before they could prove that the war against the Al'Anter had been a crime against humanity. What could they have learned from those aliens? They had clearly been more developed, especially socio-culturally. But this opportunity had been destroyed by the Kazeruns' fear of everything foreign, because they had reacted with old reflexes firmly wired over millennia of wars and conflicts. For nearly twenty years they had lived in the boundary zone above Taak, and yet nothing had changed. Was their species simply lost? Was there no way out of the spiral of violence and mutual distrust? The endless segregation of "us against them"?

The work distracted her from her pain but could not hide the fact that she was as torn up inside as she thought of her parents. Her mother had been murdered, and her father had betrayed everything they believed in to protect her. She didn't know how to reconcile it, didn't know whether to be angry or compassionate—or even grateful. More than once, she stood in front of one of the many airlocks used to receive resupply shipments, some of which were now arriving weekly. Again and again she thought about entering one and pressing the emergency exit so it would all be over, so she wouldn't have to face the demons in her head.

In the end, she didn't for two reasons: Zelva was still alive and might need her, and her father Ultrak was out there somewhere, struggling with the pain of losing his wife and not knowing how his daughter was doing.

So, she spent every single day crawling through the maintenance tunnels and getting dirty, going to her house where she was thrown together with several men and women from the One Kazerun movement, and ten soldiers who constantly mistreated her. Occasional kicks and pushes were still the most harmless thing they did, and it was something to which one became cruelly accustomed. It got worse when one of the mostly young men in their insect-like armor started drinking and making fun of "the dirty pacifists." Then they would start shoving and hitting individuals to provoke a violent reaction and thus force them to abandon their beliefs.

"You just want us to be as inhumane as you are so you can feel better and justify your base instincts," she had once said, earning herself a broken nose and getting three teeth knocked out. She never saw a medic. She witnessed other taunts and acts of pure meanness. Sometimes they took away her evening rations or peed in her water bottle, and sometimes they tripped her on her way to the bathroom. Her life was constant torture, and yet she didn't give up and somehow continued to function.

After a year of servitude, a year where she lost so much weight that she was little more than skin and bones, she was sent to one of the clinics set up to treat the wounded from the ongoing conflicts around the former boundary zone to be force-fed. It was where she met Zelva again, who, as a medic, had to take on the abhorrent night shifts when the light tube in the habitat dimmed to a moonlight analog.

"How are you holding up?" her best friend asked quietly

as she inserted the feeding tube after Dakhra gave her a weak nod. Her face showed how much pain it cost. They were alone except for the physician on duty, a gray-haired veteran of the battle for Kulptra fifty years ago, out in the asteroid belt. He was a tired-looking man who did his work like a robot, his eyes vacant and his voice quiet. Even his stooped gait was one of someone who had resigned himself to a fate he never chose for himself, who was always alienated. What would his life have been like if he had not been forced into a rigid, militaristic system? Would he have devoted himself to art? Or education?

"I have to be force-fed because they don't have enough engineers." She squeezed her voice past the tiny tube scraping against her throat. "How do you think I'm holding up."

"Just hang on for another week, will you?"

"A week?" Dakhra frowned. "Why a week?"

Zelva leaned over her, lowering her voice again as she pretended to inspect one of the IV ports on her neck. It was probably unnecessary because the clinic was almost empty in this area. Most of the lights were off and the beeps from the machines, otherwise barely audible, seemed almost intrusive in the silence.

"I found an entry in my data consciousness that is not mine," her friend whispered.

"How could that be? Unless..."

"... Someone has a superior code. Exactly."

"What did it say?"

"That I should be ready on Tzarday. Starting at five o'clock standard time, an Alliance offensive is to begin. Its goal is to wipe out the habitats in order to destroy the Coalition's logistical beachhead."

"But that means that someone from the Alliance leaked that message to you."

"Yes. Someone of high rank." Zelva peered over her shoulder, through the transparent walls into the office of the clinic director, who was sitting at his desk with his back bent, scrolling through virtual reports with his hands. His eyes were closed as he did so.

"You think he's...?"

"Shh, the walls here have ears. Just listen to me. Whatever happens on Tzarday, I'll let as many of us know as I can. At least the ones I'm sure haven't given up their ideals." Zelva faltered. "Despite... despite everything. If we can break out, we must try. If the Alliance does launch a major offensive targeting the habitats, the resulting chaos may offer us the only opportunity to escape this horror."

"But how?" Dakhra whispered. "We lost over five hundred of those who once served in the military before joining our movement. They were the only ones who knew what to do in a situation like this."

"I know we don't have any pilots. But for all that, we still have the will to put an end to this. We'd all rather die than be treated like animals for another year and slowly perish. Despair can be more powerful than any military training, believe me."

Dakhra did not answer, just nodded silently. Her friend was right.

"But that means you have to eat from now on." Before she could respond, Zelva continued, hissing, "I know they took everything from you, but from now on you have to be like them, you understand? Take anything you can from them. Stuff everything you can find inside you. Wait until they're asleep—I don't care! But you've got to get your strength back before it starts on Tzarday."

Again, Dakhra nodded.

"And I know what you're wondering; if it's all a hoax, so be it. But if there's something to this, and someone from the Alliance or in contact with the Alliance has given us a chance, we have to be ready. You understand that, right?"

Another nod.

"Good."

Dakhra spent her time until Tzarday going about her work until she completed all her duties. The maintenance bots that followed her at every turn constantly reminded her of her work just in case she thought of resting. By now, she hated them with a passion that frightened even her. In the evenings, when she returned from her rounds, she behaved even more inconspicuously than usual, simply agreeing with soldiers when they insulted or challenged her so they quickly lost interest, like predators bored with prey that offered no resistance.

Once the men were asleep, she stole back the rations they had taken from her and the other forced labor activists and ate what she could before sharing as much as she could with the others. While she couldn't tell them anything about what she was preparing for, she had the feeling they knew something was going on. Every morning they woke before the soldiers and went about their chores so that they could escape the wrath caused by the missing rations.

Then one evening, she felt relief. A new platoon was billeted with them. In her weaker moments she rejoiced at the thought that the previous men had been killed in action, only to condemn herself for it. It was so easy to give in to the desire for revenge and so infinitely difficult to put herself in their boots and wonder why these people had become so hard and mean. They were hardly born that way. She was sure it was the oppressive, warmongering system and the violence that had held their civilization in a stranglehold for millennia that increasingly made them unable to conceive of any other way. Violent parents, traumatizing training at the point of a gun, abuse at the hands of superiors, or horrific experiences in war—the list of ways a good person could become a monster was long. Would she have become something else if she had had to live the lives of these people? What if her parents had not brought her, with the courage of despair, to the only place that had come close to promising something like peace in the last two decades? It had been like living in the eye of a megastorm whirling with thunderous forces while everything remained calm inside.

She knew Zelva's informant was telling the truth when she was awakened on Tzarday by a blaring alarm that she had not known even existed. An unpleasantly high-pitched howl filled the huge habitat. She rushed out onto the terrace with the other sleepy activists and saw the artificial sun that stretched along the center of the gigantic drum glowing red, alternately fading and increasing in intensity. It was a terrifying sight and made the curved landscape appear bizarre and nightmarish. Every tree became a clawed hand, and every blade of grass turned into the diseased finger of an entombed corpse trying to excavate its way to the surface. Over the past eight days, her anticipation of this moment had increased with each passing hour, the moment when it would finally happen, when she would finally have a chance to change her life or mercifully end it. Yet now that it was here, she only felt fear.

But she acted, and held her group together as the soldiers rushed half-dressed out of the house, weapons in hand, and descended through the floor hatches leading to the transit passageways that would quickly take them to one of the hundreds of shuttles that were docked along the outer hull like dark, blood-bloated leeches on the body of a wild animal brought down by hunters.

"It's starting," she whispered and winced at an ear-splitting crash of thunder.

The light from the blinking, mile-long tube far above their heads flickered briefly. Dakhra looked along the curve of the landscape. She tilted her head back and located the green grasslands above their heads, many miles away on the other side of the artificial sun. Something like a volcano appeared to have formed there, its edges jagged. Its center, however, spewed no red lava, but rather it yawned in deep blackness. Even at that great distance, she could see the violent storm spreading around the crater as it began to engulf everything. After a few seconds of horrified hesitation a light wind started to blow and tug at her stained overalls.

"Come on!" she shouted to the others. They didn't move.

"What's that?" asked Mikratz, the little cyber-mechatronics girl from the Jokraatz family.

"A hull breach!"

The horrified looks of her fellow activists were enough to ensure her that they would follow her. Dakhra wordlessly turned on her heel and sprinted toward Zelva's clinic. The wind gained strength every second, expanding into a full-blown storm before they were even halfway across the gravel road. The surface pebbles rolled northward, skipping across the grass. A few of them were lifted from the ground and started floating in the direction of the light tube. Dakhra's hair whipped painfully in her face, and the clothes of her running companions rattled violently as the decompression storm snatched at them. Through the whirling chaos, the uprooted sod and branches nearly struck her several times, but she barely noticed the second worst effect brought on by the dramatic loss of atmosphere: diminishing breathable air. Not only were trees, plants, and rocks uprooted, filling the air on their tornado-like path to the hole in the hull, but so were the millions of gas molecules that allowed them to breathe. The light flickered with increasing frequency. In the creepy, unsteady twilight, she saw roof tiles in the distance flying upward, first one by one, then as a swarm, followed shortly by fragments of wall and pieces of furniture.

Just before the wind grew so strong that she feared she would not be able to stay on her feet, they reached an emergency maintenance access hatch. She used her priority code via data consciousness to trigger the unlock command and ordered her companions inside with frantic hand movements. Her impatient shouts were carried away by the deafening howl of the dying habitat. Not a single syllable penetrated the roar.

Inside the narrow tunnel, only the combined forces of five people managed to close the hatch again and shoot the manual steel bolt into place—and even then it rattled.

"Follow me!" she urged her companions, scrambling northward. As she did so, she had her data consciousness project a virtual hologram of the maze of tunnels and the clinic ahead so she would take the correct turns. Dull thunder rang out, again and again, shaking the metal walls and causing their hands and knees to vibrate. Then, gasping for breath, they reached the clinic's basement.

Dakhra kicked in the security grate covering the ventilation shaft that provided air to the clinic and slipped into a large storage room lined with narrow drawers filled with medical supplies.

To her horror, she was not alone. Standing in front of a small display, was the doctor she had seen last week when

Zelva had told her about the secret message. He wheeled around and stared at her, startled, but quickly relaxed.

"A-2 through A-17," he said in a raspy voice, gesturing to the left wall before turning back to his display and making frantic entries. At the same moment, their connection to the habitat's datasphere broke.

"The server room's been hit," she blurted.

She ran to the labeled drawers and yanked one open. Inside were two emergency pressure masks, which she passed to her utterly terrified companions. Only when they were all masked did she take one of the remaining two from A-17 and pulled the nanonic strips over her head. The mask covered her entire face and formed an air-tight seal. Then she ran to the doctor with the other one and held it out to him. He donned his without hesitation and visibly breathed a sigh of relief. The small tube connected to the fist-sized compressor tank, which dangled an arm's length below, wiggled with each breath like a transparent trunk.

"I sent Zelva to the lower level," the old man gasped. "You'd better hurry! If you don't, she'll die waiting for you rather than go without you."

"Why are you doing this?" Dakhra asked. A violent jolt nearly knocked her off her feet. Many of the drawers opened and nearly broke from their frames. People screamed.

"Because you have a chance to make it and I've been watching what you've done here for twenty years," the doctor replied, pointing to an open hatch beside him. "We got a strange signal from a Coalition cruiser that I intercepted before it went to the central computer. Make something of it."

"Are you coming with us?"

"No. My journey ends here. My old bones have been through enough. Go now. Zelva knows everything you need to know." With that, he shooed her away like a pesky insect, and she wasted no more time as another hit to the habitat sent her tumbling. As soon as everyone reached the next basement level, a visibly excited Zelva leaped out of the single door leading to a waiting vacuum capsule where cold white light flickered ominously.

"Come on! Hurry! Go, go, go!"

Dakhra did not linger and quickly proceeded through the hatch. The capsule was oval-shaped and had thirty seats, but no one seemed willing to sit down. Not even the twenty or so frightened and rag-clad activists already waiting there. It warmed her heart to see her house companions immediately join them, hugging and clinging to each other like a herd of sheep.

Her friend was the last to step inside as another blow rocked the capsule. Judging by her absent look, she was making a few final entries before the bulkhead closed and the capsule shot off north through the vacuum tube.

"The doctor, he—"

"Helped us, I know." Zelva nodded.

"So, what are we going to do now? There really is a battle raging out there, isn't there?"

"Yes. I've been listening in on the military channels. Supposedly, it's a major offensive with over five thousand Alliance battleships." The intern physician waved in dismissal. "But none of that matters. One of the Coalition cruisers sent a strange message to the station."

"Strange how?" Dakhra winced as the capsule was knocked aside and sparks flew past a window, but it continued on its course. "What do you mean?"

"It shared its position with us and said it would remain there for the next eighteen minutes."

"And that's "

"Unusual, yes. That's what the doc assured me. It could be that it's a transmission error, but if not..."

"... it could be addressed to us."

"Yes, and that cruiser is only two clicks from here."

"You don't want to..."

"Yes, I do." Zelva pointed to the small suitcase sitting next to the bulkhead that Dakhra hadn't noticed. "We have to."

The ride ended shortly after at one of the spaceports that protruded like great stalagmites from the gigantic tube that formed the habitat. They ran after Zelva into the sprawling hall filled with switches and floor markings, continued to the passenger elevators that took them to the top of the port, and finally into the last airlock designated for the largest warships. Those vessels were too large and too difficult to maneuver to dock closer to the hull, where their exhaust flares would have caused serious damage.

No one said anything in the elevator car, and it was silent except for the occasional rumble when another jolt shook the walls. Each time they wondered if it would be the critical hit that might suck them into the vacuum of space. Yet, they pressed on, hugging each other tightly in small groups, doing the only thing they could: providing comfort and security where there was none.

Zelva and Dakhra were the first to disembark when they reached the top of the port after what felt like an eternity. They had reached the very end of the four-hundred-meter-long starscraper where numerous airlocks lined its base. Due to the rotation of the habitat, the gravitational acceleration at the far end of the centrifugal push was slightly higher than a G, which they noticed in their heavier than usual legs.

"Straight ahead to the airlock, but before that, I have to

distribute the infusers to raise our body temperature," her friend explained and then suddenly froze. Dakhra blinked as she saw a single figure in full black armor standing before them. Its red visor eyes were fixed on their large group, which had fanned out into a semicircle. They stared back at the soldier. He held his rifle down at an angle and had not yet raised it, but the peril of the situation was physically palpable.

"We're not going to fight you," she said firmly, swallowing her fear. The words that followed were infinitely more difficult for her to speak, and yet they felt right and contained a trace of pride. "If you have to shoot us, then so be it."

"You want to escape," echoed through the speaker diaphragm on the soldier's neck.

Zelva nodded. "Why are you alone? There are no more shuttles docked here."

The soldier did not answer her.

"They left you behind or you were too late." She saw the man's hand tighten around the grip of the gun, a sign of indecision. So, with all the honesty she could put into her voice, she continued, "You can come with us, but in exchange you'll have to leave your weapons behind. Forever."

She knew that some of her companions, despite their convictions, must have found it difficult not to protest after more than a year of mistreatment and harassment by soldiers like him. He was indistinguishable from all the other hooded men and women who had made their lives here hell and treated them like animals. But no one objected. That made her proud because she realized that their ideals were not yet dead. In retrospect, this was one of the moments that had most shaped and strengthened her convictions, showed her what power laid in them. It was infinitely harder to feel compassion than hate, she could not deny that, but it was worthwhile and ultimately liberating because it signified a willingness to break with those seemingly fixed patterns of behavior to which one did not surrender without a struggle.

Then the miracle happened, the soldier threw away his rifle along with the rocket pistol and knife strapped to his thighs. He pulled off the helmet. Its ring hinge opened with a loud hiss as the entire spaceport shook and screeched as the structural metal struts above their heads announced the habitat's imminent end. A frighteningly young face with freckles and a long forehead crowned by red hair emerged.

They approached him and an activist handed him a respirator as he began to gasp for air without his helmet. Tears rolled down his cheeks.

"I'll hand out regulators now. Inject them into the carotid artery," Zelva said, her voice distorted by her mask. "The ship whose message we intercepted is on a fixed course, which it shared with us. If we fly through that airlock in exactly four minutes, reaching about twenty microclicks per unit of ten, we should hit the right dorsal hangar bay."

"What if it's locked?" someone asked.

"Then we're dead." She noticed the startled trepidation and paused briefly as she handed out the injectors. "My guess is that the crew of the ship is trying to help us and is correct, or we're going to die out there. The only alternative is that we die in here."

There were no further objections.

"We have five minutes before we freeze to death despite the regulators. The respirators will equalize the pressure for three minutes, then your lungs and capillaries will begin to empty. You'll lose consciousness after a minute or two. Don't try to orient yourself, just keep breathing in a controlled manner and wait to see what happens. Don't row your arms, don't move at all. Got it?"

The group nodded.

"Good." Zelva's gaze unfocused. "One minute to go."

They walked to the airlock and stood close together in a long line, three abreast. "Best close your eyes. See you on the other side."

Dakhra, aware of the ambiguity of her statement, gulped and took a deep breath—until her friend activated the emergency release of the large, gate-shaped airlock.

Everything seemed to happen at the same time. The inner and outer doors opened simultaneously, and the explosive decompression pulled her body into space like a broken doll. She kept her hands close to her body and her legs stretched out with her feet together, so the tips of her toes touched. She shot through the vacuum like a fish. Her mask began to mist from the bottom up. The cold was so extreme that her skin, paradoxically, felt like it was on fire. Supported by the regulator drugs rushing through her veins, her body worked at maximum strength to keep its core temperature supernaturally resistant. She flew along in complete silence, rotating slightly around her longitudinal axis but unable to do anything about it.

Below her, the habitat came into view, a huge gray toroid that reflected Taak's eternal storm bands. Dozens, if not hundreds, of wounds gaped in the spiked hull. Fires whipped through cracks and holes, instantly smothered by the vacuum, reduced to short-lived lightning flares. All around, the battle between Alliance and Coalition raged. Thousands of shining dots, visible whenever shots were fired, faced each other or tangled across unimaginable distances. Explosions flashed up and down her entire field of vision like fireworks gone wild. A powerful cruiser flew past and was ripped apart by green plasma lances that melted the hull in several places before the reactor exploded, turning the debris into a short-lived second sun. Unconsciously, Dakhra's mind calculated numbers on how much radiation she was being exposed to during her suicidal flight through space, whether from the antimatter annihilation she had just witnessed or the constant bombardment from the atmosphere of the gas giant that formed the backdrop of this man-made madness, a giant disk of brown hues. Hundreds were dying every minute in this mutual massacre, trillions of credits evaporated in the form of melted or ruptured shells and reactors. It was a picture of the madness to which their entire species had degenerated, an eruption of the irrational that preferred to destroy rather than create and was trapped within itself like a tragic protagonist.

Dakhra's chest began to tighten noticeably, and the mask began to squeak, which her ears interpreted from the vibrations through her skull bones, and which impacted her like a warning siren. She could do nothing but crane her head back and widen her eyes in fear when she saw the massive shadow above her, entering her field of vision from left to right. It was quite obviously the battlecruiser Zelva had told her about, a colossus several hundred meters long. Its hull was dotted with propellant tanks except for a frighteningly small opening awaiting the swarm of unprotected bodies flying toward it. In the gap between four tanks, a section of the spinning crew toroid below gaped. Its massive, armored gates were locked open. She realized it was a hangar large enough for four fighters to land simultaneously, and yet the perspective and general size of the cruiser made the opening a seemingly tiny target that they could hardly hope to hit.

So, she was not only relieved, but also extremely surprised, when she saw the edges of the door pass her diminishing field of vision, closing under the assault of black pulses, and felt gravity suddenly take hold again. She slammed hard onto cold metal and ripped the mask that had transformed from refuge to death trap from her head. She gasped loudly and sucked greedily at the ozone-scented air that surrounded her as she lay helpless and panting on her back.

After that, everything happened so fast that her mind could hardly keep up. Her body felt like some fruit squeezed dry of juice. She was hot and cold at the same time as her vascular system panicked and tried to adjust to normal pressure and temperature conditions again. She broke out in a sweat even though she wanted to shiver from the chill.

Soon, she was carried away on a stretcher and she saw the faces of the paramedics to her right and left as if in a hazy dream. They walked through corridors where red combat lights constantly blinked and flickered. Now and then, the ship would shake or crack, but the men and women at her side seemed unfazed and got her to an infirmary where she finally lost consciousness, but not before she saw the young soldier who had joined them beside her. He was crying uncontrollably while a medibot cut open his armor to gain access to his body.

About a week later, when she was able to move again after three days in an induced coma and four more in a meditank, she was led into a large assembly room with the twenty other survivors of their daring escape. About as many had not made it because they had been pulled out of the airlock at the wrong angle during decompression, or could not be saved once on board. Dakhra had not known most of them, and yet it filled her with sadness that they had not survived.

She sat in the front row, leaning against Zelva with a blanket around her shoulders. She felt drained and tired until her father entered. She quickly realized that he was the captain of the battlecruiser. Undecided what to do, she just sat there with her mouth open, torn between wanting to fall around his neck like the little girl she felt she was to him and a deep dislike for the disheveled uniform he wore that stood for everything she and her movement despised. He gave her a look that was so melancholy and yet determined that it further confused her. She simply sat frozen in her seat. She had never forgotten the words he spoke then.

"Dear friends, we have made it. We are free because we have made choices. I have made choices that I cannot undo, but which I accept and stand by despite everything, even though they will haunt me for the rest of my life. It is a consequence that you are sitting before me today, that my beloved daughter is sitting before me. To achieve this, I have had to bear blood on my hands, blood I had sworn never to shed so that we might break the endless spiral of hatred and violence. I failed in that, but I succeeded in something else, winning over the crew of this battlecruiser to our cause and, within a year, building a network of loyal soldiers who are also fed up with a life of constant conflict and the incessant fear of death. They are soldiers, they have known nothing else, but they have risked everything to gradually take over sixty-four ships and prepare for the great battle for Taak, where we could bring our people back. One Kazerun lives, but it has changed. In addition to eighteen thousand of us that we were able to liberate from the habitats, there are now over four thousand soldiers, Kazerun, who want to break out of the cycle but never learned what you all here drank of with your mother's milk. I wish very much that you will show them how we want to live, without constantly reproaching them with where they come from, or how we *don't* want to live. Our future must be a positive one, and that's why we need a better plan than just setting an example."

He told them about the plan and all the ships of their fleet flying together toward the asteroid belt. Because of the extreme losses on both sides after the battle for Taak, which had apparently ended with the destruction of the habitats and a Pyrrhic victory for the Alliance, they were not pursued. After all, a bruised but still operational fleet of over sixty battlecruisers was nothing to disregard, but at the same time they were aware that they were being watched and would be immediately pursued as soon as a sufficiently powerful fleet could be dispatched.

Despite these gloomy expectations, their subsequent course through the asteroid belt, where the ships dispersed and spent months flying erratic courses until they finally rendezvoused in orbit around the plundered moon of Kulptra, turned out to be unnecessary. Neither Alliance nor Coalition seemed willing to be the first to expend ships and resources to hunt down activists who posed no threat anyway because of their nonviolent philosophy. And the longer they remained undetected, the less interest the two power blocs seemed to have in seeking out and eliminating a small, half-destroyed fleet of pacifists.

So, little by little, her father's plan unfolded according to the idea he had shared with them that day, as if a higher power had interceded to make sure everything went smoothly. It involved remaining unpredictable so as not to risk any more lives while they extracted resources from less productive asteroids overlooked by the major consortia, so they could organize equipment and supplies. Independent traders and black-market gangsters were plentiful in the system, so time quickly became their ally. With the first proceeds from selling the reactors of half their fleet, they acquired cryostasis capsules for all of them, allowing them to work in four shifts in the shadow of Kulptra. Three shifts slept for a decade, while one flew about in small shuttle spheres gathering resources, maintained the capsules, and proceeded with their largest project, converting the remaining thirty-three ships for interstellar travel to a Kazerun-compatible planet they named Staris, after the mythological paradise of their ancestors.

It was a long, energy-sapping job in zero gravity. They had to detach the tanks of the ships now lacking reactors and weld them to the other ships to provide enough propellant storage for a journey of over a hundred years.

Dakhra remembered years of toiling in a spacesuit as if it were a fever dream that just would not go away. The constant flash of welding equipment, the zero-G bots flying about her like fish in water doing the heavy lifting while she laid cables and soldered fuses together.

What helped her during this time, when she had little sleep and no opportunity for distraction or diversion, was the very plan they were following and the cohesion and fierce determination of her fellow activists. In particular, the former soldiers her father was able to recruit to their cause proved remarkably motivated and industrious at the prospect of a new beginning among the stars. Many worried whether such a journey, which had never been ventured before, could succeed at all, but the calculations inspired optimism.

A great fear remained, of course, that they might be

pursued—sooner or later, at least—but Dakhra did not share this fear. She knew how obsessed her home world was with conflict strategy and, thus, how little a bloc dared to break cover and commit resources to such a chase. Such a move would be seen as weakness, make themselves vulnerable, and bring about the downfall that the autocratic leadership feared more than anything else.

After more than a hundred years, during which they repeatedly had to interrupt or postpone resource extraction in the belt to avoid detection, the ships were finally ready. Patched together from the remnants of the abandoned half of their fleet, of which only skeletons now remained suspended in vacuum, they assembled their arks for the great journey. Each was equipped with many hundred cryostasis capsules and housing units for two hundred crew members for their breakout from the system and their eventual arrival in the Staris System.

Her father planned to leave their species' sphere of influence by the most direct route, which meant using their weapons one last time—but only against robots. The moon Klaash, in orbit around the gas giant Nuuk, was a Coalition outpost used as an automated supply point in the heart of their sphere of influence, and it was defended by automated defense systems. It was a gamble on whether the old transponder codes would still work, but to make sure they weren't blasted out of the sky before they could break out, Ultrak planned on one last battle, firing whatever weapons they could repair as they prepared to flee. After that, they would finally be free and could remove all their weapons systems, before they could be tempted to another compromise and betray their principles after all.

19

James pulled the VR goggles and headphones from his head and stared in disbelief at the displays in front of him. It took a while before he could match the excited voices around him to his friends.

There was Mila with her gold-framed face, Mette with her rosy cheeks, a worried-looking Justus, and Vincent looking at the screens frozen in a freeze frame of what James had last seen through eyes that were his and yet not his—the beginning of the shelling of Klaash by the Activist fleet. He had seen it as Dakhra had experienced it on the bridge of her ship, alongside her father, who had become a stranger to her, something she was inwardly ashamed of. Even if he had not directly shared her bodily sensations, his brain had managed to fill in the appropriate gaps.

He was drained and weak after what felt like a lifetime that had passed in his brain. It was not quite what he had experienced back on Al'Antis when the Avatar had implanted all its knowledge and memories, but it had still overloaded his senses and synapses. Now his friends were all talking, even Adrian, whom he could not make out among the many faces that pressed in on all sides.

"That was incredible."

"Was it real?"

"Did you know these Activists existed?"

"Can we trust her?"

"What did you feel?"

"God, how long did that last?"

"Please," he interrupted the storm of questions and weakly raised both hands, still clad in the hacker's feedback gloves. Their owner had just pushed Mette aside and was looking at him urgently.

"It's indescribable, isn't it?" the young man said looking feverish, ruffling his hair, "I've seen it a dozen times."

"Yes," James breathed, closing his eyes for a moment to collect his thoughts.

"I modified the transmission to run certain visuals from it in the form of moving and static images on the displays in parallel, to give an impression of what Dakhra experienced up until she arrived in our solar system. I wanted to make it understandable to the world, but how do I do that? No matter how many times I work on it, it always remains just a movie that can't make you aware of how real everything was. Only the whole VR experience makes that possible. But nobody has that equipment anymore!" Frustrated, Gabriel slammed his fist into his open palm.

"We have to stop them."

"The Activists?" Mette asked, irritated.

"No." James shook his head. "The UN. They have to have noticed by now that they're not being fired on, even though the fleet has long been in weapons range after crossing Mars's orbit. They could have fired from Neptune orbit if they had wanted to, but they can't. Their weapons systems have long since been deactivated and dismantled. We have to stop them from getting blown out of space."

"What if it's a ruse?" Adrian asked. James still couldn't see him, but his voice came from somewhere behind Mila.

"It's not a ruse."

"You once said yourself that the Kazerun can't be trusted. They were devious and vicious and always looking out for their own advantage," objected the cosmonaut.

"That's true, but I fell into a typical human trap in the process." He sighed. "I generalized. I was sure they were what they were without seeing that there are always exceptions, that civilizations contain many kinds of people."

"But how do you know that what you saw is real?"

"I can't know one hundred percent, but I've felt and seen what I've felt and seen, and when we get back out here and see that we're not being shot at, we'll have still more evidence. The people on those ships would have no reason to fear us. With their weapons, they could sweep away whatever defenses the UN put up, just like that"—he snapped his fingers—"long before we could even react."

"That's an argument," Mila agreed.

"He's right," Justus said, hesitantly.

"But what are we supposed to do with this information? No one will believe us."

"We humans from Earth are also capable of empathy," Mette said. "We empathize when we see something, and that's the best way to access our humanity. If enough people see this, they will change their thinking. I'm sure of it. Precisely because the whole world has been so rigidly fixated on the fact that it will come to a fight that we may not be able to win. This recording will calm them even more when the Kazerun don't attack, and a peaceful resolution that was thought impossible suddenly becomes realistic. If there's one thing we humans of Earth have proven in our history, it's quick rethinking when it's needed, and always when the need is great enough to force us to it and leaves no other alternative open. The preparatory militarization is, after all, paradoxically, just another example of exactly that."

James merely nodded and turned to Gabriel. "Is that the whole signal?"

"No." The man shook his head, frantically typed something on his keyboard, then pointed to one of the screens, which now displayed a repeating frequency pattern. "That right there is the main signal that's been sent over and over for the last two years. A huge data packet that took me exactly two years to download and decode using keys provided by an anonymous member of the hacking board."

"And what are these spikes in between?" asked Mila, pointing to the much smaller and shorter spikes in the graph that resembled a human EKG.

"That's Dakhra."

"What do you mean, 'that's Dakhra'?"

"She's desperately trying to make contact with our world and start a conversation, but, so far, I'm the only one talking to her, as far as I know. She wants to contact the one who decoded the message," the hacker replied.

"So, she knows about this 'anonymous member of the hacking board' and that it wasn't actually you who succeeded in decoding it?" James asked.

"Yes."

"And was contact made?"

"Yes, three weeks ago. But nothing has happened since then, and Dakhra only checks in briefly. She tells me that she's waiting for those who have been chosen to contact her to speak with her."

"Chosen?"

He nodded mutely.

James looked to Mila, who swallowed and nodded imperceptibly.

"The Avatar," he breathed. "It's already talked to Dakhra and has known we were coming. If she meant us, at least."

"Either that," Vincent said, "or we'll soon be getting a visit from those she really meant."

A shudder went through the group.

"We need to contact Norton somehow." James looked at Gabriel. "Can you connect to an American phone number from here?"

"Not a chance." The young man shook his head decisively. "The satellite phones are undetectable and the rest runs through coded local towers, which I can't even get into with my hardware. Remember, all this shit is ancient. With the right parts your countries supply, I might have cracked the original signal in less than a month, but as things are…"

"Then we have to go back to the soldiers and ask them…"

"Soldiers?" squeaked the hacker, jumping back from the keyboard.

"They're here to protect us, not…"

"Wait a minute," Adrian interrupted him. "Weren't they going to storm this place after half an hour if they didn't hear from us?"

"Yes, as a matter of fact, that's what they said. How much time has passed?" James asked.

"Almost four hours," Mila explained.

"I'll go out and see," the cosmonaut stated. "Justus, are you coming?"

The German nodded tensely.

"We're going to see if anything happened to them or…

anything else has happened." Adrian hesitated. "You guys stay in here until we find out!"

With that, they both disappeared through the door.

"I don't know about those soldiers," Gabriel said, pointing to another display where a new sine wave with smaller spikes appeared, "but this is something new."

"Something new?"

"Yes!"

"What is it?"

"A damned signal!" The young man became agitated and typed wildly on one of the keyboards before entering long lines of code into an input console that seemed to start running several programs at once.

"It doesn't sound like you're very pleased about it," James said.

"It's outside the schedule. The others have always come in at the same time every three days. The last one was yesterday, so there shouldn't be any today. Now I have to hurry and aim the antenna at the right position, so I don't lose it." A loud snort.

"What is it?"

"Quite a coincidence. You show up here after a year, and right now, for the first time, we receive an unscheduled contact transmission."

James had to stop himself from pressing the young man further. He could see that Gabriel was frantically trying not to lose the signal and hopefully connect with Dakhra.

"It knows we're here," James whispered to Mila, and the others looked at him with serious expressions. "The Avatar."

"And so does this Activist, apparently. Or it's already in direct contact with her. That would be irritatingly absurd and yet entirely probable. While we're thinking that we can track it down, it's already a dozen steps ahead of us and has planned for everything."

"Well?" James asked over Mette's head in Gabriel's direction, who had lifted a headset and was holding it to one ear.

"I've got it." The hacker paused triumphantly before slowly turning and eyeing James as if seeing him for the very first time. Simultaneously, on all the displays, a tired face appeared, accompanied by static noise. It was a face he now felt he knew as well as his own.

"Dakhra."

"Who are you?" Gabriel whispered, handing him the headphones, while Adrian and Justus returned. "She wants to talk to you."

20

"Dakhra," James said in a strained voice.

"Hello, James," the Kazeruni replied. Her voice was lighter than he remembered, which made sense, since he had lived through her experiences, through her perceptions, and, accordingly, had only been able to hear her in his voice. Her face looked tired, but her expression was as determined as he imagined her to be.

"You know my name? How?"

"Our mutual friend told me."

"The Avatar," he whispered.

To his surprise, she frowned.

"I am not familiar with that name, but one of you returned our contact and assured us that he wished to avoid bloodshed. He told me someone had sent a group of people to a secret location to possibly contact me. In the process, I was given the name James Hamilton."

James looked at his friends.

"Whoever the Avatar is, it even knows about this mission," he said.

"Is it true that you and the people next to you visited

Al'Antis?" Dakhra asked with a look of melancholy and disbelief.

He merely nodded.

"Is it..."

Again, he nodded, and the Kazeruni's shoulders slumped. Her eyes closed for a moment, and the corners of her mouth dropped as if it had lost all tension.

"It is a tragic crime that I'm ashamed of."

"You had nothing to do with it," he assured her. "I saw the memories you sent."

"I wasn't alive at the time of the war, it was millennia before, and yet it shames me. What I would have given to have known those people."

"They were unique," he replied, tensing as memories of the Al'Anter's evolution tried to push back into his mind. As though he was reflecting on a past life he had never lived and yet had experienced more deeply than almost anything he remembered. He gestured gruffly to the hacker to turn on the speakers.

"I would like to make sure nothing like that ever happens again," Dakhra said. "Not with you Earthlings and, if possible, not with our fleet."

"When you started out, you didn't know about us because your telescopic images were so old that Earth hadn't fully industrialized yet, am I right?"

"Yes. We thought it was a Kazerun-compatible world. Nitrogen-oxygen atmosphere, a protective magnetosphere, and about the same mass as our home planet. Never did we think it would be an identical celestial body."

"But you knew about Al'Antis," Mila said, confused. If Dakhra hadn't expected anyone else to speak she didn't let it show.

"What do you mean?"

"Al'Antis was also identical to Kazerun and Earth."

"No, we didn't know that. All the public talked about was an alien threat that was detected by the teleporter."

"I guess they also led you to believe that the teleporter was Kazerunian technology?" James asked, snorting when she nodded. "Why does that just sound so familiar?"

"When the ship's systems detected signs of an advanced civilization, some of us were awakened prematurely from cryostasis. Our ships' AIs are programmed to detect early threats, especially military threats, and respond accordingly. However, since we had disabled and mostly destroyed our weapons systems even before we left the heliosphere of our system, they woke us instead of taking action themselves. Basically, they needed us to troubleshoot. That was ten years ago."

"Ten years ago? So, you've been awake for ten years?"

Dakhra nodded, and now James noticed that she looked older than he had imagined her to be.

"We debated for a long time how to deal with the new situation," she continued. "Some of us felt that we should destroy ourselves so as not to interact with your civilization and thereby possibly disturb it, others wanted to make contact with you in the hope that you would be different from our kind. Then we found out that you were most likely humans, like us. At least, that's what the television signals you've sent traveling through space suggested."

"Your appearance *has* changed our world," James admitted, sighing slowly, "and not for the better—though many would debate that point. However, that is not your fault, but our own."

Dakhra looked downcast and her lips thinned. "It wouldn't have happened without us, though."

"Who knows? There have been enough dark periods in

our history that had nothing to do with alien spaceships approaching us. No"—he shook his head—"creating dark futures is something we've always been able to do all by ourselves."

"We've been trying to contact you for years to convince you that our intentions were peaceful and to ask for asylum, but we received no response and doubted whether you could even hear us. Even after decoding your language, nothing came back."

Only now did James realize that they had been speaking in English the whole time, and the Kazeruni had an indistinct accent, but it was otherwise flawless.

"That was quick."

"With all the radio signals you broadcast, it wasn't particularly difficult." Dakhra's gaze tightened, and she looked him straight in the eye. "Are you speaking for your planet?"

"Uh, no."

She looked confused.

"But this Avatar you spoke of has assured us that you represent Earth."

James looked at Mila and the others and blinked in confusion.

"It said that?"

"Yes."

"Did we miss anything?" Adrian wanted to know, rubbing his chin thoughtfully as he stood in front of the screens and raised a finger. "Let's go over everything again. The Avatar seems to know us and arranged for us to come here to talk to Dakhra."

James nodded. "All preplanned. That would fit. The Avatar on Al'Antis always had the foresight to make complex decisions, too—Nasaku was one of them."

"But if it's been directing us all along, why haven't we been aware of it?" Justus asked. "After all, it must have enough influence to pull the necessary strings."

"Norton," James said, first in disbelief, then in frustration. He slapped his forehead. "Of course! Norton's the Avatar!"

"What?" Mila frowned. "What are you talking about?"

"It's obvious, isn't it? How could I have been so blind!"

"Could you please include us in your train of thought?"

He looked at her and grabbed her hand.

"I know from the Avatar on Al'Antis that it had inhabited bodies before its self-imposed digitization. It kept jumping from one person to another, although I can't tell you exactly how that was done. The fact is that it was forced to do so at a certain point once the Al'Anter had evolved. An immortal, semi-synthetic human walking among them would have been noticed. So, it found a way to weave itself into the DNA and minds of host bodies and subtly influence them. For a long time, it didn't interfere, but instead acted as a passive observer, soaking up everything its hosts experienced."

"So, it could always be with those who changed history or caused profound changes at critical points." Justus nodded vigorously. "That makes sense."

"Such a point was the discovery of the teleporter—if not that, then what?" James looked around at his friends, who were beginning to understand but still didn't seem fully convinced. "He was the military chief of the project, subordinate to Pavar, but still always near the teleporter, while the politician constantly had to fly to Washington and spent most of her time on the surface in her office. A major who was quite old for his rank. Anyone who hasn't reached a higher rank by his early fifties will probably never be a general. But thirty years later, he's one of the most influential officers in the US, a candidate for the Military Council the next time one a post is vacated. Steep career trajectory for someone who, after more than thirty years before that, never rose above the rank of major."

"That could be a misconnection. Maybe he just got smart," Adrian said.

"You really think so?" James shook his head. "No, he also made sure we got through every crisis at the beginning of the project. He protected us from Pavar, made sure we could help Nasaku, and made sure we got to Al'Antis before the facility shut down."

"But then why did he task us with finding the Avatar after we returned, if he himself *is* the Avatar?" Mette asked.

"Maybe he wanted to find out how good his cover was. Or maybe he wanted to keep us from disappearing into military service because he still needed us." He turned to Meeks. "And then there's this business about the memory block that was slipped to you at work by your talkative colleague. Quite a coincidence that something like that wouldn't happen for a year, but then uncovered just before discovering that a hacker in Bolivia had cracked the Kazerun's signal, don't you think?"

"Okay, let's assume it's really him," Mila said. "Let's play it out. He doesn't reveal himself to us but sends us here, into the jungle, to make contact with Dakhra so that she can then clue us into the fact that he's the Avatar, an ancient, intelligent being who has made it his business to observe and record Earth's evolution for his creators, who have long since become so ancient that they've either digitized themselves or live in a technology-free preserve they've built for themselves. He even organizes us as a team, the first to use the teleporter and experience an odyssey across the galaxy, only to end up here with a few soldiers, meet with this hacker, and hear about Dakhra and her Activists. Why?"

"She's right. Why didn't he just tell us, 'Hey, I'm the Avatar, and the Kazerun ships coming at us aren't a threat because they're persecuted pacifists? Here are Dakhra's memories. Check them out and then off on stage with you, James.'" Meeks looked around questioningly. "That would have been more efficient."

"On stage?" Mila asked.

"The Military Council has made James its poster boy, roaming the country as a teleporter hero to boost morale."

"No, not just to boost morale." James looked up. "As someone to incur fear and anger by warning people against the Kazerun because I fervently hated them for what they did to the Al'Anter. Not only that, I've seen what they are capable of and I'm afraid for Earth, afraid that what I witnessed through the eyes of the Avatar of Al'Antis might happen to us here."

"So, if he had put you on stage with this new information, no one would have believed you because you were famous as the one person who had seen the enemy. Your news played into the hands of the Military Council, but if you suddenly went before the public with the opposite message, not only would it have sounded implausible, the leadership would have made you disappear into a dark hole forever."

"Yes. That's it. He *couldn't* tell me. But then why did he let me go on if he did know for so long? Why did he let me continue to stir up sentiment against the Kazerun and stoke fear of the supposed invasion fleet?" he asked.

"Who knows what an Avatar has in its mind?" Mila said.

"It wouldn't have been merely implausible," Adrian said. "James wouldn't have believed it just because Norton told him. And he wouldn't have believed the general either if he'd said, 'Oh, by the way, I'm the Avatar.'"

The cosmonaut gave everyone the usual piercing look he employed when he wanted to make an specific point.

"Think about it. What's happened up to this point was the only way it could work. Norton has been making sure all along that it all comes down to this moment. The meeting with Private Ruby that just happened to coincide with your presence at the Air Force base? When you told me about it, I thought that was pretty weird, but it was just another piece of the puzzle in his game."

"But why all this here? Time is running out, the ships will arrive soon and we're crawling around in the jungle, away from a global public who should be seeing this. Away from the Military Council and the UN. The fact that we're talking to Dakhra is good because it's opened eyes that were shut by our entrenched fear of the Kazerun. But none of this is doing the planet any good." James sighed, frustrated. Then he stiffened as he remembered his last conversation with Lieutenant Lacey. "Have you examined your equipment?"

"What do you mean?" Mila asked, tugging at her bullet-proof vest. "This stuff?"

"Yes. All the soldiers are equipped with microcameras because mission control is tracking everything live," he explained impatiently. "But what if we're equipped with them, too? Then Norton would have recordings of my authentic change of heart. Demonstrably, not fake, entirely genuine, and a symbol of contrast to the statements I've previously made to everyone I've spoken to."

Without waiting for his friends' reactions, he pulled off his vest and searched it. It wasn't long before he spotted lenses the size of a pinhead in the thickened hinges of the vest's various zippers. They could only be seen at all if someone was specifically looking for them, otherwise they could have passed for over as tiny rivets. He also found some on his helmet.

"Well, fuck me!" Meeks showed them what he had discovered. As it turned out, they were both fitted with over a dozen such cameras, while Mila, Mette, Adrian and Justus could find none. This, again, suggested that it had to be Norton's doing since his radius of action certainly ended. or at least dramatically diminished, at the borders of the United States.

"He's been using us all along."

"Yes, but think about it," Mila said, laying a hand on his shoulder. "If he had involved us from the beginning, I'm sure things would have been different than they are now. Maybe we wouldn't have believed Dakhra because we would have felt like we were being controlled by someone. Norton did the only thing he could. He nudged us in the direction of the truth so we could discover it for ourselves. How would you have done it?"

"Exactly the same," James admitted after a moment's hesitation. "I would have done it exactly the same way."

"Wait a minute—" the hacker cut in. He'd been so quiet that James was surprised he was still there. "That means you guys have recorded all this? Bloody hell!"

"Believe me, this is a good thing. You have to do something for us."

"Have you guys gone completely insane? First, you ambush me here, then it turns out Dakhra was expecting you, and now you're bugged!"

"Hey, take it easy." Mette tried to calm the upset man, placating him with slow gestures as if she were trying to tame a wild animal. "There are no UN satellites here, you said so yourself."

"But—"

"I must confess that I didn't understand half of what you said," Dakhra said, "but you seem worried."

"The Elders created six worlds. They were the first human-type beings, and billions of years ago they were probably the first intelligent species in the Milky Way. Their greatest scientific project was the directed evolution of six identical planets in six identical solar systems. To document what happened and answer the question of whether the emergence of humans and human evolution are preordained, they placed an Avatar on each planet, an immortal, quasi-human being who witnessed and recorded everything and regularly transmitted their findings. These Avatars functioned as the creators' microscopes, if you will. The Avatars don't normally interfere, but the conflict between Al'Antis and Kazerun triggered something in the Al'Antis Avatar. Perhaps some sort of emergency program that prioritizes the survival of local humanity over external interference. When the Earth Avatar learned of this, the same mechanism may have been triggered in him once the existence of your fleet became known. Norton appears to be that Earth Avatar, at least currently."

"And he's been moving you back and forth like chess pieces on a board," Dakhra concluded. "Now you're trying to figure out what move you need to make to complete his plan and checkmate the other side."

"A somewhat martial analogy, but yes."

"Who is the opposition anyway? The Military Council? Or Earth's entire, warmongering society?" Meeks asked.

"We shouldn't be too hard on people," James said. "For thirty years they've all believed that a threat from space was intending to wipe us out, and that we all had to work together to defend our home world. Who can blame them for that? I, myself, was part of it and went along with it. It's not their fault that they wanted to take action and prepare."

"You're probably right."

"But the question remains: What do we do now? What's the final step in Norton's plan?" Mila asked.

"What's important is not what Norton's plan is, but what *we* do," Justus said. "After all, *that* was his real plan, wasn't it? To nudge us in the right direction and hope that we would act authentically and genuinely. He interfered as little as he could and left how things would work out completely up to humans. It makes sense."

"Well, the first thing we need to do is get the recorded footage out of the cameras, and then we need to make it available worldwide," James said. He looked at the hacker, who was as pale as if he had seen a ghost. "We need you to help us. How can we get the data?"

"There must be a receiver somewhere that converts the raw data into an audio and video format via a codec. For a live transmission, you would need a powerful broadcasting device, which it doesn't look like you have."

"Then why the panic just now?" Adrian asked. Gabriel didn't answer, but instead took James's armored vest and began scanning it.

"There's one more thing we need," James said.

"A way to distribute the data globally, like you said," Mila said. "But that won't be easy, I think."

"It might be easy if we knew how to transmit the appropriate signal to every e-pal in the world. There may not be any in South America or Africa, but then they're not armed to the teeth and determined to fire all their guns at space visitors." Adrian rubbed his chin thoughtfully before suddenly stopping and grabbing the hacker by the shoulder. "Hey, you're in contact with the Avatar on this forum, aren't you?"

"Hacking board."

"Whatever. You need to contact him and say that we need the encryption frequencies of American e-pals, and the European and Asian ones as well, if possible. If we have those, couldn't we use the ships of Dakhra's fleet as transmitters? They're far enough away to have a large broadcast arc, and they could cover the entire surface of Earth within twenty-four hours as Earth rotates. With the right broadcast frequency, they would reach every single device without activating a firewall."

"Like a text message," Mette said.

"In principle, yes."

"But how do we get the data to Dakhra?"

"We're talking to her now, too, aren't we," James said.

"Not a chance." The hacker shook his head as he tore out the inner lining of the vest with a jerk. The polyester in his hand tore in protest. He reached into a small recess in the back of the vest and pulled out a small device the size of a matchbox and eyed it triumphantly. "We don't have that much bandwidth available here. It would take weeks."

"What about ALMA, the Atacama Large Millimeter Array?" Justus said. "In northern Chile? It's comprised of a large array of radio telescopes in the Atacama Desert. Each telescope has a dish twelve meters in diameter. If we point them correctly, we should be able to send quite a bit of data. Assuming we can get the frequencies from Norton. Otherwise, there would be no point."

"And assuming our babysitters out there play along. Without their helicopters, we'll never make it there in time."

21

"They've been in there for two hours now," the leader of the Russian task force said in a heavy accent, scowling. "We agreed on half an hour."

"Right," Lacey said. He was sitting with his back against one of the fallen logs, his hands on the shock pad of his assault rifle like a shepherd holding his staff. "But we got a message to give them more time. They're not in any danger."

"And how would they know that?"

"I don't. My boss obviously does, though."

"Does your *boss* happen to be around here somewhere and know everything that's going on? Or did I miss something?"

Preston Lacey would have preferred to laugh as he looked into the angry face of the Federation soldier. His Slavic features with their high cheekbones and small eyes lent him the look of a rather tensed-up Rumpelstiltskin. Instead of immediately answering, he pointed to the man's insignia on the left upper sleeve of his uniform. It bore the new UN logo.

"We're playing on the same team, see? And my boss is

running this operation, so he's kind of your boss too, *Starshina*."

"I think you misunderstand me," growled his Eurasian colleague, whose expression turned even more somber at the emphasis on his rank, which was roughly equivalent to a sergeant first class, and thus merely an NCO.

Always that pride, Lacey thought, sighing to himself. *It just gets in people's way when they should be relaxed.*

"So, enlighten me, *Starshina*."

"My mission order is to protect the two Russian Federation nationals who are part of the team."

"And you're doing an outstanding job." Lacey gave a thumbs up. "They're still alive, after all."

"And how would I know that? You can't just change the mission parameters at will."

"I didn't. My boss did."

"General Norton." The Russian, Vladimirovich, snorted.

"That's right. He has overall command of this operation." When his counterpart seemed about to say something disapproving again, Lacey rolled his eyes. "Come on, man. We're supposed to wait, so we wait!"

"Wait for what?"

"We'll see. You're an elite soldier with the Spetsnaz. Don't tell me you are unfamiliar with these types of situations." He pointed to the man's four comrades, who were lying under cover nearby, not taking their eyes off the hacker's hiding place below them in the valley. The Europeans had moved to the other side on the ridge to ensure better visual coverage, while his own four men were playing cards to his left, teasing each other in hushed voices. "Your units are the equivalent of Navy SEALs. In our country, at least, they're given the utmost respect for their self-control and coolness."

Vladimirovich shook his head. "'Spetsnaz' is the general Russian term for special forces. I was part of the Independent Naval Reconnaissance Spetsnaz of the Russian Navy, but I wouldn't expect an American to know the difference."

"See?" Lacey said lightly, winking. "It had spetsnaz in it."

The Russian shook his head again and went back to his men and talked quietly to them, probably letting loose a barrage of not particularly complimentary remarks about him, but Lacey didn't care. Whether it was because the Soviet image of the enemy of the past century had woven itself so deeply into Western DNA, or because he'd been influenced by movies and television, he didn't know, but he had always found the Russians too serious and cool.

Let them fret a bit.

Since there was virtually no reception out in the jungle and the Pentagon had not been able—or willing—to spare any of its communications satellites for this operation, the message from General Norton that said they should wait indefinitely had come in via his military analog ticker, which he wore on his wrist like an old-fashioned pedometer. The signal came from the helicopter, which acted as a relay station of sorts—another reason why he had had to land so far away in a clearing on a mountain instead of bringing them closer to their destination. How the general knew they should wait was beyond him, but one of the advantages of serving as a Special Forces soldier was that you got significantly less gray hair because you didn't have to think too much. So, he took advantage of it and relaxed for the next two hours, trying to ignore the throaty Russian conversations that kept wafting over to him.

While he waited, he sent a short text message over his ticker to the pilots in the helicopter, who replied that the Kazerun fleet had still not opened fire and was continuing its braking maneuver toward Earth. He always found it disturbingly strange that the UN had decided not to make any contact with the alien ships. Since the many televised appearances of this Hamilton guy, they all knew they were beings from another planet that were extremely aggressive and hostile—at least if you wanted to believe the guy—but they were still people. Shouldn't they call at least once and ask "Hey, nice of you to stop by, but what do you actually want?" He understood the reflex not to allow any contact lest they fall victim to a cyberattack they had no means to counter, but even to him, a full-blooded soldier, the desire to talk first was natural.

A shrill, rising beep snapped him out of his thoughts, and it took him a moment to realize it was the satellite phone in his backpack. It was used only for extreme emergencies since no satellite had been diverted for this mission. That seemed to have changed.

His comrades and the Russian team quickly became aware of this fact. All eyes turned to him as he turned over and opened his backpack, which he had been using as a pillow. Cards were discarded, conversations ended, and silence fell, except for the ubiquitous concert of jungle noises, as he pressed the green button.

"Renegade Bravo here," he reported as per mission protocol.

"I'm connecting with Fleet Admiral Jones," a female voice said, and Lacey involuntarily stiffened, something his men noticed immediately.

"Renegade," said a worn voice that sounded like someone had thrown rusty nails into a metal bucket.

"Fleet Admiral Jones," he replied, making no effort to hide his surprise.

"The Military Council?" he heard Sergeant Fox ask. Specialist Jenkins silenced him with a hissed "Shh!"

"It has come to my attention that you did not follow the mission parameters. You were to neutralize the target upon your arrival!" Jones said sternly.

"Sir, we were under orders to give the civilians a half-hour head start. That period has been extended indefinitely." Lacey frowned and turned his head so he could see the hideout in the valley. He was just able to make out some sort of building there.

"Negative, Renegade. The target must be taken out!"

"The general has—"

"His order is countermanded!" the Fleet Admiral interrupted him gruffly. "Execute! Now! And don't bring any additional passengers back with you!"

"Roger that, sir!"

The connection was broken, and the phone went dead.

"Lieutenant?" Jenkins asked, who had joined him with the others and was looking at him expectantly over her weapon.

"That was the fleet admiral. We're supposed to take out the hacker, and we're supposed to do it now."

"But what about Norton's order?" wanted Fox to know.

"Countermanded."

"That stinks big time!" The sergeant snorted, and Lacey couldn't blame him. They had worked with Norton since their training in Special Forces and trusted the old warhorse as unconditionally as only working together for twenty-plus years made possible. The general had made it abundantly clear before their departure that the mission was a personal matter for him and that he trusted Hamilton and Meeks. Supposedly, Hamilton had saved his life once, although he couldn't imagine that. In their home barracks, their team had often been derided as Norton's dogs because they worked so closely with him. And now the Military Council was ordering them to override his standing order, even though it was his mission.

"They've taken over," Jenkins grumbled.

"Not only that"—Fox pointed upward through the dense canopy—"it means they repositioned a satellite specifically to reach us. So, a mission that they might not have even been aware of has suddenly become worth a lot of effort to them. Why's that?"

"There's another possibility," Lacey said, "the satellite could have been there all along and they didn't want the general to get wind of the Military Council's interest."

"But why?"

"I don't know; I don't give a shit about politics." He shrugged his shoulders. "But orders are orders."

"We can't leave the general hanging!" protested Jenkins, and the rest of the team also nodded in agreement.

"We're not going to leave him hanging. We're following the orders of our country's top commanders," Lacey corrected them sternly. "That's our job, and you'd better remember it, fast. We're going to go down there and take out the target. Period. The general will understand because he has to. Do I think this whole stunt sucks? Yes! Is there anything we can do about it? No."

"There you go," Vladimirovich sneered as he approached them from the side and openly loaded his weapon. "At least your superiors were able to set your head straight."

Lacy didn't respond to the provocation and waved to his men to get ready. A short time later they advanced down the slope with their Russian mission mates, splitting up so they stayed under cover of the trees and covered the entire south side of the valley.

"I don't like this number at all, Lieutenant," Jenkins muttered to the soldier next to him. They were circling old tree stump that was completely rotted and home to populations of various insects.

"What about it, exactly?"

"Everything. A satellite we didn't know about, our boss being passed over, the Military Council taking over without prior warning, and the timing."

"The timing?"

"The fleet passes Mars orbit and nothing happens, despite everyone thinking they would open fire from there, at the latest. The civilians have been in there much longer than anyone figured, but Norton doesn't seem concerned and says we should give them more time. How does he even know they're not in danger? Then the Russians get restless and urge us to go in, and two hours later the fleet admiral is on the phone ordering us to take out the hacker *right now*." The soldier snorted and looked somber. "*That* timing."

"I see." Lacey shrugged. "Maybe."

"Maybe? What about the Russians? They definitely have their satellite orbiting above us. Why else this sudden pressure to finally move in? It's our mission, that's why they've been holding back, but under normal circumstances, they could have just sat back without complaining. Don't tell me they care about their two civilians."

"Smailov was a fighter pilot and cosmonaut. They're kind of like folk heroes with the Russians," he objected.

"That may have been true in the past, but now he's a civilian."

"Well, let's assume they have their own agenda. What does that change for us? Nothing!"

"I'd rather listen to Norton."

"Careful, Specialist," he warned her. Although they had become close friends over the years, there were boundaries he had to maintain to keep them functioning as a military unit.

"They're cutting him off at the knees. He'll never be elevated to the Military Council after this stunt. And we're the saw in their hand," the soldier insisted stubbornly.

"Maybe so, but we're not politicians, and I have no desire to see that change."

"We're here and they're in Arlington."

"What are you saying, *Specialist*?" Lacey asked in a dangerously calm voice. While he knew the cameras and microphones in their equipment were not transmitting live, they would be evaluated after the mission. Jenkins was already in trouble, and he didn't want her executed or even deported upon their return.

"Nothing, sir." She cleared her throat as if only now realizing what she had done, and stuck her chin out. "Only that we are operating as the Military Council's scalpel, doing their work here because they have more important things to do at home."

"Wonderful. Now, full concentration. We're supposedly dealing with only one target, but you never know what's waiting for us down there."

They made their way down the densely overgrown slope, and Lacey kept trying to reach the leader of the European unit, Sergeant Major Reuter, but he got no response. It didn't worry him much, because given the geographic conditions they might have simply been in a radio shadow. While constant contact was essential on a special ops mission, their comrades from the EU also knew that they had only been sent in their strength because none of the three power blocs within the UN wanted to back down or act as a junior partner, however little they believed in the importance of this mission.

When they arrived at the west side of the ancient, half-ruined, house he gestured for his soldiers to position themselves at the windows and see if they could spot anything. He only got a general shake of the head in response. They crept toward the entrance, where the Russians had already opened the door and were entering with their weapons drawn.

So much for agreed procedure, Lacey thought, annoyed. That the Russian leader didn't like him had become obvious, but that he would just rush in like that, although other operational arrangements were in place, was simply unprofessional, if there were no other reason—

So, they pressed themselves in behind the Spetsnaz soldiers and entered an anteroom filled with broken furniture that had suffered so much from time and mold that it apparently could no longer hold its own weight. The signs of decay could be seen everywhere he looked over his rifle barrel. Due to the onset of darkness outside and the lack of any light source within, he had to turn on his underbarrel flashlight, which cast a circle of light varying in size as it scanned the different areas like a stage spotlight. There were faded pictures with ghostly faces, broken glass covered in mold, and a rough patina on every object. Tattered scraps of newspaper, damp leaves, and many-legged creatures seemed to scatter from the light as if rudely driven from their homes. Lacey had seen a lot and was not the type who was particularly jumpy or easily frightened, or else he would never have been ordered into a reconnaissance unit, but this place made the hairs on the back of his neck stand on end.

Using quick hand signals, they searched the entire ground floor until it became clear there was no one was there. But since they knew with a fair degree of certainty that the civilians hadn't just disappeared—since they hadn't come back out through the door—there had to be either a hiding place or another exit. They did not find the latter after several minutes of careful searching. They removed two of the weathered picture frames, tapped the walls, and even poked the ceiling with their rifle barrels. All that was left was to look at the floor and proceed as they had until a hollow *thud* sounded from Sergeant Fox's position in the living room. They and the Russians joined him quickly and uncovered a hatch. A small depression in the hatch allowed them to pull it up.

Lacey nodded at him, and they all aimed their weapons at the gap that appeared when the sergeant opened the hatch.

"Jenkins, you—" he started, but Vladimirovich beat him to it, shouldering his weapon and sliding down the ladder like a fireman.

"What an asshole," he whispered, pushing ahead of the other Russians who were about to follow their leader. He ignored the muttered Russian curses.

Below, they found themselves in a tiny room with just enough space for the ladder. Muffled voices could be heard through a door to his right. He believed they were speaking English.

Vladimirovich reacted with an extremely calm expression. Lacey looked at him seriously as the Russian thrust his rifle forward on his way through the door.

They went along a short corridor and reached a large room with displays on the opposite wall. Someone was sitting in the only chair in front of it, and the group of motley civilians they had brought on the mission were engaged in an animated conversation. They didn't notice the soldiers. A quick examination revealed that there was only one stranger present, presumably the hacker, who was working at several keyboards while standing. One of the monitors showed a progress bar, like one displayed while a program was installing, or data was uploading.

"Hey!" Vladimirovich shouted rather unoriginally and took two quick steps to the right to make room for his team to follow him in. He aimed his weapon at the hacker, a man with shoulder-length, stringy hair. The target wheeled around startled, panic in his eyes. The civilians, on the other hand, were just as surprised, but in the very next breath they seemed more angry than scared.

Lacey moved left and gestured for his men to come up behind him so they formed one-half of a semicircle. His gun raised, he also aimed at the target, who quickly raised his hands.

"Everybody out of here!" he barked at his charges, looking at Meeks, the big engineer with the Colorado accent. Hamilton, too, came into view; he was the person sitting in the chair. On his lap was the armored vest Lacey had given him—turned inside out with the lining ripped out. So, he had discovered the camera systems and the storage unit. That did not surprise him.

"What's going on?" Meeks objected loudly. "There's no problem here!"

"VNIZ!" Vladimirovich roared as Mila Shaparova placed herself in the line of fire.

"Nyet," replied the resolute woman, releasing a torrent of Russian. She sounded upset.

"You don't understand," Hamilton said in Lacey's direction. "This man wants to help us. We're looking at this whole Kazerun thing all wrong! They don't want to destroy us and they're not planning an invasion!"

"Clear the line of fire," he demanded without apology as another man stood and got in his way.

"Our information is wrong!"

"So?" Lacey asked.

"They are seeking asylum! They are persecuted refugees from their home system. That's also why they haven't fired on Earth. If they had wanted to, they could have already done so from the edge of the solar system!"

Lacey exchanged a glance with Jenkins, who looked at him across her rifle and bared her teeth. Every weapon was still aimed at the hacker and the civilians standing in the way. They stood shoulder to shoulder, hands raised, their faces filled with equal measures of fear and determination.

"You mean to tell me the Kazerun aren't a threat?" he finally asked Hamilton, snorting. "*You*, who's been getting on my nerves for almost a year now with your endless, televised rallying cries and war speeches against the invaders? *You*, who supposedly witnessed firsthand how evil and devious the enemy is?"

"Yes."

"Quiet now!" Vladimirovich barked. "Out of the way! We're ordered to neutralize the criminal and if you don't drop to the ground right now, we'll just shoot right through you!"

"No, you won't!" Lacey said harshly to his Russian colleague, still eyeing Hamilton with disapproval.

"Lieutenant," Jenkins interjected, "I don't know what's going on here, but if Norton's poster boy has suddenly changed his mind, we should at least listen to him, right?"

"Our orders—" Vladimirovich started.

"—were issued based on information available to our

mission control. They might be missing something," he interrupted the Russian. Then to Hamilton, "You have two minutes to convince me. The clock is ticking."

"Lieutenant, this—"

"—is normal procedure in the field! We're improvising according to the current operational situation!" Lacey hissed. He was quickly running out of patience.

Hamilton's face was white now. He seemed to be aware of how critical the situation was. Good.

"Talk! Now!"

"We have made contact with Dakhra. She is the daughter of the commander of the flagship of the Kazerun fleet." The gaunt man's voice almost stuttered with the frantic speed of his words. "They are persecuted on their home world and do not want war. They just want to live in peace."

"Well, this planet is already occupied."

"But they didn't know that when they set off!" Hamilton pleaded, his face contorting as if in physical pain. "They would fly on if we don't grant them asylum, but to do that they must first complete their pre-programmed braking maneuver, which will take them into a Lunar orbit. After that, they could replenish their reaction and propellant mass at Jupiter and get onto another course if they have to. Think about it, Lieutenant. Why would the Kazerun risk flying to within range of our defenses when they could have fired on us long ago?"

"Malfunctions, short range... what do I know?"

"I understand you don't believe me, but if you take a little more time, you can see it all for yourself. You can witness Dakhra's memories that led to her journey here. They are on these computers." Hamilton pointed behind him.

"Even if I were convinced," Lacey said, chewing on his lower lip, "how would we convince the Military Council?"

"We don't have to! We'll just show all the citizens what I've seen and experienced. The whole United States. knows me, and if they'll believe anyone, it'll be me because I have been the country's loudest demagogue when it comes to fighting the Kazerun."

"And how are you going to do that?" Jenkins asked, but Lacey could already tell from her voice that she was convinced enough to put their kill order on hold. He was inclined to feel the same way. This matter was too big to make a foolish decision now without looking at all the facts.

"I have all the footage from my video equipment here." Hamilton held up the small memory box Lacey himself had inserted into the lining of the armored vest. "We copy the data, convert it, and send it to every household we can reach."

He exchanged another glance with Jenkins, who barely nodded. Fox, Luis, and Bradford also signaled their agreement. While he hadn't specifically asked them for it, he was someone who liked to get the opinions of his people.

Finally, he nodded and lowered his rifle. With a hand extended to his side, he gestured for his subordinates to do the same.

"Show me."

22

James breathed a sigh of relief. For a moment he had thought that these trigger-happy men and women, fanned out across the entire width of the suspended room, would simply mow them down. But apparently what they said about Special Forces soldiers was true, they were not hotheads, but intelligent, self-possessed contemporaries who could weigh things wisely and were quite able to improvise.

As he was about to bring his hands down, his cheeks puffing out a breath, he caught a movement out of the corner of his eye an instant before he heard a deafening blast of thunder. His left hand, which was holding the small data storage device and was connected by a cable to the hacker's computer, turned into a cloud of blood.

As if in slow motion, his face turned to the mangled stump where his forearm now ended. His face was wet and there was a metallic taste between his lips. Through the red haze settling before his eyes, the Russian soldiers swung their rifles around and took down the five Americans, who didn't realize what was happening. Before Lacey and the others could even look to their right, they were already riddled with bullets. Dense splashes of blood slapped against the server racks, painting them red as the twitching bodies fell to the ground.

James did not scream, did not even sense that he was hurt. Instead, he stared open-mouthed at the terrifying explosion of violence, transfixed by the volume of the rattling guns until someone threw himself on top of him and he fell under the weight. Dazed, he watched as Mila, Mette, and Justus also dropped, just before the Russian commander stepped forward and fired past them into the computers under the table. Blue and yellow sparks flew and crackled loud enough to drown out the crash of automatic gunfire as Vladimirovich also turned the displays into electrical debris.

What's happening? James thought. He was in shock and felt as if he was being alternately showered with lava and ice water. He was powerless to act as he watched another Russian soldier walked up to the completely terrified hacker, shoved him roughly against the wall, and put a bullet into his forehead. The man's eyes, wide with surprise, burst, and he slumped like a wet sack against the wall, leaving behind a long red smear.

"No," he breathed as he realized they had lost their only chance to avert the war. Now they couldn't reach Dakhra, couldn't show the Americans and the other UN citizens what he had seen, couldn't stop a trigger-happy world government from destroying a fleet of pacifist space refugees who wouldn't even fight back when the time came.

That's it, he thought numbly. His head felt as if someone had softened and sucked out his brain and then filled the cavity with cement. His whole world was dull and slow. *They're destroying the evidence because they have to. It's just what the military leaders need, an enemy that doesn't fight back, that they can destroy, so they can say they were right, and their severe leadership was worth it because it was the only way they could protect humanity. Once the fleet is turned into a nebula of debris, their power will be consolidated forever.*

"*Voz'mi ikh s soboy,*" the Russian commander ordered. James could barely hear him over the ringing in his ears. Mila and Mette rushed to James and pressed something against the stump of his arm. He hardly felt anything, except for the hint of a faraway horror that tried to fight its way to the surface from the depths of his consciousness, but lost the energy it needed to break through.

"James!" Mila shouted angrily, wrapping something that looked like a belt around his arm below the elbow. Her next words were lost among the barked orders of one of the Russians, who roughly tore them apart and began tying his friends' hands behind their backs one by one. James was the last to be lifted to his feet and he almost fell again when his knees gave way. His eyes fell on the slain US soldiers lying in the growing pools of blood in front of the server racks. Dark smoke rose from numerous holes in the blood-spattered glass doors and gathered under the low ceiling. It reeked of ozone and burned cables.

He was led away, limping as if half asleep, behind his friends, who kept giving him worried and horrified looks over their shoulders that he didn't quite understand.

It's only a hand, he thought lamely. The Russians split into two groups. Three men went ahead through the narrow corridor and two followed behind, presumably pointing their guns at them. On the main floor, they were forced to wait in the room leading to the outer door and squat silently on the floor, which reeked of mold and rotting biomass. A soldier slipped out, returned after five minutes and hurriedly waved at them. They marched single file into the jungle and disappeared under the green canopy that enveloped them like a suffocating blanket.

The screech of insects and birds filled James's head, creating an almost physical pressure that kept increasing and nearly drove him out of his mind.

After what felt like an eternity of climbing over the same wet roots and fallen tree trunks, wading through bushes and creepers and mud, and trying to fend off mosquitoes, they took a short break.

One of the soldiers doctored the stump of his arm while the others drank water. The soldier was not particularly squeamish about it, more like a robot with a pre-programmed task to do, unencumbered by things like compassion or gentleness. James felt the pain from the amputated hand, like it was on fire, even though it wasn't there anymore. Still worse, though, was the knowledge that he had only one hand left. His mind could not—or would not—come to terms with the thought of losing something seemingly inseparable from his body. And yet there was an inner voice that assured him that it hadn't even been his. It belonged to the clone body he had inhabited for the past year, as interchangeable as any he had possessed before. His real one, after all, had long since been cremated after the artificial coma could no longer be maintained.

Worse was the shock of the sudden violence and multiple murders that had taken place right before his eyes. In some ways, it had been more terrifying than facing the monster on Al'Antis because that had been a nightmarish creature that triggered his primal fears. But there was something much more disturbing about the brutal murder of people by other people, something *wrong* that shook him to his core.

"James, I'm so sorry!" Mila came over to him as the soldier professionally doctored the stump—or professionally enough considering the overall situation. At first, the man wouldn't let her approach him, but after a brief angry exchange of words, he finally did. She pressed up against his side and kissed him on his sweaty forehead. "Everything's going to be okay."

"You seem more distraught than I do," he said, bravely wrestling a smile onto his face. He could almost sense that he looked as pale as a piece of paper, and now that his mind was slowly realizing what had happened to him he felt like he'd been put through a meat grinder.

"Those damn bastards," she growled in frustration. "They just... just..."

"I know," he interrupted her and sighed, "It's over now. All we can do now is watch them blast Dakhra and the Activists out of the sky."

"Shh! That's not important right now."

"What could be more important?" he grumbled.

"These men, the Spetsnaz soldiers," she whispered, "they're not to be trifled with. I'm not even sure who they are."

"What do you mean?"

"They have a Chechen accent and don't exactly talk like any Special Forces soldiers I've met so far. Those were calm, circumspect guys, whereas these seem more like paramilitary *thugs* to me."

"Thugs?" He shook his head weakly. "*Thugs* don't mow down a Special Forces team."

"You don't understand!" She silenced him with her typical hawk-like look, quickly glanced over her shoulder, and then quickly continued talking, "Not much has changed in Russia, as far as the rule of law is concerned, unlike in your country. The oligarchs still hold the power, under the president of course. Many of them have infiltrated their own paramilitaries into the Special Forces. Tough guys with lots of combat experience, loyal to their boss, like in a mafia syndicate. If it's true, which I think it is, one of them may have pushed to get his people on this mission. Unless the Kremlin gave it a high priority, the chances were good."

"And what does that mean?" he asked cautiously.

"It means that we cannot assume they are acting on behalf of my government. The oligarchs always have their own agenda, and the first thing on it is always maintaining power."

"Seems to be the same everywhere." James shooed away a large bug with a frightening number of legs under its wings that was about to land on his bandage, which was slowly staining with blood where the tourniquet was squeezing the veins.

"You still don't understand. They don't play by the rules. Have you seen the Europeans anywhere?"

"No." He blinked and looked around. "That's right, they weren't at the house."

"They probably killed them, too," Mila whispered grimly.

"How?"

"I don't know."

"And what are they going to do with us?"

"I don't know that, either. Since they haven't killed us yet, I think they—"

"O chem ty govorish?" shouted one of the soldiers, who had just emerged from behind a tree and was fastening his fly. *"Otoydi ot nego!"*

Mila took a step back. "Hang in there!"

James nodded silently.

Soon, they continued walking. As time passed they had to crowd closer and closer together to get enough light from the soldiers' flashlights. The density of the undergrowth made it difficult to move reasonably fast, and their captors' constant shoving and cursing at them didn't help them avoid obstacles or keep their eyes open to avoid stepping on a snake or scorpion. So, their only hope was to create enough noise to drive the creatures off before they got too close. James stumbled repeatedly, and the others lost their balance here and there or tripped over something that made them stumble. This made the soldiers more and more impatient, and it wasn't long before they were delivering furious blows to the team members with their rifle butts and threatening blows to anyone who yelled at them about it. Mila, in particular, was unusually loud and verbal and never missed an opportunity to take issue with her countrymen, and the usually level-headed Adrian backed her up and joined the intermittent exchanges in Russian. Soon they both had black eyes and bruises on their arms, which infuriated James. The only thing worse was the injustice that rendered him helpless to step in and protect them, as futile as that gesture would have been. He was simply too drained and his mind too befuddled by his injury to be able to do more than make a pitiful protest.

They reached the helicopters sometime during the night, completely exhausted, while the soldiers still appeared as agile and focused as before. The three helicopters stood in the suggestion of a semicircle in the large moonlit clearing, perched on the ridge like a saddle on a thick coat. Three tents were pitched in front of them, and their camouflage patterns made it very difficult to see them, especially since the Russian soldiers turned off their flashlights and gagged James and his companions before continuing up the slope, which gave became a meadow that gradually flattened out. The pilots were still asleep and there was still no sign of the European commandos.

The Russian commander hand-signaled two of his men to approach the American pilots' tent, at least that's what James thought it was since it was set up directly in front of the US helicopter. Quietly, with their rifles angled, they neared the entrance as a red flame appeared in the open door of the European helicopter, dimly illuminating an angular face. He believed it was the German leader of the EU team, with whom he had not exchanged a single word.

"There you are," the man said in English, taking a drag on his cigarette. James saw an uncertain expression pass over the Russian commander's face, who was now standing almost right next to him. His eyes darted around, gleaming in the sparse light, no doubt searching for the other European soldiers, but unless he possessed better eyes than James, he was unable to find anyone. "I was beginning to think something had happened to you, Vitali."

"Yeah, you could say that," the man said hesitantly, licking his lips. His men, who had paused on their way to the pilot's tent, looked back at him. "We lost the lieutenant and his team when we stormed the hacker's hideout."

Vladimirovich approached the German.

Run away! Shoot him! James wanted to shout, but the European sat calmly on the helicopter cabin floor, smoking his cigarette. *Get out of here! It's a trap! He's going to kill you!*

"How did you guys get here so fast? We could have used your support in there!" said the Russian.

"Radio was down. Very strange."

"Happened to us, too, when we got closer to the hideout. Must have been that son of a bitch's jamming equipment."

"*Ach, so.* Hey, you." The German waved to the two

soldiers standing near the US pilots' tent. His gaze lingered on Vladimirovich as he did so. "Best let them sleep. They're supposed to be rested when we fly out of here. What about the civilians? Why aren't they saying anything?"

"They're completely exhausted from the forced march here. Civilians, you know."

"Sure."

"Where are your boys?"

"Them?" James thought he saw him shrug between the moonlight and the glow of the cigarette. "I spread them out on the edge of the woods to cover us. Didn't know if we'd get visitors or if you'd be followed."

Again, Vladimirovich thought, trying to fathom if the European soldiers had seen them when they arrived and what that meant for the situation they were in. The Russians were beginning to get restless, and he could hear them handling their rifles.

"Two of the civilians you've bound and gagged are European citizens. Two of the others are Americans; good friends of ours." The German paused and carelessly flicked the cigarette away. It flew in a high arc into the grass like a stray shooting star. "Release them."

Silence.

"You have three seconds."

"How did you know?" Vladimirovich growled.

"Took a peek in your backpack when we were on the slope, and you were arguing with the lieutenant. Your satellite phone was active. You've had a satellite in orbit with an active connection. That made me wonder. Also, one of your fellow civilians tipped me off to be careful with you guys. I didn't think to take them seriously at first, but then there was the matter of the satellite phone…" The leader of the

EU team looked down at his wrist. "Nice talk, but the three seconds are long gone, I'm afraid."

A shot rang out, and James flinched as Vladimirovich's head jerked forward at the same moment. His body fell forward into the grass, hitting with a dull *thud*.

"As for you," the German said, glancing at the Russian soldiers who raised their weapons and looked around indecisively, "I'll give you a chance to throw down your guns."

The soldiers talked wildly to each other in Russian, and a moment later more shots rang out, followed by several shouts, then all was silent.

"I'm Sergeant Major Reuter." The commander of the Europeans introduced himself as he approached them and briefly knelt beside each of the bodies to check their pulse. "They are safe now. Hannah, Mika, good shots. Maxim, Letty, get the pilots, tell them to get the engines ready. Now, for you people."

Reuter freed them from their cable ties, one by one. They had cut deep into their wrists and, in James's case, his elbows. Next came the gags.

"I need to know exactly what happened, understand?"

Mila was the first to regain her speech as James tried to expel the dryness from his mouth. It was as if someone had made him suck on sand.

"They murdered the US team! The hacker we found actually decoded Dakhra's signal an—"

"Dakhra?"

"She's speaking for the Kazerun fleet. It's different than we thought. They're running from their own people, and they don't have any working weapons on board. They want to negotiate a way to live with us, or collect the necessary resources so they can move on. Without a war."

The master sergeant raised an eyebrow.

"Look, that probably sounds crazy," James said, trying to support her.

"A slight understatement on your part."

"But it's true! We have records of how Dakhra—"

"We *had* records," Justus interrupted dejectedly.

"That's not quite right," Meeks said, who had remained silent all this time and now pushed his way between them. "We don't have the records of Dakhra's memories anymore, and we don't have the records from James's surveillance stuff, but we do have something else."

The engineer undid the Velcro straps of his armored vest and ripped out the lining, revealing a small indentation in the back holding a small device James had seen before.

"We have records of the records," Meeks continued. "We even have something better than before to show people, you know? If we want to show authentically how James's views changed and what contact with Dakhra triggered in him, then it makes much more sense to extract my video and audio data so everyone can see him and his famous face."

"You're right! So, we have to go to Chile after all!"

"Wait a minute," Reuter interjected. "Chile?"

23

Timothy Norton straightened his black uniform and left the conference room. It had looked more like a tribunal: the Military Council at one end of the long mahogany table and him at the other, flanked by two guards from the Black Marines, grim-faced men who were almost fanatically devoted to their leadership. The discussion had been as brief as it was brusque once he had complained that the Council, without informing him, had deployed a communications satellite over Bolivia. Only his paternal mentor, General Booker of the Air Force, had been conspicuously silent. So, he had been outvoted on the matter.

That the Council had bypassed his authority for this mission was something akin to a withdrawal of trust. They had called him in merely to inform him that they had decided to play it safe and take out the hacker. The whole affair was basically a reprimand. That told him something, too. The Council had only approved the half hour Norton had given his team to find out more about the signal because, in their eyes, it would not be enough time for his "civilians," as one Council member called them, disdainfully, to obtain any meaningful information.

Outside in the corridor, his aide-de-camp, Major Bolton, was waiting for him.

"Well?"

Norton didn't answer, instead putting on a face that feigned controlled anger. It wasn't until they arrived at his old office in the Pentagon's West Wing that he emitted a long, drawn-out sigh and turned on the white-noise generator he'd had installed. While it was against regulations, his position within the military allowed him some liberties, which he deliberately took. Even though the small device made eavesdropping virtually impossible, he had preferred not to go to his new office, which he had moved into a year ago and which was right next to General Knowles's. He had never felt comfortable there, since it had only been given to him for political reasons, to show everyone he was number five in the country, right after the four members of the Military Council. The first successor. That move alone had ensured that a whole new set of doors in the United States' halls of power were now open to him. He, of course, had never been under the illusion that he was now at the main playing table. While it was clear that Booker had made his mark by choosing him as his successor, after all, the Air Force general was no spring chicken at eighty-two, and the gap between the nation's four highest-ranking officers and the next-highest place below the Council was vast.

"What happened in there?" Bolton asked after he closed the door.

"I'm not sure." Norton sighed again and rubbed his hands over his face. They were rough and old. Von Booker already seemed an old man to him. Although Norton was the same age, he felt considerably younger than his mentor looked. He still had a few years left in his bones, but there weren't many. "They obviously took more interest in the mission than they admitted."

"How did they reveal that?"

"They had a communication satellite over the mission area the whole time and didn't tell me about it. They said t that they didn't want to expend any resources and were just going to assign me an Air Force reconnaissance team that I could use. It seemed to me that they were merely doing me a favor because of my position, not really giving a damn about the mission."

"It seems you were wrong about that," the major said.

"Yes. But why go behind my back?"

"That depends."

Norton raised his eyebrows and looked at his aide.

"It depends on what your people found out in Bolivia, doesn't it?"

"The Kazerun..." He paused and thought. Finally, he shook his head. He could trust Bolton after working together for over twenty years . No, he *had* to trust him, because otherwise the entire plan would be moot. "The signal revealed that the Kazerun have come with peaceful intentions and are not interested in a fight. They probably aren't even in a position to fight because they don't have any weapons systems."

"Ah, I'm not surprised," Bolton replied unexpectedly, settling into one of the two chairs on the other side of the desk, where he crossed his legs and folded his hands on his knee.

"No?"

"Well, that they've come with peaceful intentions—I didn't expect that. But I'm not particularly surprised because I've felt there was something wrong with the official view of the danger confronting us."

"Why?"

"Because you've been spending a conspicuous amount of time with the brigades under your command for the past few months. You've always done that, but not with the lower ranks. And you've had two battalions of Special Reconnaissance moved here to Arlington to put on a special parade for the anniversary of the founding of the Military Council." Bolton smiled mirthlessly. "You've never been a military pomp man, so I figured you were expecting trouble and you want your people around."

"This is a dangerous conversation we're having here," Norton said quietly.

"You are exceedingly popular among the troops, which is the only advantage you have over the members of the Military Council. They're as distant from the rest of the serving population as a brain from its feet."

"What are your conclusions?"

"That you didn't disclose to the Council exactly why you launched the mission. So, you basically double-crossed the Council, and the Council double-crossed you at the same time. A game in the shadows. Politics, that's what it is. The stuff you hate," the major said. "You gave your team more time than you officially granted them to find out the truth about the Kazerun fleet. The Council didn't like that because not having the big war would jeopardize their power base. So, they stepped out of the shadows and slapped you on the wrist. Without Booker's protective hand, you might have even faced serious consequences. But in the absence of those, I'm assuming there's some confusion on the Council about what your actions meant."

Norton nodded appreciatively. He knew exactly why he had never let Bolton go as his aide-de-camp.

"So, what are you going to do now, General?"

"My team in Bolivia—I've lost contact with them, and I won't be able to get access to the satellite. Get in touch with General Kohlhammer in Munich. Maybe he can help us."

Bolton nodded. "Through the team he sent along. Will do. What do we do if Kohlhammer agrees? He'll smell a rat even across the Atlantic."

"He's a good friend."

"Well, then."

"There's one more thing, Major. We've got to get a code to our people in Bolivia."

"A code?"

"The access code to our national e-pal frequencies for nationwide emergencies." Norton paused to let the words sink in. That his aide didn't argue made him more than a little proud. "That's where you come in, isn't it?"

"You know perfectly well I can get my hands on it." Bolton smiled wanly. "You're a good strategist, General, and I don't regret letting you set me up as a pawn on your side of the board. Just assure me that you've thought through what will happen once I have the codes."

"I have," Norton confirmed, nodding. "If all goes well, there will be no need to move my queen because all positions will be blocked by pawns. But just in case, she's standing by to checkmate the king."

"You seem very confident, which is unlike you."

"It's a matter of necessity."

He leaned back and for a moment looked out through the open slats of the office blinds into the open-plan office filled with analysts. Dressed in their uniforms, they resembled an ant colony. The colony functioned smoothly and around the clock in different shifts that could hardly be distinguished from each other. The machine was well-oiled, and it was hard to imagine any grating in its gears. But that was exactly what would have to happen for his plan to work. He had feared the satellite might come into play, but he had still been surprised by how vehemently the Military Council had dragged his secret out of the closet. They were scared, and sooner than expected. That was dangerous.

"Everything now depends on whether my team in Bolivia can find a way to get to Chile and put their plan into action," he muttered.

"Their plan, or *your* plan?" Bolton said almost accusingly.

"In the best case, the two are one and the same. Major?"

"Really?"

"Be careful, but proceed with haste. Our window of opportunity is small, no more than a few hours, but it could be the most important in the recent history of our nation and our world. Do whatever it takes. Start now. There are no do-overs on this one, so failure is not an option. Understood?"

"Understood, sir." Bolton stood, smoothed his already immaculate uniform, and then straightened before snapping a salute.

Norton crisply returned the salute and shooed the major out of his office.

24

"Please, Sergeant!" James almost pleaded, but Reuter's expression remained hard as stone. The tall German sat across from him on the Eurocopter's bench seat with his rifle across his knees. The headset he wore looked like a Christmas decoration on a weathered fir tree.

"Sergeant Major."

"Sergeant Major, excuse me. Don't you see what's at stake here?"

"Yes, I do see. But I'm a soldier, Mr. Hamilton, and as a soldier, I carry out orders. My mission orders from the beginning were to protect our citizens and support Lieutenant Lacey."

"But that doesn't matter at all!" Meeks said. "The issue here is war or peace."

"Perhaps, but I am not so presumptuous as to usurp such decisions."

"You decided to take out the Russian team on your own," Mila said.

Reuter shrugged. "I did that because civilians were in danger. Among them, some from the EU and the US."

"Improvised, then. I'm sure that wasn't in your mission orders."

"Protection of civilians is always in the mission order."

"Oh, for Christ's sake!" James mussed his hair with his remaining hand and pursed his mouth. "Don't be so damned stubborn! We can't afford to wait any longer. We're flying east when we should be flying southwest! Every extra mile is taking us in the wrong direction, man!"

"Listen," Justus tried in German. "We really appreciate you getting us out of there. We really do. But it's not enough. There's too much at stake here for us to stick to the chain of command."

"The chain of command is the one thing that should never be compromised," the sergeant major objected impassively. "And now—"

"Sergeant Major?" one of the co-pilots shouted. "General Kohlhammer on two for you."

"Are we in range of Guiana yet? Patch it through." Reuter raised a hand to stop them all from trying to talk to him. "Reuter here. Yes. No. We had to neutralize the Russian team. No, General. They took the civilians hostage and killed the American soldiers. I know. Yes. Excuse me?" The soldier frowned. "Can you repeat that? Yes, General. *Nein, Herr General*, no problem."

Reuter clicked his tongue and leaned forward to peer through the narrow passageway to the cockpit.

"Change of plans!" he shouted. "I'm giving you coordinates for a new destination." He listened to someone on the radio, then nodded. "Do that."

"What's going on?" asked James.

"Good news for you. My commander has ordered me to fly you wherever you want to go."

"He did what?"

"He gave me an order, and I'm going to carry it out. But first we have to refuel because otherwise, we won't make it to Chile," the German explained, giving James a penetrating look. "Do you still want me to be a soldier who disobeys his orders now that it fits your purpose?"

James fell silent, embarrassed.

The pain in the stump of his left arm had been reduced to a dull throb after the European team medic had given him some painkillers, but the ebb of the adrenaline and the shock made his attention wander more and more, uncomfortably dominating his conscious thoughts.

"We'll have to do something about that soon," said the commando soldier tending to his horrible wound. He was a wiry little man with a protruding, hooked nose, and surprisingly kind eyes for someone trained to kill. He pointed needlessly at the bandaged stump.

"Do what?" James asked, swallowing hard.

"Putting it in a tourniquet was the right thing to do, but I removed the belt right away for a reason. Due to how long that the forearm was ligated, a large part has already died, or rather is no longer salvageable. I will have to amputate as soon as possible to avoid blood poisoning and too much necrotic tissue. I've already told the sergeant major that we will stay at the military base in French Guiana."

"No!"

"I have to operate on you. There's no way around it."

"Then do what you have to do on the way, but I have to go with you to Chile!" insisted James.

The paramedic looked at Reuter, who shrugged.

"Suit yourself. But a helicopter, even with the proper emergency equipment, is not the best place for surgery, not least because of the motion, lack of sterility and—"

"I consent to that."

"I'm not sure you know the risk. You could die within a day or two if the surgery is not a success."

"Then that's that." He caught a scowl from Mila, and she seemed to want to say something, but she clenched her teeth and remained silent.

The paramedic shrugged. "Your call. I'm not a doctor, but I'm trained to do field surgeries like this, so you're in capable hands, even if I can't replace a good surgeon. But you should know the risks."

James waved his hand.

"I'll put a Ringer's solution in you as an IV, including blood and a broad-spectrum antibiotic. Then you'll get an inhalable anesthetic and be intubated for ventilation before I make a clean incision below the elbow and cauterize the blood vessels. After that, I'll sew everything together and, hopefully, everything will go well. The MedEvac even has a monitor for EKG and oxygen monitoring."

"That sounds pretty good to me."

"That's because you have no idea. We have cramped quarters here, dirty passengers nearby, lots of movement, which means contaminated incisions, bad sutures, and no assistance during the procedure. If all goes well, you can get a good prosthesis in a few months and regain normal use with a few restrictions. I put the chance at fifty percent—because I'm an optimist. If it doesn't go well…"

"You don't have to—"

"Then I'll have to start above the elbow, and the prosthetics will be more complicated, even in the best of bad cases. If it goes really bad, there's sepsis, which I can't stop, and if it comes after a few hours without me detecting it soon enough, then you're dead in a day or two." The matter-of-fact way the paramedic said this made James go cold.

"Maybe you should—" Mila started, but he didn't let her finish.

"No. My chances have been worse. I survived the Al'Antis death zone and the radiation I suffered after the Tokamaku. I'll survive a little flight surgery like this, don't worry." He tried to smile at her, but got nothing more than a sour look and a sigh in response. "That's how we'll do it, Doc."

"All right. That's the fastest you'll ever lose weight." The paramedic grinned and winked at him as if now that the matter settled it constituted an amusing diversion.

It was still two hours to the base in French Guiana. Two hours during which he felt extremely restless. Not because he was worried about the surgery, but because it meant an additional two hours to get to Chile and to the telescope Justus had talked about.

What if Dakhra drew the wrong conclusions from the sudden disruption in communication? They wouldn't change their minds, would they? Her father had proven before that he could put his principles aside when it came to survival, just as James would do if the situation called for it and he could save someone he loved. Would the Kazerun leader do it again? Could the fleet power up its weapons after all? He felt the urgency of what they were about to do like an uncomfortable tickle on the back of his neck, and it was only getting worse.

At the airbase, they changed clothes while changing helicopters and were generously disinfected with large spray bottles before entering the readied French MedEvac, complete with a fresh crew. Inside was a stretcher with all sorts of medical equipment and only four seats, so there was not enough room for everyone. It was extremely cramped, and since the paramedic immediately had him sit on the stretcher, he felt like a test subject surrounded by medical students. He saw fear and concern on the faces of his friends, while the soldiers looked rather bored, as if everything happening was the most normal thing in the world. Ironically, their attitude calmed him, and he decided to keep his gaze on the soldiers or the cabin ceiling after the helicopter took off and thundered toward the southwest.

The helicopter vibrated badly as they ascended through the low cloud cover and to a cruising altitude high enough to escape notice from naked eyes on the ground. Countries were supposedly aware of their overflight, but the pilots apparently didn't want to take any chances or hoped the higher altitude would cause less turbulence. They were professionals, so he tried not to think about it.

Then the paramedic began the surgery. He was wrapped in a white overcoat with a hood, mouth guard and splash goggles. Mila squatted next to James and held his good hand.

"I'll see you in a minute, and then everything will be fine," she assured him. But he noticed her eyes were as moist as shiny pearls.

Waking up was a process that went neither quickly nor slowly—at least from James's point of view. He saw blurred faces, felt an indistinct pain pass through him like a distant storm on the horizon, threatening and dark, and yet without the urgent distress it would have caused if was much nearer. There was Mila, her face streaked with tears, Adrian looking very serious, and Vincent, Justus, and Mette with expressions that were sometimes worried and sometimes composed. Then, suddenly, they were all gone except for

Mila, who remained at his side, next to a hooded figure with a blood-spattered mask. Only his eyes were visible behind the goggles.

"What's going on?" he asked in his hazy stupor. "Where am I?"

"You're still in the helicopter," Mila said, squeezing his right hand.

"Why aren't we moving?"

Slowly, memories of their mission to Chile returned, but only fragments stubbornly resisting his memory as if he were trying to fish for a speck of dust in a jar of honey. He could see it, but whenever his fingers approached, it slipped away in the liquid.

"We arrived at ALMA an hour ago," she said.

"We're at the telescope!" James tried to raise himself up, but his body only managed a feeble jerk. Mila easily managed to stop him with a hand on his chest before he could sit up.

"Adrian and the sergeant major went in with the others. They know what they have to do."

"But I have to—"

"No, you don't have to do anything, James." Mila suppressed a sniffle. What on earth was wrong with her? Why was she so sad?

"It's everything," he said, groaning as he tried again to sit up, but as he did a sharp pain cracked through his left arm like a bolt of lightning, and he fell back onto the cot like a wet sack. "OW!"

She shook her head and stroked his forehead. "It's not your fight, James. Not this time."

"I—"

"I know you always want to be up front, but you can't this time."

"The surgery... It didn't go well, did it?"

She shook her head. "No."

"How does it look?"

"We shouldn't—"

He turned directly to the paramedic, who pulled his mouth-nose guard under his chin and eyed him carefully. "Doc?"

"Twenty-four hours, then you'll die of the sepsis I couldn't prevent. I'm sorry."

"Not your fault." James swallowed. *Twenty-four hours. Then it's over. Just like that.*

"I'll put you back to sleep now, Mr. Hamilton."

"No, I need to know—"

"They've transferred the data to Dakhra," Mila assured him. Her gaze was empty before she refocused on him and smiled bravely. "And we got the code for the e-pal frequencies from Norton. Now all Dakhra has to do is transmit her message and then all the Americans will see what we saw."

"And what about the rest of the world?" he asked weakly.

"I'm sure your general is in contact with our commander. Otherwise, he would never have sent us here to the telescope." The medic sounded sure as he nodded to his right.

James turned his head with difficulty and saw several telescope dishes set in a clear pattern amid an extremely dry, brown landscape. At the same moment, he spotted several silhouettes racing toward them. He was about to say something to change his sudden excitement into a warning to Mila and the medic, but then a dark shadow swooped down from the sky and enveloped the telescope dishes in a gigantic explosion. The helicopter shook and the wave of heat that reached them made the air crackle and his skin glow.

25

"Come on," Norton muttered. He had been staring at his e-pal for half an hour now. The Military Council's Founder's Day parade was drawing to a close and still the little device remained silent. It was his private one, which he usually never used, but for this purpose, it was just the thing.

His two battalions of Special Reconnaissance troopers, loyal elite soldiers, could already be seen at the rear of the missile force formation, and in the next five minutes would march past the grandstand where he was sitting, graciously waving a raised hand at regular intervals. The whole idea of holding such a parade while an allegedly hostile fleet of aliens was on Earth's interstellar doorstep was utterly absurd. If he had not learned that they posed no threat—something the Military Council did not know or did not want to know—he would have done everything in his power to prevent this farce. It served only to propagandize and supposedly raise morale.

And the preservation of power, he thought, sighing inwardly as he waved to the mobile launcher drivers, who saluted artfully in the direction of the military leadership on the upper tiers. The crowd lining the streets on the right and left cheered with excitement, waving American flags and those of the new UN.

An Army television crew at the foot of the heavily guarded bleachers panned in his direction and he smiled as graciously as he could without losing the serious expression in his eyes.

"Are you all right, Timothy?" asked Fleet Admiral Jones beside him, not pausing in his waving. His steel-gray eyes flashed toward his e-pal.

"Yes." Norton straightened and nodded his expression unchanged. *Get on with it, James! What's taking you so long?*

"A good day for the armed forces," the Chief of Naval Operations continued, as more and more mobile launchers passed by like streamlined snails with outsized shells on their backs. The accompanying soldiers, striding along beside the massive machines, saluted simultaneously once they reached the center of the stand and looked up to their right as if in response to an inaudible command.

Chants of "U-S-A!" resounded from hundreds of throats and the crowd cheered even more frenetically. Norton's guts tightened at that.

"A good day for America and the world," he replied, and Jones frowned for a brief moment.

"Of course. Our strength is their strength, and vice versa. Ah." The Admiral nodded to his left. Norton's battalions approached. Men and women dressed in dark patch camouflage who, unlike the parade regiments, were not identical in height and wore no parade uniforms, but wore full combat gear with closed helmet systems and composite fiber-reinforced armor. They looked like insects, their rifles carried in front of their chests and maintaining a steady stride that lacked the crisp perfection of the polished soldiers who had dominated the parade so far and had been specially trained for show.

"There are your people," Jones said with a hint of scorn. "Interesting outfits."

"It seemed appropriate to show some soldiers as they would go into battle, in addition to soldiers in parade dress. After all, it also shows our battle-ready face."

"Would?" the fleet admiral echoed disdainfully. He spoke softly., yet despite the loud background noise, his voice, which sounded like two iron bars rubbing together, was clearly audible. "More likely, *will*."

"Of course," Norton said noncommittally.

His e-pal finally stirred to life, flashing red three times to indicate that the central military service was displaying an urgent message that switched every other function of the small computer into background mode with a priority code. As a result, the message could not be turned off, deleted, or otherwise blocked because the frequency on which it was broadcast was reserved for national and global emergencies that required every citizen to be reached immediately.

The noise of the spectators lining Washington Avenue broke off immediately. The parade participants marched a little further while he waved to his battalion commanders. The Military Council and every officer in the stands stared at their e-pals and the footage they played, as did everyone present.

The transmission showed James in the hacker's lair.

Norton's gaze swept beyond the image. Normally, ammunition was taken from each soldier before they participated in the parade to ensure no weapon was loaded. This was meticulously checked by designated personnel, but on this day, Norton had taken over this job for his men after he had intimidated the master sergeant who normally handled the procedure.

By the time the two battalions broke from their formation, each five hundred strong, they had emerged at the left end of the stands, catching the Rangers assigned to protect them off guard. They surprised the soldiers while they were trying to understand what was going on, eyes fixed either on their e-pals or the leadership behind and above them, looking for an answer to what everyone was wondering: A priority message from the Military Council that merely showed a popular hero sitting in front of displays and pulling VR goggles over his head as the image panned to the monitors. It only took a few seconds for Special Reconnaissance to disarm the Rangers and surround the bleachers. Several dozen of Norton's men rushed through the stands, causing a commotion among those officers they had to push aside to continue upward. The confusion was so great that many still did not realize what was happening.

"What is the meaning of this?" Admiral Jones asked as he frowned and looked up from the hologram above his wristband and noticed the heavily armored soldiers. Many of the jostled officers along the stairs took no notice of them as they continued to stare at their e-pals, listening to James's and Dakhra's voices, trying to make sense of what seemingly made no sense at all.

"We'll see when the news has ended," Norton said neutrally. At the same moment four of his most loyal officers, two from each battalion, appeared in front of his row and posted themselves in before of the four members of the Military Council. They raised their rifles very slightly, just enough for the warning to be unmistakable to the Council members while appearing to act as bodyguards to onlookers. After all, he wanted to allow them to save face in case they decided to act more reasonably than he expected.

"Explain yourself!" Jones commanded the special ops officers hidden behind their closed visors. "That's an order!"

None of the four men responded.

"General?" The Fleet Admiral looked at him menacingly. "What is the meaning of this?"

Norton pointed to the image above the Navy commander's e-pal.

"See for yourself, then you'll know."

A deep silence settled over all of Washington and Arlington and the rest of the United States and Europe. After some delay, and illegal routing, the footage also reached Russia and China and found its way to every pair of eyes and ears in the UN, spreading the silence. Everyone listened to James Hamilton's change of heart, the face of the heroic first teleport team that the Military Council itself had built into an icon of human resistance. Ironically, that very icon was now poised to topple everything they had built—at least Norton hoped so. He firmly believed that reason and compassion, though in the end more quietly expressed than the baser instincts, were fundamentally much more common among his fellow humans than one might think.

EPILOGUE

James sat on the lush green grass and wiggled his bare toes where the larger blades tickled them. The two suns sent a pleasant warmth through his skin and he smiled. Mila leaned against his shoulder and sighed contentedly.

"Can I see it again?" he asked gleefully, wrapping his right arm around her as he supported himself on his left.

"You mean the explosion, right?" Meeks said beside him.

"Yes!" Justus confirmed, unusually relaxed. "You mean the one when the telescopes were destroyed and blew us over, and then, like Hollywood heroes, calmly got back up and patted the dust off our shoulders before climbing into the helicopter to fly off into the sunset after rescuing everyone?"

"I'm sure that's what he means," Mette crowed happily. "That moment when we managed to send the signal at the last second."

"He must mean that." James could hear Adrian grinning behind him.

"Come on, people! You were there, but I was lying... where actually?"

"In the memory cache on our side," God replied. The construct grinned broadly under its white, ruffled beard and rearranged its toga. James wished it would stop making fun of Earthly beliefs, but he was apparently the only one. His friends seemed to find the digitized personality conglomerate's humor rather amusing.

"Okay, you all survived the explosion, we flew back to Guiana and then we were flown to Wyoming. Norton made sure to save me the only possible way there was: I was put in the teleporter in a coma and I was sent in the direction of the master teleporter—that construct. Now I'm just... what, actually? Data?"

"If it makes you feel any better, that's what you were before," Adrian said. "And then you were a clone. You can be that again."

"At least I have experience with that. And you came along for the ride."

"Once a team, always a team," Mila said smiling.

"And what happened to Dakhra? I would like to see it all again."

"Ask and you shall receive!" the construct intoned, raising a hand. The suns quickly sank behind the horizon and the stars emerged, twinkling in the sky. A large image appeared over the meadow like an ethereal movie screen.

The scene was in North Africa, in the northern Saharan foothills, and showed tens of thousands of people standing in front of a cordoned-off area of several square kilometers. The footage was shot from a helicopter slowly approaching the crowd.

The image jumped to eye level, showing General Norton in civilian clothes next to other world dignitaries looking skyward. Right next to him were the head of the EU Commission and the Russian and Chinese presidents. The camera panned to where they were looking and focused on several shooting stars falling out of the blue sky. They were soon revealed to be small, dark dots that quickly grew into thirty-three landing craft. They were cylindrical spaceships that looked like an Airbus A380 with its wings clipped off.

Before they landed, stubby appendages extended from the fuselages and changed into thrusters, and blue exhaust flames braked their plunge into the atmosphere. They kicked up a lot of dust in the last hundred meters, but that didn't seem to bother the waiting crowd. There a silence filled with a tense anticipation that seemed caught between fear and hope, but unable to find an outlet.

The space shuttles landed several dozen meters from the waiting onlookers, and as the desert sands slowly settled like a brown glittering rain in the sun, even the murmur of the gentle wind seemed to halt, as if it recognized the significance of this moment.

An opening in the lead shuttle appeared and a ramp formed, bridging the gap to the ground like a tiny plank at the base of a skyscraper. It appeared to be steaming from the heat of atmospheric friction. A lone figure emerged and walked tentatively down the ramp, shielding her eyes from the glare of the sun. Others followed her and more emerged from the other shuttles. The visitors merged into a single stream that advanced over the desert floor. Some went down on their knees and let the hot sand run through their fingers, others fell into each other's arms. But the person in front continued straight ahead until James recognized her as Dakhra. Dakhra from his memories, which in reality had been *hers*. Dakhra from the display in Bolivia, as if he were reliving a faded dream. She walked straight toward Norton.

They stood silently for a few moments while the crowd of tense and exhausted Activists grew behind her.

Then it happened: the general extended a hand. Dakhra eyed it briefly, confused, then grasped it somewhat clumsily yet resolutely, and the waiting crowd erupted in cheers as tension and anticipation dissolved into a collective frenzy of joy.

"So simple," James murmured, tears gathering in his eyes. He didn't care.

"Nothing about it was simple. But sometimes it's the smallest symbols that give us hope," Mila said against his shoulder. "That right there is just a handshake, but it's probably the best start to the future we could have wished for."

"It all started with Mother Russia," Adrian said. "When the official there discovered that the Russian Spetsnaz team was being paid by an oligarch who had enriched himself from the drastic increase in arms spending during the last few decades and had no interest in avoiding the approaching conflict, action was swift. The Kremlin locked him up and apologized to its allies."

"That's something to build on," Mette agreed. "Whether the Kazerun stay or move on is now a question for the future."

"And that's a good thing," Justus said. "For the future has become many times brighter this day than it has been the entire thirty years before."

"Do you think we'll learn from each other?"

"I'm sure," said Adrian, expressing this unusual optimism.

"Am I the only one who feels like I've been robbed of the fireworks? The epic finale? Thirty years of preparation and then: nothing. Not a single shot, instead, just a simple handshake that we weren't even there for," Meeks grumbled but winked all the same.

"I'm already quite happy not feeling like a protagonist in an action movie for once."

"But it doesn't matter to you anymore, does it?" asked God/the construct, a smile spreading across its face.

"No." James nodded in relief.

"Now that you have escaped death and your friends have escaped their home world, where there was nothing left for them," the white-bearded male figure said, "I wonder if you have made a decision? Do you want to go on to our world and live a simple but fulfilling life? Or would you like to go to a world connected to the teleporters? We have a few inhabited with your settlers."

"Deportees," Meeks corrected him.

"Unjustly deported," James said. "Australia was colonized by convicts, and today they're some of the nicest people around."

"That convict story is also just a persistent myth," his American friend snorted.

"You can also return to the Tokamaku," God suggested. "Or you can stay here in the memory cache of our construct and do whatever you want."

James turned to his friends and pulled Mila close, grinning. "You know what? I feel like this is the first time we're under no pressure to do anything. Why don't we just take our time for this decision?"

Mette clapped her hands. "Amen."

"I love you guys," James said suddenly emotional. He saw the same expression on his friends' faces. "You are my family, and no matter where we go, we go together."

AFTERWORD

Dear reader,

Thus ends the tale *Teleport*—for the time being, at least. I think the ending provides closure without any cliffhangers. Yet, if the desire should arise—on your part or mine—there is certainly room for further adventures. After all, we have used only two of the six teleporters so far.

If you enjoyed this book, I would be very happy to see a star rating at the end of this e-book or a short review on Amazon. That's the best way to help authors like me keep writing exciting books in the future. If you want to get in touch with me directly, you can do that. Just write to: Joshua@joshuatcalvert.com—I answer every email!

If you subscribe to my newsletter, I'll regularly tell you a bit about myself, and my writing, and discuss the great themes

Afterword

of science fiction. Plus, as a thank you, you'll receive my e-book *Rift: The Transition* exclusively and for free: www.joshuatcalvert.com

Warm regards,
    Joshua T. Calvert

Printed in Great Britain
by Amazon